GETTING LUCKY

GETTING LUCKY

A Jail Bait Novel

MIA STORM

Getting Lucky

This is a work of fiction.

Cover Design: Sarah Hansen, Okay Creations

Dedication

To everyone who has ever been in love

with the "wrong person."

CHAPTER 1

Tro

I squint against the glare of the megawatt stage lights reflecting off the shiny cover of the *Rolling Stone* issue Jimmy Fallon is holding up for *The Tonight Show* cameras. There's a ripple of excited chatter from the live audience and a girl near the back shouts, "Marry me, Tro!"

On the screen at stage right, I watch as the TV monitor pans in on the cover, a full frontal of me totally nude except for the black and red Schector C-1 Hellraiser hanging from the strap around my neck and covering the part of me that would have made the cover X-rated otherwise. She's my baby—my first electric guitar and the only thing I own that I truly give a shit about.

Jimmy flips his hand at the image. "It's pretty safe to say you're comfortable in the limelight, but some people say you're over the top."

I almost never agree to interviews. First, you sort of have to be sober for them, and second, they're bullshit. But Jimmy's pretty cool, and my manager was pissed that I'd turned down every other promotional opportunity leading up to this tour, so here I am.

I loop my arm over the back of the chair next to his desk and slouch into it, crossing one black-booted ankle over the other knee. "Balls out, man. That's how I live my life. I know some people find that offensive, but…" I give the audience my best I-don't-give-a-shit smirk. "Who the fuck cares?"

There's a mix of chuckles and gasps from the studio audience, and the girl in the back yells out, "I love you!"

Jimmy cringes. "And…that's why we do these segments on tape," he says, scratching the top of his head. He leans on his elbows toward me. "So balls out."

I nod. "I live life on my own terms. Otherwise, what's the point? I march to someone else's orders, then I'm living someone else's life. I'm not gonna waste my time worrying about what other people think. I do my thing, they do theirs, and everyone's happy. That's all it's gotta be."

A wry smile curves Jimmy's mouth as his fingers drum the desk. "That's pretty philosophical for a guy whose first big hit was about getting lucky in the middle of a barroom brawl."

I pull myself up straighter. "Let it be, let it be, let it be, oh let it be," I sing, doing my best John Lennon. Girls in the audience scream. "That was a from guy whose first hit was all about begging some chick to love him." I plant my elbow into the arm of the chair and lean toward Jimmy. "And as for nailing someone in the middle of a brawl, the deeper symbolism there is that life is all about finding the positive in adverse situations—looking for the silver lining, and all that shit. So that song might have been a little more philosophical than you're giving it credit for."

He cuts an amused glance backstage. "Got your finger ready on that bleeper, Pete?"

That's part of living balls out. I live in the moment and never apologize for any of it. Ever

Or regret it.

I spent way too much time doing that before I learned that the only thing that really matters is right now. My *real* life started six years ago, when I walked away from what I *thought* was life. I never look back at all the shit that came before. None of it matters.

"So, I've got to ask," Jimmy says, setting the *Rolling Stone* issue face down on his desk. "How sick do you get of the paparazzi and the tabloids? You must feel like you're living in a fishbowl most of the time."

He's right but, "I don't really give a shit."

My manager, Ray, called me last night while I was kicking back at the hotel with the guys to ask me what the fuck I was thinking. Apparently, last night's episode of *Access Hollywood* had someone's iPhone footage of me banging some actress I don't even remember meeting on a table at the Sunset Lounge. I was pretty fucked up at that after-party, but just because I don't remember it doesn't mean I doubt it happened.

"The way I see it, they're just doing their job, trying to make a buck. Why anyone would want to read or watch that shit is beyond me, but as long as there's a market, I can't really get too pissed about it."

"You don't feel like you're entitled to a private life?" he asks.

I give him half a shrug. "Nothing they do is going to change anything I do. I'm just living my life. If they feel compelled to capture that on film, so be it."

"That attitude will probably save your sanity." He scoops a copy of Roadkill's latest studio CD off his desk and holds it up for the camera. On the cover, I've got this sort of deranged psycho-killer look in my eye and the guys are in the shadows behind me. Totally fucking sinister.

"Speaking of which, the lead single off your new CD, 'Insane,' debuted at number one on the rock charts last month."

"Yeah." I send an appreciative wave toward the audience. "Thanks, guys."

A handful of girls scream my name and the rest of the audience applauds.

"Fuck me, Tro!" the girl in the back shouts.

I shield my eyes with my forearm and squint through the lights to a seat near the back where two security guards are converging. "Be right there, doll." I flick a hand at Jimmy. "Just give me a sec to finish up what I'm doing here."

Jimmy rolls his eyes and tosses his note cards. "We're going to be able to air like three words from this entire interview."

"It's all good, man," I say with a wave as they haul the girl off.

He swivels his chair. "So, Roadkill kicks off your world tour tomorrow night with two sold out shows at Madison Square Garden."

I nod. "We've got nine weeks touring the U.S. and Canada, then we head to Europe and Asia for another eight."

He whistles through his teeth. "That's long time on the road."

"Got nowhere better to be," I say with a shrug.

And it's true.

I've got apartments in L.A, Austin, and London, but there's really no one who would miss me if I never set foot in any of those places again. Besides, I like being on the road—the rush of waking up somewhere and having no fucking clue where I am. I show up, play my gig, then do whatever or whoever the fuck I feel like doing. The next day, I get up and move on. No strings, no accountability.

Jimmy sets the CD down. "It's got to feel good that your shows are selling out worldwide within minutes of tickets going on sale."

"Pumped that people are digging what we're doing," I say, bobbing a nod.

"Well, they're going to hear some of that now, right, guys?" Jimmy says, looking toward his house band, The Roots, with raised eyebrows.

"On it, man," their drummer says into the mic.

Jimmy looks into the camera and holds the CD up again. "We'll be right back with Tro Gunnison and The Roots' schoolroom instruments rendition of 'Insane'."

CHAPTER 2

Shiloh

They say be careful what you wish for, but when your wildest dream comes true, never in a million years do you expect to regret it. And I don't.

Mostly.

It's just that I don't belong to me anymore. Everywhere I go, every second of every day, somebody wants a piece of me. I'm starting to feel more like a thing than a person.

I got a break from the talk show circuit for a few months when we were in the studios recording, but since the new singles started releasing, it's been non-stop radio and TV shows. Today is the big one: we're kicking off the start of our North American tour with an appearance on *The Tonight Show*.

I sit still, despite the compulsion to squirm out from under the makeup artist who's touching up my face, and watch the screen in the corner of the Green Room. Tro Gunnison, the frontman for Roadkill, the tour headliner, is setting up with Jimmy Fallon and The Roots to tape a schoolroom instruments version of the Roadkill single that's been sitting atop every rock chart for the last three weeks. Jimmy starts the beat box. It sets the breakneck rhythm Roadkill is known for. He starts pounding out the melody on the xylophone then nods at Tro, who shakes his maracas and blends into the mix. A devil's smile flashes over Tro's face, making his deep dimples pop, as he opens his mouth and starts singing the lyrics.

His voice is like smoke over gravel, the type of sound that seeps through every cell in your body and becomes part of you. A shiver runs down my spine at the first note. There are certain voices that will do that to me every time. Tro Gunnison's is one of them.

The Roots accompany Tro and Jimmy with the pound of tambourines, the hum of kazoos, and the clang of cow bells, and it almost sounds better than the original. With just the acoustic schoolroom instruments, Tro's vocals carry the show. I close my eyes with the rush as my skin pebbles into goose bumps.

"I need them open to touch up your mascara, sweetie," Tammy, or Tony, or whatever the makeup lady's name is, says.

I open them and fight to keep them that way as she nearly blinds me raking the brush over my lashes. I'd never worn makeup before *The Voice*, and even after a year, I'm still not used to it.

"All done," she says, pulling off the paper bib she put on me to keep from dusting my clothes with the heavy powder.

I chance a glance in the mirror. They never match my coffee-with-too-much-cream skin tone very well, but this one did better than most. No one knows my ethnicity because no one knows who my parents are, but on every state form I've ever seen it says Hispanic. I'm thinking one of my parents must have been black, though, because my hair is a copper afro if I let it go. I slick a few strands back into my tight ponytail and slip off the chair. "Thanks."

"Ten minutes," Billie, my manager, warns when she catches me preparing to duck out of the room.

After they finish taping the song, I'm supposed to do an interview with Jimmy to promote the tour. When I glance over my shoulder, Billie's face is fixed in the maternal scowl she always wears.

She's forty and has no kids of her own, so she's sort of adopted me. I shouldn't complain, but it's been years since I was in anything but a group home, and let's just say the foster families I lived with before that weren't in it for the love of children. I'm not used to having to answer to anyone, and Billie is like an overprotective mama bear. But I'm living in her world now. She gets how it works and handles everything so I don't have to. For that alone, she's worth her weight in gold.

My head nods automatically as I slip out the door into a short hallway that leads backstage. In an alcove around the corner from the sound and light boards, I spotted a stack of crates on my way in. On each side the square crates are stacked three high, but in the middle there are only two, forming a recess. I test them and decide they're sturdy enough to hold my hundred and ten pounds. I find hand and foot holds, climb the middle stack, and tuck into the shadows, sliding back against the wall and pulling my knees up to my chest. My arms wrap around them and I melt into the massive twist of cords, speakers, and other various sound equipment spilling from the crates.

The first thing I do now when I walk onto a set or a studio is scope out spots like this where I can vanish when there's downtime. Billie calls me Diva because she thinks I think I'm too good to mingle with the rabble in the Green Room. It has nothing to do with that. If anything, it's the opposite. I've met some of the hugest stars in Hollywood in Green Rooms over the last seven months, and it's me who clearly doesn't belong.

It really has everything to do with just being Shiloh Luck for a few minutes, instead of the sixteen-year-old phenom who won *The Voice* last winter.

The concrete wall feels cool against my back and I drink it in. In about five minutes, I'll be roasting under the blaring stage lights. I close my eyes and lean back, letting the music from the stage vibrate through the wall into my bones. This is what it's all about, I remind myself. I wanted my life to be all about music, and now it is.

I guess I should feel lucky that it's been seven months and I seem to be building a fan base instead of seeing mine dwindle the way so many before me have. *The Voice* runs a winter and spring season and Billie says the spring winner, who was crowned the new Voice only a month ago, is already forgotten. She says I have staying power because I'm the most unique and talented winner to ever come out of *The Voice*.

I don't believe her.

The first two singles off my CD released in March and May, ahead of the launch of the full CD this month. Both hit the top ten on *Billboard's* charts and they've been holding. I'm the opening act for the North American leg of Roadkill's world tour, thanks to the record label I share with them. Considering they're the hottest thing out there right now, I should be over the fucking moon.

But the only track on my entire CD that I feel good about is the original song I sang in the finals of *The Voice*. My best friend Lilah has a gift for writing music that's amazing but not the same as everything that's already out there. It's the reason everyone's so convinced I'm unique. I gave the producer five more of my favorites of Lilah's, the ones we used to sing together in the BART stations of San Francisco. He rejected every single one. Instead, they gave me a bunch of vanilla fluff. Nothing stands out. Nothing is going to keep listeners coming back.

It's only a matter of time before people realize I'm nothing special and give up on me.

On the other side of the wall, Jimmy and Tro wrap up with flurry on the xylophone, triangle, and cowbells. A lingering kazoo hits the final note and I hear the crew cut to a break. They'll insert a commercial in this spot when they air the show tonight.

I pull my back off the wall and lean my forehead onto my bent knees.

One. Two. Three deep breaths, pumping myself up for what comes next. People I'm supposed to smile at. Questions I'm supposed to answer wittily. Hundreds of eyes on me that I'm not supposed to be affected by. No big deal that if I fuck up and say the wrong thing, game over.

"That bad?"

The deep male voice rumbles through me, smooth in the middle but rough all around the edges.

And close.

My eyes snap open and my gaze darts through the backstage gloom as a dark form materializes out of the shadows next to the stack of crates I'm sitting on. The red cherry of a lit cigarette glows a streak across the dim as he lifts it to his mouth and takes a long drag. As the glowing tip brightens, it illuminates a mass of dark curls that stick up at every angle and appear to only ever have been combed by the multitude of women's fists that have been twisted into them. Thick dark brows arch over deep-set eyes so intense I'm convinced I feel them burning a hole through mine. A slightly crooked nose leads my eyes to a square jaw covered in dark scruff, and a pair of firm red lips that are currently smirking at me.

Tro Gunnison.

I nearly fall off my crate. He's the guy every woman in the world wants to fuck right now. His nude *Rolling Stone* cover last fall made sure of that. He's outrageous in everything he does and notorious for the long list of celebrity hearts he's left broken in the two years since Roadkill exploded onto the music charts.

My eyes trail down the tattoos on his neck to the black T-shirt covering what I know is an incredible body. (Yes, I've seen the *Rolling Stone* cover.) But I catch my wits and pull my eyes away, refusing to give him the satisfaction of seeing me ogle. I've spent enough time around his type in the last few months to know that's what they get off on.

"If I said yes?"

He blows out a long stream of smoke and stalks around to the front of my crate, leaning his elbows onto it and staring up at me. "Then I'd be compelled to ask why."

"And if I told you it was none of your fucking business?" I challenge.

His mouth pulls into a crooked smile and a little bit of devil flashes in his dark eyes. "Then I'd think you're not only hot, but mysterious too."

A sudden whoosh of butterflies in my chest sends a rush through me that tightens my groin. I mentally crush them into dust because I'm not letting Tro Gunnison turn me into some swooning groupie. I'm way the fuck smarter than that. Growing up in the system means you grow up fast. I know how the game is played, which makes me hard to play. If I fuck him, it's going to be on my terms.

"Whatever," I say with a roll of my eyes.

"You'll be at the show tomorrow?" he asks, taking another drag off his cigarette. "I could get you backstage."

I feel my eyes start to widen with surprise and stop them. He doesn't know I'm his opener. Guess he's too fucking high and mighty to concern himself with the rabble and hangers on. But when I get past feeling a little pissed off, I realize something about him not recognizing me is liberating.

I lean back against the wall and decide to have some fun with it. "What show?"

He gives me a curious look—the same one I nearly gave him a minute ago. But then his eyes rake down my body and the corner of his mouth curves into that devilish smile again. "Better idea. What are you doing right now?"

I can hear them doing sound checks on the other side of the wall, which means they'll be ready to tape our segment in a few minutes. They'll be calling for us any second. "Working."

He drops his smoke and grinds it out with the heel of his biker boot, then pulls a pack of Dentyne Fire from his pocket and offers me the open end. I slide out a stick and fold it into my mouth.

He does the same then shoves the pack back into his pocket. "C'mon."

I slide to the edge of the crate. "Where we going?"

"Somewhere that's not here," he says, holding out his hand to me.

A wave of nostalgia makes me shudder. This feels like something me and Lilah would have done back in the day. I know it sounds backward, but I miss no one giving a shit about me. I miss doing whatever I wanted, whenever I wanted. Now that I'm everybody's paycheck, they monitor everything I do. Image is everything, after all.

I hop down and take his hand, feeling more than a little dangerous as he leads me toward a door at the back of the sound room. He glances over his shoulder at the crew scrambling around the fringes of the set before punching the panic bar.

"No alarm. That's good," he says, stepping through.

"Shiloh!" I hear Billie call from somewhere backstage. "You're on in three!"

Tro tows me through the door into a dimly lit storeroom without slowing down. Course, he has no clue that Billie was calling for *me*. Tro's supposed to be out there too for our segment, and if I didn't know he's probably going to catch more shit than me for this, I'd be shaking.

"What's your name?" he asks as he strides past racks of props and stage gear, my hand still in his.

"Lo."

"I'm Trotte." He glances back at me, where he's towing me along like a dingy. "Don't ask."

"Tell me about your name," I say with a smirk when he ducks behind the shelves in the back of the room.

He spins me up against the wall and pins me there by the upper arms. "I'll give you the whole story only if you trade me something for it."

"Trade you something…?" I repeat, wondering what I've gotten myself into.

He's not quite a foot taller than my five-foot-three and probably outweighs me by a hundred pounds, but I'm not afraid. I learned how to defend myself against perverts and creeps on the streets of San Francisco before I was ten. If he turns out to be one of those, he's going down.

He nods and lets go of my arms, but doesn't back away. "A story for a story. I want to know how someone as hot as you ended up a stage rat. They've got you hauling sound equipment or whatever when you should be on the other end of the camera."

"Why are you so sure I'm a stage rat?"

He shrugs and leans a shoulder into the wall next to me. "Who else would be hiding in the sound crates?"

"Someone who was trying to pull her shit together."

"Boyfriend shit?" he asks with a questioning raise of one dark eyebrow.

I shake my head. "Don't have time for that."

His wicked smile is back. "Knew I liked you."

"How? You've known me for thirty seconds."

"Call it a sixth sense," he says, leaning closer.

His breath feathers across my cheek and I force myself to keep my cool. I refuse to give him the reaction he's looking for. I'm sure he's shocked I haven't dropped to my knees and unzipped his jeans yet. "So, you knowing you like me before you have a single fucking clue what I'm all about has nothing to do with me being hot, then?"

"I never said that." He rolls off the wall and plants a hand on either side of my head. "You *are* scorching, by the way. Feel like I'm standing five inches from the fucking sun right now. But I also like your attitude. Most people wouldn't just walk out on their job because a stranger asked them to. Which means we must not be strangers."

I shove him away, ignoring how solid his biceps feel under my hands. "We are *definitely* strangers."

He shakes his head as a smile ghosts over his face. "I know your name, and that you're tough and tenacious and you know what you want and aren't afraid to do what it takes to get it."

"Why would you think that?" I ask, suddenly wary he really does know who I am and he's playing the same game with me that I am with him.

"Because you're young, but you've managed to land a job at one of the biggest studios in New York," he says with a shrug of his shoulder at the door we came through. "This is the big time, little girl."

"Tell me about your name and I'll tell you what I was doing backstage," I say.

He leans wearily against the wall next to me. "My mom was the hometown rodeo queen. Guess she thought Trotte was clever."

"You're a country boy?" I ask, my eyes raking over the open plaid button down hanging loose over a black T-shirt, torn black jeans, and black biker boots. "Never would have guessed."

"Nope," he says with a stiff shake of his head. "Left that behind years ago."

"Your family?" My heart lodges in my throat at the thought of having a family and walking away. "Why would you do that?"

His voice drops lower and something dark clouds his face. "Sometimes, family's not all it's cracked up to be."

"I wouldn't know," I say, my irritation coming through loud and clear. All these fucking people who bitch about their families just piss me off.

"You're better off." He leans a shoulder heavily against the wall. "Course, you end up with my gig," he adds, waving an arm at the door we came through, "every fucking person in the world wants to be your family."

He stops talking and his eyebrows shoot up when he realizes he just blew his cover.

"So why do you go by Tro?" I ask.

His smile turns skeptical. "You knew who I was this whole time."

It's not a question, so I don't answer.

His eyes flick over my face, catching for a moment on my lips. He licks his. "And here I thought we were connecting like normal people do."

"Huh," I say, scratching my head. "That's what we were doing? Connecting? 'Cause it felt more like hooking up."

"I'm all for hooking up, but…" His eyes darken as they lift to mine. "Yeah. Seemed like there might have been something clicking."

"You could tell that in thirty seconds?"

He leans closer and traps me in his gaze. "I could tell that in three."

"Shiloh!" Billie's frantic voice from the other side of the door shakes me out of his spell.

"Got to get back to work," I say, pushing past him. I round the corner of the shelves and march toward the door just as it opens.

"What the hell are you—" Billie's eyes widen when they shift over my shoulder, and that's how I know Tro is following me. I brush past her into the studio and she holds the door after I pass. "Mr. Gunnison," she says behind me. "I'm Billie Sinclair, Shiloh's manager."

She's still talking as I head for the set, but I don't slow down to listen.

The producer I met in the Green Room when we came in stops me at the stage curtain. "Thought we lost you," he says with a tight smile.

"Sorry," I say. "Was in the bathroom."

His smile softens. "It happens. That's the beauty of taping. We won't miss a beat when the show airs tonight." He holds his hand up over my shoulder just as I catch the scent of cinnamon. "Ready, Tro?"

"Yeah, Pete." Tro's thick hand knuckle bumps him from over my shoulder. "Good to go, man."

"Head on out and take the seat next to Jimmy's desk," Pete tells him, pulling a tissue from his pocket and holding it out. At first I'm confused, but when Tro deposits his gum into it, I do the same. "When Shiloh comes out, you move one seat to the right and she'll take the seat between you and Jimmy."

I look over my shoulder at Tro as Pete jump shots the tissue in the trash can in the corner. He gives me a shake of his head and that devil's smile. "Got it, boss."

He steps through the curtain and strides toward the indicated seat to squeals of "I want to have your babies, Tro!" from the girls in the audience.

The sound guys get both of us wired, and after a quick mic check, Pete says, "All set back here, Jimmy," into his headset.

Up front, Jimmy introduces me and Pete pulls open the curtain. I walk out and wave at the audience like I totally belong here. I ignore the applause and the girls still screaming for Tro. I ignore the hundreds of prying eyes just waiting for me to fuck up. I ignore the hottest man I've ever met, standing near Jimmy's desk, watching me with wolf's eyes. I might make him feel like he's standing five inches from the sun, but he's got his own gravitational pull. My heart pounds harder with every step closer to him I take.

His fingertips glide over my waist as he moves to the side and makes room for me to sit between him and Jimmy. I fight the shudder as I shake Jimmy's hand, then Tro's. We all settle into seats and it takes another minute for the stage managers, now holding up their "quiet" signs, to get the girls in the audience to stop their declarations of undying love for Tro.

Jimmy's first few questions are predictable, mostly about my path from orphan to recording phenom and how it's changed my life. They play of clip of me singing my final song on *The Voice* finale, then cut to the moment I won. I'm crying a little and my mascara is all running down my face.

I hate that clip.

The whole time, I can't help sneaking glances at Tro. I'm just now realizing his presence is impossible to ignore. His eyes are on the screen and his crooked smile is making my insides fizzle like a lit fuse. When his gaze slips to mine, it's like a nuclear bomb goes off in my chest.

The clip finishes and Jimmy looks past me to Tro. "So, what do you think about the whole *Voice* thing?"

The smoky timbre of Tro's chuckle causes a tingle to ripple up my spine and tightens my nipples. "I'm thinking about doing it just to get pointers from Adam Levine."

"We had Maroon 5 on earlier this season," Jimmy says. "So talented—like your opening act." He turns his gaze back to me. "Your first single, the one we just heard a snippet of from the finals of *The Voice*, spent seventeen weeks in Billboard's top ten, and everything you've released since has debuted in the top five. That's got to be pretty exciting."

I want to sound all kickass and confident, but I hate those last two singles. Course, I can't say that without pissing off everyone at my label, so I nod. "My whole team has been really amazing, and Universal's done a great job with promotion, so…"

God, that was a stupid answer.

"But I'm nothing like Roadkill," I add to deflect the attention from me. "Their first CD went double platinum in like a week."

"Uh-uh," Tro says with a shake of his head. "Our first CD was recorded in the basement of a crack house in Louisiana when I was seventeen. No one's ever heard that 'cept a few drunks at the seedy bars we played who we persuaded to part with ten bucks. That was Roadkill's first three years."

"You mean, this one?" Jimmy says, and when I turn to him, he's holding up a CD with a picture of three mangy guys on the cover. The one in the middle is a much younger Tro. He's probably close to my age in that picture.

"Well, fuck me," Tro says with a shake of his head. "Where'd you find that?"

"Apparently, one of those drunks was selling it on eBay," Jimmy answers with a grin. "There's not a whole lot we can play off this, but here's a clip of the title track."

The music's mostly drums and bass but Tro's voice is no less incredible. He slouches back and scratches his nose as the clip finishes. "Wow…"

"That was something, all right," Jimmy says, tapping his finger on the CD case.

"Something that should be put out of its misery and buried in the back yard," Tro says with a shake of his head.

"It wasn't horrible," I say, and Tro's eyes snap to mine. "I mean, with a remix and a decent guitar line, that could be really good."

Tro leans his elbow onto the arm of my chair and raises an eyebrow. "Maybe you can help me with that."

"An original duet," Jimmy says with a grin.

At the word duet, my stomach cramps. My head's already shaking when I say, "Not gonna happen," at the same time as Tro says, "You bet your sweet ass."

Jimmy grins. "This should be quite the tour."

Tro smiles at me again—this cocky, crooked thing that should not be causing everything between my legs to ache. "I just met her for the first time backstage, but there's definite chemistry. We're going to crush it on tour for the next nine weeks..." He reaches for my hand and I'm so shocked when he scoops it off my knee that I don't have the presence of mind to pull it out of his grasp. "...and get to know each other a whole lot better."

Jimmy looks at our hands and raises his eyebrows at Tro. "Careful there, Tro. You might not want to rock that cradle too hard, if you catch my meaning."

CHAPTER 3

Tro

It takes me a sec to get what Jimmy's saying, and the instant it clicks my gut tightens. But I keep the shock off my face. Always. Cool as a fucking cucumber.

But this chick I'm all hard for is under-fucking-age.

Fuck.

I look at her again and there's nothing innocent about her. She's tiny, but totally fuckable: all legs and curves topped with a heart shaped face and flawless skin the color of caramel. Her shiny red lips are wearing a smirk that makes my cock take notice, and there's a demon with all kinds of depraved ideas shining out through whiskey-colored eyes that don't miss much.

A fucking succubus.

But she's just a kid.

I feel the southern gentleman that I've spent the last six years burying beneath countless women and truckloads of booze tugging at my gut. But I didn't get where I am by doing the right thing. I got here by doing exactly what I wanted, and the more outrageous the better. The supermarket rags call me player, man-whore, lady killer. Industry rags call me rebel, pioneer, visionary. They all think I'm some kind of genius and I'm good with that. The only one who's ever called me shit-for-brains is my old man.

"Guess I'll just have to wait till the tour hits Kentucky then," I say with a wink.

"Or until hell freezes over," comes one of the sexiest voices I've ever heard. It's all gravel and fire. My cock, which has been hard as a fucking rock since I had her pressed up against the storeroom wall, threatens to bust clean through the zipper of my ripped jeans.

The truth is, I don't pay much attention to the supermarket rags, or any of the rest of it, which is why I didn't know this little succubus was my tour opener. But I can't say I'm disappointed. How did they introduce her? Shiloh Luck? Then I plan on spending the next two months before we leave our U.S. opener behind and head to Europe getting Lucky.

"We'll see," I say directly to her, ignoring the audience's blend of gasps and snickers.

"Hey Pete!" Jimmy calls toward backstage. "Can we get someone to change the marquis on the street to *The Dating Game*?"

There's a drum roll from the band, but I don't let Lucky's eyes go. She doesn't melt under my gaze the way every other woman before her has. She holds my eyes, and if anything, hers harden and become more determined.

"No," she says defiantly. "*You'll* see. *We* aren't doing anything."

I send her every watt of my charm. "Nine weeks is a long time, Lucky."

"Take us through the schedule," Jimmy says to Lucky, bringing me back to the room. I'd been so lost in those whiskey eyes I'd forgotten where we were.

She blinks as if to clear her head then takes him through the next week of shows. I'm so wrapped up in watching her mouth, the way it puckers on certain words, and the way just the tip of her pink tongue slips over her lower lip with others, that I don't hear a word she says.

"Well," Jimmy says, "this is going to be an explosive tour, that much is clear."

"We're going to blow it off the hinges," I say as Lucky's scorching gaze burns a hole through me.

Jimmy turns to the audience. "Be sure to look for Tro Gunnison and Roadkill, featuring *The Voice* winner, Shiloh Luck in a city near you this summer. Stick around. We'll be back after the break with Channing Tatum.

They cut, and before Jimmy can even stand and hold out his hand for a shake, Lucky is gone. She storms off the stage the way we came in.

"Guess she's a little pissed," I tell Jimmy as I shake his hand.

His eyebrows go up. "You think?"

"Thanks, man. And send me a link to that schoolroom tape." I grin. "Might want to take some of that shit on the road."

I head backstage and poke my head into the Green Room. There's some actor I've seen in some stuff back there with his entourage, but no Lucky.

"Great take, Tro."

I turn and find Pete coming up the hall toward me. "Yeah, thanks," I say, looking over his shoulder toward the elevators.

"Can we get you back here after your next release?" he asks.

"Sure, man," I say, taking his outstretched hand and shaking. "Hey, you know where Lucky went?"

He cracks a grin. "Lucky?"

"Yeah, the girl who's—"

"I know who you mean, dude, and she slammed out the door and was on an elevator less than a second after we cut."

"Guess I might have pissed her off a little."

He cracks up. "A little maybe."

I turn for the elevators and give him a wave over my shoulder. "Guess I'll just have to find a way to make it up to her."

The one I'm thinking of at the moment involves pinning her up against a backstage wall again. And with just the thought, I'm hard as stone for her.

I can't even remember the last time I had blue balls, but fucking Lucky is giving me the worst case I've ever had, and we just fucking met.

CHAPTER 4

Shiloh

I yank open the door to the waiting limo and dive in the back before the driver can even react. I find out Billie is right behind me when I start to slam the door and it jerks out of my grasp.

"Well, that was a nice little temper tantrum," she scolds. "You over it now?"

I press into the seat and fold my arms over my chest. "He totally humiliated me."

She turns to the driver, who's now standing behind her in the door. "Take us back to the hotel, please." She shoves me over and slides in next to me. "He's just trying to get into your head so you don't upstage him on tour. Marking his territory, like peeing on a fire hydrant."

"And I'm the hydrant in this scenario?" I ask with a glare.

She gives me an exasperated look. "My point is, just treat him like a big, stupid dog. He's doing it to get a rise out of you. If you don't react, he'll stop."

"That was *The Tonight Show*!" I say with a fling of my hand at Rockefeller Center as we pull onto the street. "How many people watch that? Thousands? Hundreds of thousands? And that douche made me look like an idiot."

"You were fine, Shiloh," she says, looping her arm over my shoulders and tugging me close. "But in this business, you're going to have to grow a thicker skin. So far you're a media darling, but at some point, people are going to start criticizing. If you show weakness, they go for the jugular and it becomes a feeding frenzy. Whether it's someone like Tro Gunnison, who's just looking for publicity, or some other artist who's jealous of your success, or your producers who aren't with you artistically, or the media just looking for a story, you have to learn to let the jabs and criticism roll off and don't take the negative to heart."

I tip my head back and grind my teeth. "I hate him."

She presses her lips to my temple. "Guess you're not over that tantrum after all."

I don't move except to settle into her a little. We weave our slow way through New York City traffic. It's only a few blocks to the hotel, but it takes forever.

"What would you think if I filed for legal guardianship?" Billie asks as we sit at a light.

Her words send a jolt of…what? Panic? Not exactly. But not excitement either.

Hope. Her words send a jolt of hope through me that makes me feel like I'm going to throw up.

When I was little, I used to fantasize that my mom would come for me. I used to waste hours imaging our happy reunion and how we'd leave San Francisco and live in a white house with a big yard and have a dog. I think I got that from watching too much Nickelodeon.

I thought I was too old for that stupid fantasy now.

"Why would you want to do that?" I ask without looking at her.

She peels me off, though I now seem to have a death grip on her, and looks into my eyes. "You don't want me to?"

I breathe deeply when I realized I've stopped. I'm long past thinking there's any chance my real mom is coming for me, and Billie's the closest thing I've ever had. She's been fair and I know she cares about me.

"It's just something I've been thinking about for a while," she says when I don't answer. "You're still a minor, and a ward of the state. There are a lot of moving parts in this business and it just seems like it would un-complicate things if you had someone other than the State of California who was legally responsible for you." She pulls me back to her side and says, her lips against my temple, "And if I could have picked a daughter, it would have been you."

The ice in my heart melts a little and my suspicion melts with it. "Remember it's me you're dealing with. You may regret it."

I feel her head shake slightly against mine. "Never. Now let's go celebrate the start of an incredible career!"

#

Billie's been in the bathroom throwing up all night. A bad scallop in the Coquilles Saint Jacques at the swanky French restaurant we went to after *The Tonight Show* taping, she thinks. But that's not what's keeping me awake. How are you supposed to sleep when the biggest thing that's ever happened to you is about to happen?

Madison Square Garden. Sold out. I know they're all coming to see Roadkill, but still.

At the thought of his band, a pair of wolfish eyes stalk into my mind.

Tro fucking Gunnison.

He's like that bad scallop you can't get rid of no matter how many times you puke. I haven't been able to shake him out of my head.

I know Billie's right. This is what he wants, to get under my skin. I hate myself for letting him. And the truth is, I never have to see him again. I open for him. There's at least twenty minutes between my act and his while the roadies break down our equipment and set up Roadkill's. Once we're out of New York City, Billie's contracted a tour bus for us, so after our set, I can escape to my own space. I'll be long gone before Tro fucking Gunnison ever graces the audience with his presence.

But something about running and hiding rubs me the wrong way. It's not in my DNA. I grew up on the streets of San Francisco, the castoff daughter of two junkies. Tro is nothing compared to what I had to deal with out there. But unless I want this tour to blow up in my face, it's probably the best strategy.

The clock says three AM when I glance at it. I shove the sheets aside and grab my guitar on the way to the balcony.

Billie rolls to look at me. "I'm so sorry, sweetie. I should have gotten my own room. This just hit me out of the blue."

"It's not you," I tell her. "I wouldn't be sleeping anyway."

She pulls herself up to sit against the headboard. "Nervous?"

"A huge stadium full of Roadkill fans?" I say, hugging the guitar to my chest. "What have I got to be nervous about?"

She bunches her pillow under her head. "You're going to win them over, kiddo. I know it."

"What if they boo and start throwing shit? You know Tro's girls have done that to openers before."

She swings to sit on the edge of the bed. "They're going to love you," she says, but her face looks anything but sure. A second later, she's running for the bathroom again.

While she wretches over the toilet bowl, I slip out the glass door onto the balcony. New York isn't like San Francisco. Even in early June, the night air is heavy and thick. I set my guitar on the small glass table and go to the rail.

We're a few blocks away, and I'm pretty sure our room faces the wrong way, so I can't see Madison Square Garden, but I know it's out there. I remember thinking on the night of *The Voice* finals that nothing could ever top it—that everything depended on winning. Now I know that was only the beginning.

Everything depends on everything.

Everything I ever wanted is balancing on a tightrope and there is no safety net. Every interview has to be kickass. Every move I make, perfect. Every outfit, daring. Every hairstyle, classy. Everybody has to love me because the bottom line is that every record has to sell. One wrong turn, one false move, and show over. And the only thing waiting for me then is the streets where I started. After having everything, I don't want to go back to nothing.

So I'll toe the line; avoid Tro Gunnison and sing my ass off.

I'll make them love me.

I lower myself into one of the two chairs and pull my guitar into my lap. I close my eyes and, in my mind, I go back to the BART stations of San Francisco. Music starts in my head, and I finger the melody of Lilah's songs out on my guitar. I feel my only real friend at my side, hear her hum out the harmony to the music she wrote. Then I open my mouth and sing quietly to myself. I need to settle my nerves and this is the only thing that calms me down when I'm this wired. I let myself go home, where I was never really safe, but at least I knew what was what.

Because here, I'm totally lost.

CHAPTER 5

Tro

I've seen hot. Hot girls throw themselves at me on a daily basis. All the fucking time. Case in point: the blonde under my left arm and the redhead under my right.

Our road parties have gotten smaller over the last year, mostly because it got too expensive to reimburse the hotel for all the damage, so now it's just the band, some of the backline guys, our closest friends, and a dozen or so handpicked girls.

We're in the city, so the lot is hotter than average. These two are scorching.

But the face I can't shake from my head isn't just hot, it's different—heart-shaped with wide-set whiskey eyes, smooth caramel skin, full red lips. Lucky's heat is more than skin deep. It comes from inside and radiates for miles, like a nuclear reactor ready to blow.

No matter how much I want to focus on the blonde's fingers, dancing over the zipper of my jeans, or the redhead's tongue in my ear, all I can think about is that girl.

I'm not going to fuck her—partly because we have to work together and partly because she's just a kid—but I can't help fucking *with* her.

From my drummer Jamie's Bose speaker across the room, Eddie Van Halen launches into a guitar riff that has me about an inch from coming. Grim, my bassist, cranks the volume, then starts on air guitar, like any of us could touch the great Eddie.

Grim is the oldest of us by far, probably pushing forty. Years of hard living show in lines around his eyes and deep creases across his forehead. Living large the last few years has tacked a beer gut onto the package. But none of that has slowed him down. His long blond hair is thinner on top than when I first met him six years ago, but he's still a chick magnet...as evidenced by the three twenty-something girls who are instantly on their feet, dancing with him. I crack a smile when he drains his beer, then grabs one of them by the ass.

Truth is, Grim is the reason I'm here. His real name is Jim Grimsby and he and some guys he was playing random gigs with came into the diner I was washing dishes in when I'd first left home. He looked badass and the waitress I was fucking at the time told me he was a local legend, mostly for raising hell. I was seventeen, on the run, sleeping in my broken-down car, and had exactly nothing to lose, so I figured what the hell. Walked right up to their table, told him I played kickass guitar wrote shit too. Told him he needed me in his band. Turns out, he was getting ready to dump the others anyway. Asked what I had for original stuff. Took me back to his place and we jammed a little in his garage. I moved in with him, his girlfriend, and their kid the next week. We stole Jamie from a rival band because he's an animal on the drums, got fucked up every night and played our asses off, got some bar gigs, and that was the start of Roadkill.

The blonde at my side gets up and starts dancing, all hips and hands. The redhead stands and slinks over, pressing up against the blonde and grinding to the pounding rhythm.

Jamie whistles appreciatively at them from across the room, then staggers over and drops his mile-tall frame onto the couch next to me. He rubs a hand over his shaved head and slumps into the cushions, so totally baked his eyes are barely slits. "Dude, you gonna tap that?" he asks with a nod at the girls. "Because, fuuuuck…" He drawls the word out as his head lolls back onto the couch and he closes his bloodshot eyes.

I watch through my buzz as they dance together, and they're keeping my interest, but just barely. Until they start making out. "Yeah, I'm gonna tap that."

He leans forward and does one of the lines off the coffee table in front of me.

"I was saving that," I say, shoving him. "Pacing myself."

He shrugs and slumps back into the cushions. "Snooze, lose." When the redhead starts unbuttoning the blonde's shirt, a lazy grin splits his face and he holds up his fist for a bump. "Fuck, man, I love fucking New York."

I bump him and he watches for another minute, then hauls all six and a half feet of himself up and starts grinding against the backside of one of the girls that Grim left behind. She spins, ready to be pissed, but when she sees who it is, she smiles suggestively and starts dancing with him.

I turn my attention back to the show in front of me as, little by little, the clothes start coming off. The girls' hands and mouths are all over each other as they dance for me, and it's pretty fucking hot. When they're down to thongs, they come for me. I let them drag me off the couch. The guys catcall behind us as they pull me through the bedroom door of the honeymoon suite we booked for the weekend. Grim and Jamie's rooms are adjoining.

The whole thing goes on for an hour or so, and I lose track of who's doing what to who. When they're done with me, they both pass out on the bed. I untwist myself and I yank on my jeans, because I need a fucking smoke. I find my pack on the dresser and stagger onto the balcony.

It's three in the morning, but this city is never quiet. The muggy New York night presses down on me as the rush of traffic and blare of horns wafts up the eleven stories to where I lean against the glass door, staring over the city. And then something else wafts up from below. The quiet chords of an acoustic guitar.

It's so faint I have to strain against the noise of the city to hear it. I move to the edge of the balcony in the direction it seems to be coming from. A floor below and to my right, a girl sits on a balcony, her white T-shirt glowing against the smooth brown skin of a pair of endless legs, propped on the rail in front of her. I lean a little more to get a better look, and when she opens her mouth and starts to sing, my suspicion is confirmed.

Lucky.

I know her by voice because, after I left the taping at Rockefeller Center, I looked her up online. She grew up in foster care in San Francisco, dropped out of high school last year to be on *The Voice*, but plans to finish when her schedule slows down. She gives her best friend, Lilah Morgan, all the credit for her success, and has her seventeenth birthday coming up in a month. I also pulled her up on YouTube. I spent hours listening to every track that was posted: everything from the covers she sang when she was competing on *The Voice* to newer vids from her original CD.

She's pretty damn incredible.

But what she's singing now is nothing I heard in any of those tracks. I listen closer.

The guitar line is simple but not dull and the lyrics are synced to the backbeat. I can't make out all the words because she's murmuring, trying to be quiet, no doubt, but the melody seeps through my ears, into my bones, and settles there, causing me to shudder despite the muggy heat.

It's been a long time since music did that for me. This girl has something real.

I slide to my ass, my back propped against the glass door, and take a long drag off my smoke, feeling that silky voice of hers saturate every cell in my body along with the nicotine. She's still playing two hours later when the horizon starts to pink with the new day, and I'm still listening. Finally, the music stops. I drag my ass up and find out it's numb. When I look over the rail I find Lucky's balcony is empty, and I can't deny the disappointment that sinks like a stone in my gut.

I duck back into the room and find the girls are thankfully gone. The living room is quiet, so the party's apparently over. I drop into bed with the echo of Lucky in my mind, but while I drift off, the tune changes as the bones of a new song takes shape in my mind.

#

I never come to hear the opener. After the sound check, I usually don't show up on stage again until Jamie starts pounding out the intro to our first song on the bass drum. But tonight, I left Grim and Jamie drinking in the on-site dressing room and I'm standing in the shadows near the soundboard. I brought a few beers to keep my stage buzz on, and I drain the first as I watch Lucky wrap her second song.

She's got lead guitar and there are three guys backing her up: a bassist, drummer, and one who switches between keyboard and rhythm guitar. Her coppery kinks are up in a bushy ponytail near the top of her head and her getup is simple: a black tank top with an open men's white button-down shirt knotted at her waist, a short camo skirt, and a pair of black boots with spiky silver heels that look more like a weapon than footwear. Classy, but smokin' hot.

But, honestly, the music is nothing special—nothing I haven't heard a thousand times before from a thousand different artists. Even the lyrics are pretty pedestrian. What's crushing it is her performance. I move to the edge of the stage-side scaffolding that holds up the rigging and glance out at the crowd. The seats are only about half full, which is not unusual for the opener. But the people who are here are engaged. Many of them are on their feet, dancing in the rows and in the pit. They see what I see—for someone so tiny, Lucky's stage presence is immense. She's impossible to ignore. She plays like the guitar is an extension of herself, like she *is* the music.

I watch her move as I stand in the wings, reminding myself that she hasn't even turned seventeen yet. She's just a baby. But, fuck, she doesn't look like one—or act like one. I know firsthand that some kids grow up faster than others. I was only a few months older than Lucky when everything went down with my old man and I found myself on the run. I grew up in a matter of days. From what I read in her bio, there's no doubt this kid was looking out for herself from a very young age. From all outward appearances, not only did she grow up faster than me, but she's surpassed my twenty-three years by a few.

And one thing I know, watching her live: with the right songwriting and the right guys backing her up, she'd be unstoppable.

I glance around the stage at her band. I don't recognize a single one of these guys. I guess that's not surprising, since I've gone out of my way to distance myself from the whole music scene, but these guys are pretty green, mostly just chunking out guitar chords. Seems like there are a few veterans they could have tapped for this gig who'd at least be trying to keep up with Lucky. And whoever's writing for her has never had a creative or original thought in their lives. Her fucking producers aren't doing her any favors. They're obviously banking on her talent to do all the heavy lifting.

When I glance at the bassist, a tall, skinny Asian guy with hair all down his face like he thinks he's some anime character, I find him looking at me, and there's not the awe in his expression that I usually get from noobs. I'm having a hard time deciding what I'm seeing there, so he makes it clear for me when he moves closer to Lucky and presses his shoulder into hers as they play. Lucky smiles at him and it's like a boot to my gut.

Fuck, am I jealous of this kid?

I shake my head at myself and back toward the soundboard, but before I make the shadows, Lucky spins and sees me. I know she's a pro when I catch the expression on her face, something straddling anger and surprise, but there's no hitch in her voice or her guitar. I send her a salute and, now that I've been discovered, I cross my arms and lean against the scaffolding instead of tucking into the gloom.

For the rest of her set she shoots me furtive glances as she sings and my grin grows every fucking time. She's feeling me. By the time she intros her final song, "More Than Nothing," the house is nearly full. Some in the crowd are still finding seats, but when she hits the first guitar chords of the song I recognize from the tape I watched of *The Voice* finals, a roar goes up from the audience. The energy on the stage and in the arena turns electric, and where Lucky was killing it with the crap she was singing before, now she's stepped it up to a whole new level. The place is wired and everyone's moving. In about three seconds flat, she's got eighteen thousand people on their feet. They may have come here for Roadkill, but she's got them wrapped around her little finger.

I glance at her bass player, who's actually almost doing this song justice for a change, and find him full-on glaring at me now. He sidles up to Lucky and she presses her back against his as they play. When he turns and dips his face into the hair on top of her head, I'm about an inch from going out there and ripping him off her. But she shrugs off him and starts moving toward the edge of the stage, playing to her audience.

Lucky. How did this girl get so deep under my skin in one day?

I think back to yesterday, what it was about her that caught my attention backstage. She was curled up on the sound crates, her forehead on her knees. I couldn't even see her face, but something about her grabbed at my nuts.

Or was it my heart?

Do I even have one of those?

When she lifted her head, there was something in her expression...some mix of deep sadness and helplessness that is so opposite from every vibe she sends when she's out in the world. All her insecurities were right there on the surface. She looked so fucking vulnerable.

I wanted to help her.

But then she started with the sass and my focus took a whole new direction—went straight to my dick.

But at the root, that's what it is...the reason I feel so invested. There's no fucking question I want her, but more, I want to protect her from this world.

My world.

Me. And all the assholes just like me. Which is every fucking guy in this business, from the frontline all the way down to the riggers.

When I was her age, I'd just left home. Not too long later, I was on the road with Grim, playing seedy bars and fucking seedy women. Grim's a decent guy, but I was never anything other than an investment to him—the thing he thought was going to make him rich. The fact that he turned out to be right doesn't change the other fact. He was never really looking out for me.

No one was.

In my rational mind, I know Lucky's not alone, but does anyone really have her back? Her manager is looking out for her career, but that's because Lucky is her meal ticket. I glare out at the stage. Her band wants to fuck her and her producers would fuck her over in a New York second if it'd make them a profit.

She's like I was, wandering in the jungle without a gun. And, fuck, there were times I could have used a gun.

I take a deep breath and shove myself off the scaffolding. That's what I'm going to be for Lucky: the gun I never had.

Now I just have to figure out a way to stop wanting to fuck her senseless.

They hit their final notes to a plume of smoke from the pyro canisters and a flurry of the colored stage lighting. The crowd roars as the stage goes dark. When the lights come up a few seconds later, Lucky is just standing there, staring at the ocean of people on their feet for her. Finally, she slams her guitar in the stand and takes a lap along the edge of the stage, waving to the cheering throng. People are tossing flowers and teddy bears, and she scoops a bouquet up as she jogs toward stage left, where I'm waiting for her. Just as she reaches the wings, but before she gets to me, the bass player grabs her by the waist and pulls her into a full body hug.

"You fucking slayed them!" he yells over the roar of applause that follows them offstage.

"Thanks. You were awesome." She must know that's a lie, but she gives him a hug and a smile anyway. He tries to plant one on her, but she turns her head and his mouth lands on her cheek. The house lights come up as the roadies start pushing past them onto the stage and Lucky pulls loose from his grasp. He's slow to let her go.

"Come back to the bus and party with us," he says, still holding her arm. There's an air of desperation in his request that's pretty obvious and totally pathetic.

"Billie's got a car waiting for me," she says, backing away. I bristle, wondering who Billie is, until I remember her manager introducing herself yesterday. I feel my bunched shoulders drop from around my ears...until Lucky adds, "But I'll try to stop by for a minute."

Her smile vanishes as she turns toward me.

"What are you doing here?" she asks, her expression all suspicion.

Behind her, Max stands his ground for a minute, glaring me down, before the drummer chest bumps him and they both take off.

"Working," I say with a smirk, echoing her response from yesterday.

Her eyes roll.

"Besides, wanted to hear what you got," I confess with a nod at the stage.

"And?" A shadow of doubt passes over her face and it hits me: she actually cares what I think.

"I think the writing blows, but your performance saved it."

"Not everyone can be the infallible Tro Gunnison," she spits, her eyes narrowing, and I realize she didn't take that as the compliment it was meant to be.

I hold my hands up in surrender. "I only meant that you've got something pretty incredible going on out there," I say with a nudge of my chin at where the roadies are tearing down her band's gear. "With the right material, you're looking at world domination."

Her face changes, softens a little, then pulls into a deep cringe as she lowers her gaze. "You're right. It sucks."

"All but that last piece." I reach behind me and grab the two beers sitting on the crate there. I twist the cap off one and hand it to her—a peace offering.

She takes it and her eyes lift to mine again. "I'm screwed."

I shake my head as I crack open my beer and take a long swallow. "Not if you find someone who can write."

She throws her free hand in the air in frustration. "But that's the thing! I *have* someone who can write. That last song, the one that won *The Voice*, was written by my best friend. I've got a whole bunch more of hers that they rejected." She flings a scowl at the stage. "They gave me all that fluff instead."

The second she says it, I get what's going on. "You're young and hot," I say, and can't help my eyes from roaming over that incredible body. "They're trying to brand you pop because they think that's your audience, but you're really a rocker."

She chugs half her beer and turns back to me. "So, what do I do?"

I take a deep breath. "You're in a tough spot. What are your contract terms? Do they have you under contract for another studio album, or was that it?"

"Just that for now, but my manager's negotiating for more."

"Tell her to stop," I say. "You need to find a label that's on the same page creatively."

She takes another sip of beer. "What if no one else wants to sign me?"

I give her a slow shake of my head. "That's not going to happen."

Her eyes narrow. "You can't know that."

"I can," I say, draining my beer.

She gives me a skeptical raise of her eyebrows. "Really."

"Really."

"How?"

I shrug a shoulder. "I know some people."

Her gaze grows suspicious again, but before she can say anything, two immense hands come crashing down on my shoulders from behind.

"Gunner!" Jamie bellows, and the next second he's climbing all up my back. "Introduce me." Before I can get a word out of my mouth, he's pushed past me and is sticking his hand out toward Lucky. "I'm Jamie Harris."

Lucky stares up at him from over a foot below as his hand swallows hers. "Shiloh Luck."

"Christ, I know!" he says, pumping her arm manically. "You crushed it on *The Voice* last fall."

She squints at their hands, obviously a little uncomfortable that the handshake hasn't ended yet. "You watched that?"

"Hell, yeah," he says. "I fucking bought all your shit on iTunes so you'd get the vote bump."

"Thanks," she says, and I can see her wondering if she's ever going to get her hand back.

"Hey, Jamie," I interject into his fangirl moment. "I think you're creeping Lucky out."

His eyes grow wide and his grin wider as he stops shaking, but he doesn't let go of her hand. "Sorry. Just love your shit."

A full beer bottle cracks up against the side of Jamie's head and seems to knock some sense into him. He lets Lucky go and looks over his shoulder.

Grim is standing there, extending an arm toward both of us, a beer in each hand. "Showtime, fuckers."

I yank the beer out of his hand and glance toward the stage. The roadies are just clearing, which means we're up.

"You staying?" I ask Lucky.

She gives a vague wave toward the backstage entrance. "Billie's waiting for me."

"And Max," I say with more rancor than I intended.

Her eyes narrow.

Not sure whether that look means she's not interested, or that it's none of my business, and I don't get a chance to ask because the sound guys scramble over to get Grim, Jamie, and I wired. I take a long swallow of my beer then thrust it into Lucky's hand as the house and stage lights are doused and the crowd roars. Grim grabs Jamie and me by the scruff and huddles us up.

"You know what they're fucking here for!" he shouts. "You know what they fucking want! So let's go out there and fucking give it to them!"

We growl, then charge onto the stage.

The stage lights flash as Jamie's drums lead us into our opening song—the title single off our new CD. The crowd roars, then everyone stands and sings along. When we wrap with a flash of pyrotechnics, I glance into the wings and see Lucky is still there.

There's a crackle of electricity through my gut as my dick stirs. Despite my revelation in the wings earlier, my body hasn't quite caught up to the new agenda. Even if it had, this is the stage. Free flowing testosterone. I never hold back here. My audience would know if I did.

"New York!" I shout into the mic.

There's a deafening roar from the crowd in response.

I rip my shirt off and throw it into the pit. "We fucking love ya!"

It takes them fucking forever to quiet down.

"We're kicking off our world tour here and I wouldn't want it any other way. This is gonna be our best tour yet! And it only gets better because we've got a fucking opener that blows the fucking doors off! What'd y'all think of *Lucky*!" I shout, flinging an arm at stage left, where she's standing behind the curtain.

Another roar.

"Did she make you wanna sing?" I yell.

"Yeah!" the crowd roars.

I jump up and down on the balls of his my feet. "Did she make you wanna dance?"

"Yeah!"

"Did she make you wanna party?" I shout with a fist pump in the air.

"Yeah!" they answer.

I look Lucky's way as the stage rush crackles through me. "Did she make you wanna…" I grab my package and grind my hips in a circle as I growl into the mic. "I fucking know who I'm gonna be doing tonight!"

Her face goes slack in disbelief as screams of "Fuck me, Tro!" and "I love you!" erupt from the girls in the pit up front. As the disbelief in her expression slowly morphs to blind fury, I feel a twist in the deepest part of my chest, but I don't back down. I've got a strategy. I started the ball rolling on national television with Jimmy yesterday, so I'm just giving in a shove to keep it moving. If every other prick out there thinks I've laid claim to Lucky, they're more likely to back off.

"I've got something for you tonight that no one's ever heard." I strum my guitar with the chords I jotted down this morning, going totally off book.

When I'm writing, I know I'm onto something fucking amazing when I feel the buzz of current start to crackle through my chest. It builds as I write until I'm on fire with it. The first time I play the whole song out loud, it's like the discharge of lightning, totally electric.

I don't feel any of that now.

This isn't amazing. This is me needing to fucking vent all this pent up frustration.

I turn to the wings and stare directly at Lucky. "There's been this girl in my head and all up under my skin. While I was mid-fantasy last night, this little ditty came to me, so I wrote it down. Called 'Getting Lucky.' Only got the first coupla verses so far, but I hope you like it."

CHAPTER 6

Shiloh

I realize he's serious and this isn't part of their set list when Grim and Jamie shoot each other a baffled look. Tro starts strumming out something with their signature hard downbeat. Jamie picks up the rhythm on the drum and Grim slides in with a simple bass line.

Tro shoots me a shit-eating grin and starts singing, but it's rappier than anything else I've heard of theirs.

"Wouldn't care if I could. I'm up to no good.
Taking what I want instead of what I should.
I'm made of pure greed. There's shit that I need.
The mask is off and the demon's freed."

He stalks toward me slowly as he sings, and I listen to him tell the audience about all the depraved things he wants to do to me. When he reaches the edge of the stage, I expect him to stop, but he doesn't. He keeps coming, playing and singing, but eating me alive with his eyes. I stumble backward when it becomes clear he's not stopping until he's on me, but only end up trapped in the crates. He moves slowly forward until he's only inches from me and locks me in his gaze.

"I'm gonna get drunk.
I'm gonna get played.
I'm gonna get rich.
I'm gonna get laid.

And I'm gonna get Lucky."

"Pull it together," I hiss, shoving him away and glaring death at him.

He slowly backs toward the stage as he starts in on the second verse, but he hasn't stopped fucking me with his eyes.

I shift deeper into the shadows, but I don't leave, partly because I want to know what he wrote about me and partly because watching Tro out there is sort of like watching a slow motion train wreck. I can't believe he's doing this but I can't look away. Finally, when he finishes, I cut him a glare and spin for the backstage exit. Just before I explode out the door, I hear him bellow, "Let's tear this place down, New York!"

The walls shake as they hit the first note to their next song, and Tro's voice follows me as I weave my way through the maze of hallways.

God, I hate him.

He could have plugged my music, or said something good about my performance, but instead, he basically just told the whole world how all I am to him is a tight piece of ass.

I'm not some stupid groupie he can fuck and throw away.

After a moment of panic that, in my blind rage, I've gotten myself totally lost, I finally stumble on the door I came in. In the lot out back, near the roadies' buses, I find the driver who brought me here waiting at his big black car.

He opens the door and I'm just about to fling myself into the back when I look down the row of buses and remember I told Max I'd stop in.

"I'll be right back," I tell the driver, then work my way from bus to bus, trying to figure out which one belongs to my band mates. Our roadies are busy loading equipment into the bays of three of the seven buses, but inside most of them are quiet. Near the end, I hear muted music, and as I get closer, I see the lights are on and the whole bus is sort of rocking. The door is open, so I climb the stairs and find at least a dozen people, mostly girls, crammed into a lounge area and kitchen just behind the driver's seat.

It's a little awkward because I don't really know any of these guys. Recording studio tracks isn't how most people think. We never really played together as a band. The studio had us all lay down our tracks separately, so we only came together a few times near the end to tweak anything that wasn't exactly right. The longest I've actually spent with the band was a few days last week at the rehearsal studio while the sound guys sorted out everything for the shows.

The first familiar face I see is a round, freckled one with a glowing carrot top. My drummer, Chipper.

"Hey! You made it." Chipper flips open the cupboard above the kitchen sink. "What's your beverage?"

There are rows of bottles, everything from Absolut to Jim Beam. I nod to the beer in his hand. "You got any more of those?"

"On it," he says with a grin, turning for the fridge.

I don't really know how old any of the guys are— somewhere in their twenties, if I had to guess—but I'm pretty sure Chipper is the oldest. He seems to know the ropes, like he's done this before. He grabs a beer off the top shelf and hands it to me.

"Bottoms up!" he says, cracking his bottle against mine and drinking.

I crack open the bottle and take a long drink while I try to think of something to say.

"Thought everything went pretty well tonight," he says, clearly feeling as awkward as me.

I nod. "You guys were awesome. Thanks."

A girl comes up behind him and loops her arms around his neck. She says something in his ear that I can't hear over the music and he turns and smiles at her. "So, help yourself to whatever," he says before turning and following her toward the back of the lounge. They disappear through the door that looks like it leads to the sleeping bunks, but beyond the bunks I see there's another lounge and I catch just a glimpse of Max before the door closes.

I weave my way through the sweaty bodies toward the door and follow Chipper through. There are couples in various stages of undress going at it in a few of the bunks, and I see Chipper is already one of them. I move straight through and push out the door in the back. When I emerge into the rear lounge, I notice two things. First, there are five girls, two of whom are topless. Second, there are only two guys: Max and my rhythm guitar guy, Aram.

They're sitting in the middle of a horseshoe shaped couch that lines the back and side walls of the bus with a girl wedged between them and one more on either side. The topless ones dance with each other near the sound system.

I take a drink, trying to come off like this is no big deal. I'm not a moron. I get this is what happens on tour, so I shouldn't be surprised. But I am. I don't even know Max. But for some stupid reason I guess I thought, since he invited me, he'd be waiting for me like a monk in the corner somewhere.

Max looks up and sees me and I expect some sort of guilty reaction, but I get nothing but a welcoming smile. He says something to the girl next to him, then rakes the hair off his face and stands and comes over to me.

"I see you got a beer."

I hold it up. "Chipper set me up."

"Good man," he says. "Glad you decided to stop by."

"I can only stay for a minute," I say, realizing I should have just gone back to the hotel.

"What are you doing tomorrow?" he asks, leaning against the doorframe next to me.

"Billie's sick, so I think we'll just hang out in the room."

He nods slowly. "The Muse, right?"

I think about lying and saying no, but I nod instead.

He glances around the room, then takes my elbow and leads me back past the bunks to the press of bodies up front. "Sorry, Aram went a little crazy with the invites. It's not usually like this."

"Usually? How many times have you done this?"

His expression turns sheepish. "Okay, you got me. This is my first tour. But last night it wasn't like this."

I turn for the front of the bus and Max follows. "Well, have fun," I say with a flick of my wrist at the crowd.

He glances that way then back at me and raises his eyebrows. "I'd have more fun if you'd stay."

"Sorry, I promised Billie and I'm already late."

He nods slowly. "My loss."

"Looks like you won't have any trouble filling the void," I say with dubious glance back at the sea of girls.

He shakes his head. "They're not you. No comparison."

I don't even know what I'm supposed to say to that, so I drain my beer and set the empty on the counter, then turn and start down the steps. "I'll see you tomorrow."

"Count on it," he says.

The driver drops me at the garage entrance to the hotel and I keep my head down as I make my way up the elevator. I'm not really in the mood to deal with fans right now. My mind is still on everything that happened with Tro. He seemed almost like a real person for a few minutes just before he went onstage and made a total ass of himself.

"How'd it go?" Billie asks when I push through the door into our room. She steps through the bathroom door, all bundled into plaid flannel PJs and a bathrobe.

"It was good. Got a standing O for 'More Than Nothing.' How are you feeling?"

"Not sure I can eat yet." She moves slowly to the kitchenette and takes a cup from the microwave, dropping a teabag into it. "But I'm keeping fluids down."

"That's good." I go to my bag and pull out one of my baggy T-shirts.

"So, tell me more," she says, bobbing her teabag in the hot water.

I think about everything Tro said before he went onstage. "Do you think I should find a different label for my next CD?"

Her eyes flash to mine and her eyebrows shoot up. "Why?"

"Because I don't feel like Universal's really getting me. I have a whole crapload of songs I really want to do for my next album, but I'm pretty sure they're not going to let me do any of them."

She goes to the desk chair and lowers herself into it. "I'm not sure that's the best move right now, Shiloh. You don't want to get the reputation for being difficult this early in your career. Phillip is negotiating in good faith and I think Universal understands that your next contract is going to require they give you a little more creative say."

"Why?" I say, frustration flaring in my chest. "They didn't give me any this time."

She swirls her tea and pulls the bag out, tossing it in the trash can under the desk. "You've more than exceeded their expectations. They're going to want to keep you in-house, and to do that, they know they're going to have to keep you happy."

I take a deep breath and move toward the bathroom. "I hope you're right."

"I know I am. You've totally broken out, Shiloh. You're one of their front-list artists." She grins. "Won't be long before you're upstaging Tro and the boys. Next tour, *they'll* be opening for *you*."

"He's such a douche."

"Who?" she asks, her face scrambling in confusion. "Phillip?"

I shake my head. "Tro."

Her brows converge. "I don't like the sound of that. What happened?"

I lean into the bathroom door and pound the back of my head against it. "He just pulled some shit that pissed me off."

"Such as?"

"He told the whole arena that I made him want to…" I mimic his crotch grabbing grind. "And then he pulled this song out of his ass about getting lucky, but everyone knew it was me he was singing about."

Billie rolls her eyes wearily. "That's his gig, Shiloh. His whole image is sex. If he mentioned you at all, it's a good thing."

I shove away from the bathroom door and slam through it, then feel bad, because it's not Billie I'm pissed at. I change and get ready for bed and when I come out, Billie's in bed with a book, sipping her tea.

Her eyes widen when she sees I've changed. "You're going to bed?"

I shrug. "No reason not to."

She glances at the clock on the nightstand. "It's only nine. Let me at least call room service and get you something to eat."

"Not hungry," I say, flopping onto my bed.

She looks at me for a long minute then lifts the phone and punches a button. "Yes," she says when there's an answer on the other end. "I need the largest tub of popcorn you have and two Cokes." She nods with whatever the response is, then looks at me and adds, "Now that I think of it, bring us a pepperoni pizza too." When she hangs up, she reaches for the remote and clicks the TV on. "Saw the new Marvel movie debuts on HBO tonight. It's just starting."

I roll on my side and prop my head on my elbow, looking at her. "I don't really feel like watching a movie."

She pats the bed next to her. "This is your first major concert, the start of what is going to be an amazing career. We can't let it just go by without celebrating. If I wasn't sick, we'd be painting the town tonight."

I take a deep breath and haul myself up, sliding onto the bed next to her. I settle against her side and rest my head on her shoulder as the movie starts. She sips her tea and strokes my hair, and, slowly, my nerves settle.

"Have you thought any more about what we talked about?" she asks. "Me becoming your legal guardian?"

I think about what Tro said, how sometimes family isn't all it's cracked up to be. "What was your family like?"

"When I was your age?" she asks.

"Yeah."

She breathes a laugh through her nose. "Crazy most of the time. I have four brothers, so our mother had her hands full."

"Were you close?"

I feel her nod against the side of my head. "Still are, for the most part."

"I guess I want you to do it…" I say, "if you really want to."

"I'll see what I need to do to get the ball rolling," she answers with another nod. "I don't think it will really change anything from a business or financial standpoint. All your accounts will remain in trust until you're eighteen."

I settle more snugly into her side. "I trust you."

#

I wake to the ping of rain on the window, and when I open my eyes, I see Billie's pulled back the curtain to the balcony. I blink awake and glance at the clock. Almost eleven. I roll to find her sitting at the small table near the kitchenette with her laptop open, sipping a cup of steaming tea.

"Morning," she says, poking her head out from behind her laptop screen.

"How are you feeling?" I croak, pulling myself up to sit against the headboard.

"A little better." She turns her laptop for me to see. "The press is calling you Lucky."

There's a picture of me on stage last night with the caption "Lucky Blows the Doors Off Madison Square Garden."

I feel my face crumple. "Fucking Tro."

She scowls at me for the language. "What about Tro?"

"That's what he called me on stage last night," I say, pulling my knees up and dropping my forehead onto them. I lift my head a few seconds later to find Billie's eyes scouring the article.

"Your reviews are amazing. They loved you." Her brows press together when she gets near the bottom and she looks up at me. "And they're speculating whether there's something…romantic between you and Tro."

I take a deep breath and drop my head back against the headboard. "I told you what he did on stage."

"But it's just that, right? He hasn't tried to…touch you or anything, has he?"

I think of the first time we met, how strong his hands felt on my arms when he pinned me against the wall in that storage closet backstage at *The Tonight Show*, and I hate the shiver that skates over my skin. "No. It's all just innuendo."

Billie bites her upper lip as she thinks. "As long as it doesn't cross the line into physical, I think you should run with it. I hate to say it, but being seen as a lust object of Tro Gunnison—the man every woman is lusting over—could be your springboard."

"Maybe I *will* let him touch me." I glare at her as I throw the covers aside. "Then I can be *his* springboard. Right into jail."

"Shiloh," she says as I get up and slam through the bathroom door.

I get in the shower and let the hot water run over my clammy skin for what has to be half an hour before I even reach for the shampoo. When I finally come out of the bathroom, the rain has stopped and Billie is on the balcony, her hands braced on the rail and her head bent. She turns when she hears me in the room.

"I'm sorry," she says, slipping back into the room. "I need to start thinking more like a parent if we're really doing this guardian thing. And, as a parent, I don't want Tro Gunnison anywhere near you."

"Everyone knows Tro is all show, but I just don't want that stupid 'Lucky' thing to stick."

Her eyebrows raise. "Why not?"

"Because..." I trail off with a shake of my head, trying to find a way to explain the sick feeling in my stomach when I think about Tro calling me that. "The way he says it...I just hate it. It's a stupid nickname."

She goes to the table and flips her laptop closed. "Okay, as far as the nickname, if you really hate it, we'll do everything we can to nip it in the bud."

I drop onto my bed. "I'm just so frustrated. I feel like my whole career has been hijacked by the label and now...all this shit with Tro. I just want to be in control of *something*, you know?"

She sits next to me and loops her arm over my shoulders. "Okay, new strategy. Shiloh Luck is her own woman, so tell me about her. What parts of Shiloh do you want the world to see?"

The question ties my tongue. A knock at the door saves me from having to figure out how to answer. I get up and throw on my robe before going to the door. When I peek through the peephole, I find Max standing in the hall, shifting nervously from foot to foot.

"Who is it?" Billie asks, and Max must hear her, because his eyes widen and he assumes a more relaxed posture, one hand braced on the doorframe and the other in his jeans pocket.

I pull the door open. "Hey."

He grins. "Told you you'd see me today."

"Yeah, but I was thinking later, onstage."

"Some of the guys are heading into the city for the day. You in?"

"Umm…" I turn to look at Billie, who smiles and nudges her chin toward the door.

"You should go," she says.

"You'll be okay?"

She holds up her teacup as if toasting. "I'm fine. Go have some fun."

I take a deep breath then turn back to Max. "Yeah, okay. Just give me a sec to change."

His whole face pulls into a grin and he murmurs, "I could help with that."

I roll my eyes and close the door, then go to my bag, riffling through it for something that's not jeans and a T-shirt. All my stage and party wear is hung up, and I didn't bring much else that wasn't just for knocking around the hotel or bus. I finally come out with a tank and pair of shorts.

"You're sure you're okay with me going out?" I ask Billie as I change, half hoping she'll say no.

She sets her teacup down and stands. "You don't get many chances to just be a kid anymore. I think you need to take them when they come along."

I don't tell her I've never been a kid. The only difference is that I went from no one giving a shit about me to everyone giving a shit about me. I turn for the door.

"Just text me so I know where you are, okay?" she says from behind me.

I glance over my shoulder and nod as I pull open the door.

Max is waiting in the hall when I come out. He pushes off the wall. "Ready?"

"Yeah."

I turn for the elevators, and we're not even halfway up the hall before his hand is on my back. "You seriously kicked ass last night. Hope you know that."

I shrug as he reaches for the elevator button. "Thanks. You guys were great too."

A dubious smile pulls at his mouth as the doors in front of us slide open. "Just trying to keep up."

He gestures for me to step in ahead of him and I do. The door opens in the lobby a minute later and when we unload and I look around, I don't see anyone familiar. "Who else is coming?"

"No one. They were up late partying last night. Still passed out."

I spin on him. "Then why'd you say 'the guys'?"

His smile turns guilty. "Didn't know if your manager would let you come if it was just me."

Something tightens in the pit of my stomach. I have to work with these guys for the next two months. Things can't get weird. I don't think *I* would have let myself come if I knew it was just him. "Maybe this isn't a great idea."

He grasps my elbow as I turn, not hard enough to stop me, but just enough to convey that he *wants* to. "Listen, Shiloh, I'm not some pervert or whatever. I was just hoping we could hang out a little. That's it."

I take a deep breath. "So, what were you thinking?"

"Haven't spent much time in New York, so all I know are the touristy things: Empire State Building, Central Park." He points toward the door. "Times Square is right there, and I'm pretty sure we can get anywhere we want on the subway."

I've never spent *any* time in the city. If this is my only chance to see it, I don't want to miss it. Plus, after the morning rain, the sun is out and I haven't spent much time outdoors in months. "Let's start with Central Park and see how that goes."

He grins and guides me to the doors. We spill onto the busy sidewalk and his smile fades when he looks up and down the street. "You know where it is?"

My face scrunches as I follow his gaze. There are people everywhere, and they all look like they know where they're going. "I don't even know where *we* are."

He scratches his head then lifts his arm at a passing cab.

"I thought we were taking the subway," I say as one pulls up in front of us.

He shakes his head. "That would entail knowing what we're doing. This is easy."

We climb in the back and he tells the driver where we're going. It's not till we pull away that I realize I have no money.

"I forgot to grab cash," I say with a cringe.

He flips a wrist dismissively. "I've got it."

"Sorry. I wasn't thinking," I say, seriously wishing I'd remembered money. I don't want him thinking this is a date.

"So, tell me about Shiloh Luck," he says as we weave into the slow-moving traffic. "I only know what everyone else knows. You're an orphan who, despite all odds, somehow managed to win *The Voice*."

I shrug. "There's not much more to tell."

He looks at me a long moment, his black eyes seeming to darken in the shadows of the backseat. "Somehow I doubt that."

I turn and watch the city pass by outside my window. "This is what I've always wanted, ever since I was little and my best friend's grandma taught us to play guitar."

"How little?"

I think about the first time Lilah's grandmother took us away from the city to her place in Mendocino for the summer. My foster family had three other foster kids plus two of their own, so they were happy to pack me a bag and send me out the door. "Seven, I think. She gave Lilah her guitar the summer we were ten. When we got home, we took it to the bus stop near her house and sat on that bench playing "Knockin' On Heaven's Door" by Bob Dylan all afternoon, because that was the song her grandma had taught us that summer." I smile with the memory. "We made maybe five bucks."

"So, you're doing a little better in the income department now," he says with a grin.

I roll my eyes in self-disgust. "And making you pay."

He shrugs. "No biggie. You can get the next one."

The next one. Great.

"What about you?" I ask. "How long have you been playing bass?"

"Ever since I can remember." He settles deeper into the seat. "I come from a rock and roll family. My dad played bass for Metallica and Suicidal Tendencies."

"Have you had any gigs before this?"

He shakes his head. "I've done a lot of studio work, but no touring."

"So I'm your first." The second it's out of my mouth, I wish I could hit delete. The last thing I need is for him to think I'm sending signals.

But when I see his smile, a blend of coy and hopeful, I know I fucked up. "I saved myself for you."

I turn and look out the window again, trying to think of how to save this. "What about the other guys?" I ask, trying to move the conversation into something less personal.

"Chipper's the only one who's been on the road with a major act. He's toured with Bigfoot and Gangrene."

"How's the bus working out for you guys?"

"It's pretty descent. There's an empty bunk for you." His eyebrows rise as he grins. "Just sayin'."

I turn back to the window. "Yeah…I think Billie's made us other arrangements."

The driver slams on the brakes and honks at a horse drawn carriage. Max watches it go by and grins. "Totally that."

"You want to go on a horse?" I ask as we pull to the curb.

"After I get one of those," he says, pointing to the hot dog cart the driver pulls up next to.

We get out and he pays the cabbie, then orders two Cokes and four hot dogs from the vendor.

"I can't eat two," I protest as he pays.

"Oh, shit!" His eyes go wide in feigned surprise. "You wanted one too?"

I cut him my best glare as the vendor hands a foil-wrapped hot dog to me.

"I'm starving," he says, taking the other three in one hand.

I try to give him the hot dog in my hand but he waves me off. "I'm joking. That's yours."

We each grab a Coke, then squirt mustard and relish on our dogs, and I realize I really am having a good time. It's been so long since I've had a day where I could just kick back with someone sort of my age.

Which makes me wonder how old he is. I'm sure he's older than me, but maybe only by a few years?

He wraps his hot dogs and makes a beeline for where the horse drawn carriages are lined up on the curb. He negotiates with the driver and they must come to an agreement, because he turns to me and gestures that I should climb up.

"He's going to need your autograph for his daughter," he says once we're settled.

"Why?" I ask, and can't keep the bemusement out of my voice. I never understand autographs. Pictures, maybe, but anyone can scribble anything and say it's anyone's autograph.

"He recognized you from the poster in his daughter's bedroom. She's a fan. He cut the price nearly in half to get it."

"Fine," I say with a roll of my eyes, but I'm actually a little relieved. I've made a financial contribution to this outing. It's that much less that I feel like I owe Max.

It's turned out to be a really nice day. The air is heavy from the humidity after the rain, but it's not too hot. We scarf down our food as the driver takes us through the park, past all the sites, and tells us what we're looking at. Max finishes his three hot dogs in, like, two bites each and is done before I am.

"That's a little disgusting," I tell him as he wipes mustard from his chin with the back of his hand.

He grins and pats his stomach. "Growing boy."

As I'm watching ducks floating lazily on one of the lakes, Max's arm settles over my shoulder.

I want to shake him off, but I don't want to *piss* him off. I knew this was a bad idea. I struggle for a few minutes, trying to decide how to handle this, but when he starts to nuzzle my neck, I know I have to say something.

I slip out from under his arm. "Max, I think you're cool and all, but I'm not hooking up with anyone on this tour. We have to work together for the next nine weeks and I don't want things to get awkward between any of us."

He just stares at me blankly for a second before tipping his head in a question. "You think I'm angling for sex?"

"No...I mean..." Fuck. I knew I'd screw this up.

He grins. "Okay, I am, but not how you think. I'm not looking for one night, Shiloh. You're totally fucking amazing and there's nothing I want more than to get to know you better, so I'm going to make you love me."

All I can do is blink like an idiot.

"Do I want to sleep with you?" His dark gaze glosses over my body before coming back to my eyes. "More than anything. But I'm not expecting you to drop your shorts here and now. I'm in this for the long haul and I guarantee you before the end of this tour, you're going to want me."

"Really?" I say, crossing my arms tightly and killing him with my glare.

"I'm a great guy, Shiloh," he says with a presenting-the-obvious raise of his eyebrows. "Everybody loves me. It's only a matter of time before you do too."

My phone buzzes in my pocket and I realize I never texted Billie. I pull it out and read her, *Where are you?* then start typing, because I can't think of a single thing to say to Max other than *You're out of your mind.* I tell her we're in a carriage in Central Park and she sends me back a smiley face. On the heels of that comes another text.

You should try to be back in about an hour. Have to be at the Garden in two and you need time to change and get over there.

I tell her I will, then turn back to Max. "She wants me back at the hotel in an hour."

He nods, but there's still something in his eyes that makes me nervous.

CHAPTER 7

Tro

My grip on the balcony rail could bend steel as I watch that fucking bass player put his paws all over Lucky. I shove off the rail and rake the hair off my face. I swore to myself I was going to protect her from all the fucking douches in this business. Thought laying claim in public would do that. But that little prick's not backing off.

I pull another Marlboro from the pack and light it off the butt in my hand, then crush out the old one with my bare heel.

"Fuck," I hiss under my breath as I watch them disappear under my balcony toward the front door of the hotel.

I drop back into the chair I'd been sitting in when I saw Lucky and Max climb out of the cab and cross the street a minute ago and set my smoke in the ashtray, scooping up my guitar. My fingers play absently over the strings as I imagine what's going on downstairs right now.

"Fuck," I snarl, slamming my guitar onto the table and standing up.

I need to hit something.

Or someone.

When I push through the door into my room, the naked brunette in my bed opens her eyes and blinks at me sleepily. I storm toward her and she gives me the smile that caught my attention from the pit last night, then pushes the sheets aside.

I'm already hard. I have been since I saw Lucky in the street. Hell, I have been since I first saw her backstage at *The Tonight Show* two days ago.

The brunette lays back and runs her fingertips down her curves.

I kick my jeans off as I go and climb on.

#

I'm backstage again.

I swore to myself I wasn't going to be, but here the fuck I am. And tonight, I'm not hiding. I'm standing at the soundboard with the stage monitor engineer. Where there's no way Lucky can miss me.

And I'm so fucked up I can barely stand.

I lean against the scaffolding and watch Lucky do her thing. She's even better tonight than she was last night, looser and more comfortable now that she's got a night under her belt. I watch her and Max, trying to read the body language, because I've got to know if he fucked her. He's still all up on her, but tonight she doesn't seem to be shrugging him off the way she did last night. And every time he touches her, my guts turn to lead.

They finish their set and Lucky's eyes lock on mine as they come off the stage. She's hot in more ways than one and the sheen of sweat on her face and neck makes her glow. As she passes me, a bead trickles from the hollow of her neck down her chest and funnels into her cleavage.

And fuck, I want to lick it out.

She stops in front of me, challenging me with her hard gaze as the roadies rush past. When Max comes up behind her a second later and snakes his arm around her waist, Lucky's eyes don't budge from mine, but a smug smile ticks at the corners of her mouth.

But tonight, her manager's here with a TV crew to run interference. "Shiloh!" she calls from deeper backstage. "Over here."

Lucky gives me one last glare then pulls free of Max. "Gotta go," she tells him.

"Come party in our bus when you're done," he calls as Lucky's manager pulls her over to where the TV crew is setting up for an interview.

I lift my water bottle to my mouth, but it ain't water. The satisfying burn of the vodka grounds me. When I sway on my feet, I know I should lay off, but I can't. My head is more fucked up when I'm sober, trying to figure out what the fuck I'm supposed to be feeling for Lucky.

She glances over her shoulder at me, gives me a scowl that makes me want to rip her fucking clothes off and take her right here and now. So I down the rest of the bottle and toss it to the side.

When they wrap up taping, Lucky smiles and shakes everyone's hands. She and her manager break away from the group, and her manager says something to her before moving back to the woman who was interviewing Lucky. They leave together and Lucky's eyes lift to mine once she's alone. When she finds me watching her, she glares.

I'm getting ready to go to her, but she starts toward me instead. "You're drunk."

I crack a smile. "I'm always drunk."

Her head shakes slowly as she scrutinizes me. "Not like this. Can you even stand up?"

I only realize how heavily I'm leaning on the scaffolding when she says it. I push away and try to gain my balance, but the stage feels like it's floating on heavy waves, lurching in all directions. I grab the scaffolding before I go down.

"How are you going to perform?" she asks, her eyes narrowing in disgust.

"I always fucking perform, Lucky," I say through my best smirk. "You're gonna find that out one of these days."

The last of the roadies sweeps past us as she rolls her eyes at me, and then I hear Grim's growl from behind me. He and Jamie grab me and huddle up, saving me from my fucking self.

Or more accurately, saving Lucky from my fucked up self.

"Let's rip this motherfucker open!" Jamie shouts.

"Fucking kill it!" I yell as the stage lights go down.

We take the stage and I rip my guitar off the stand. With the first flash of the lights, we launch into our set. I find my feet after a few minutes and when the stage stops spinning, I glance into the wings and find Lucky's gone.

Which is good, because I'm a fucking shitty protector. The only person she needs protection from is me.

#

After New York, I know I can't be trusted to protect Lucky, so I decide my best strategy is to just steer clear. For the next two weeks I avoid being anywhere I know she will be, but by Toronto, pictures of Lucky and Max start to surface: cozy in the back of a Central Park carriage; standing shoulder to shoulder at the rail of the Boston Tea Party ship; laughing together at a pizza place in Pittsburg; with their heads together onstage in Montreal.

I decide I need to stick around and talk to the sound guys after our sound check in Toronto. When Lucky and her band walk in for theirs, everything inside me seizes.

I've never had this kind of reaction to a woman in my life. Especially one I've vowed to keep safe from dicks like me. I watch them go through a few songs while the front of house and stage sound guys make their adjustments, then follow her to where she racks her guitar near the stringer.

"Hey."

She looks up at me and blinks in feigned surprise. "You're sober."

I shrug. "For the moment. How's the tour going so far?"

She looks out at the arena. "Pretty good. No one's thrown rotten fruit at me or booed me off the stage yet."

I laugh at her modesty. "You crushed them in New York. I'm sure the same has happened in Cleveland, and last night in Buffalo, and will happen everywhere else we stop."

My plan is to segue into telling her I've seen pictures of her with Max and ask her what's going on, but her manager comes over from where she's talking to a local news crew.

"Hi," she says, holding her hand out toward me. "I'm Shiloh's manager, Billie. We met in New York?"

"I remember," I say, taking her hand and shaking.

"Shiloh's got an interview," she tells me but then there's a shift in her expression, as if something just dawned on her. "Any chance you'd be willing to join her?"

I glance at Lucky and her eyes widen as she gives me a nearly imperceptible shake of her head.

"Sure," I say with a grin. "Why the hell not?"

Lucky's jaw tightens as she spins for where the news crew is waiting for her.

"Special treat!" Billie tells the crew. "Tro Gunnison is still here after his sound check and has agreed to join the interview if that's okay with everyone."

The reporter gives an enthusiastic yes and introduces herself to Shiloh and me.

"So, Shiloh," she says as her cameraman gives the signal he's rolling. "What's it like touring with one of the hottest bands worldwide right now?"

I can see Lucky really wants to roll her eyes, but restrains herself. "We really don't see much of each other," she says with a dismissive flick of her wrist at me, "but I hope we're bringing the fans what they're coming out to see."

"Reviews have been stellar," the reporter answers with an enthusiastic nod. She asks several more generic questions about our music and fans and what's next from us, then turns to me. "Since I have you here, Tro, I have to ask. You caused a little bit of a stir in New York when you implied on stage that there was something…physical between you and Shiloh. Is there any truth to that?"

I let the shit-eating grin spread and look at Lucky. "I never kiss and tell."

Now Lucky can't suppress the eye roll. "What he meant to say is, *no*."

"Yet," I shoot back.

"Ever," she counters, and if looks could kill, I'd be fried by a million megawatts of hate.

And with that look, I see my new strategy.

"You are aware that Shiloh's only sixteen?" the reporter interjects, her expression deadly serious now.

I grin and raise an eyebrow at Lucky, egging her on. "Lucky for me that's the age of legal consent in Canada."

"So, you don't think that would be taking advantage of the situation?" the reporter counters, the claws of her inner feminist coming out.

I shake my head. "Hell—"

Lucky's voice is all venom when she cuts me off. "How many octaves do you think his voice would raise if I tore his balls off?"

He reporter's eyebrows shoot up.

"Because that's what will happen if he tries to touch me," Lucky adds with a smirk that goes straight to my dick. "Thinking that might not be good for his singing career."

The reporter glances at the cameraman to make sure he's getting all this just as Billie steps in.

"Let's call that a wrap," she says, holding a hand over the lens of the camera. "I think everyone's under a lot of pressure and very tired. If you could just disregard that last exchange…?"

But that's the last thing I want. I want everyone to see Lucky has teeth. They might think twice about fucking with her if they think she'll rip off their balls.

"I'm not sure I can do that," the reporter says. "This is a huge human interest story that started weeks ago. Fans want to know the real story."

Billie's stance is stone. "This is just sensationalistic journalism. No credible outlet would air that footage."

The reporter's eyes widen. "*Every* credible outlet would run it. Asking us to do anything else is censorship."

I tug Lucky's elbow as Billie continues to argue her point, trying to get her attention.

She yanks it away. "Don't touch me."

I tip my head toward the stage as I turn that direction, hoping she'll be curious enough to follow.

She does, but I find out it's because she's not done with me when she catches up to me. "That the fuck was that?" she asks, flinging her arm at where her manager is still arguing her case with the reporter.

"You showing the world that you're not some soft, pathetic girl that they can take advantage of."

"What the hell are you talking about?" she spits, bunching her hands on her hips.

"Every guy in your band, every backline guy, your producer, your manager," I say with a flip of my hand at Billie, "they're all out for themselves. Some of them want to fuck you figuratively and the others want to fuck you literally, but if they know you've got a pair of balls, they're less likely to."

The heat of her glare scouring my face leaves me feeling sunburned. "You *are* drunk."

I shake my head. "All guy musicians are whores, Lucky. Every fucking one of us. Max, me. You need to stay the hell away from all of us."

Her whiskey eyes widen in understanding at the same time as they darken with rage. "You're jealous of Max. *That's* what this is."

She's right, so I can't argue that point. Instead, I argue the bigger point. "He wants his fifteen minutes of fame. That's all you are to him, like Mark Anthony to JLo."

"Wow," she says, backing away. "You have totally lost it."

I bob a small nod. "I must have, because I'm trying to talk you *out* of letting me fuck you, which is all I've wanted to do since I met you."

Suddenly I can't read her expression. She's still pissed, but there's something else, something more feral shining out of her eyes. "Go to hell," she says, then spins back to where her manager is still fighting with the reporter.

And now I'm oh for two on great ideas, on the edge of striking out.

CHAPTER 8

Shiloh

That asshole doesn't want me to be with Max? Well, fuck him.

I storm back to Billie. "Let's go."

As we walk back to the buses, all I can think is that I wish Tro and his band were in the bus complex too. Roadkill doesn't do buses, apparently. They fly and stay in hotels. Up until now, that's been good. Easier to avoid him, but now I want him here to see what he's set in motion.

When we get to our bus, I head for the shower. I come out feeling a thousand times better. I change in my bunk, then head up front for something to eat.

Our bus is configured pretty much the same as the guys'. The bathroom and bunks are in the middle, with a sitting area and kitchen up front and a lounge in back. If there's not a day off between shows, we travel at night, but when we're on the road during the day, Billie's always at the table, right where she is now. It's her office, more or less.

"So," she says, closing the lid to her laptop. "I talked to a lawyer today while you were at your sound check. He seems to think that we could make the legal guardianship happen if you're sure that's what you want."

A cold shudder skips along my spine.

When I don't answer right away, she turns in her seat, facing me. "I only want this if it's something you want, Shiloh."

"I just don't see why you would want me. I mean, it's not like adopting a baby. I'll be seventeen next week."

She smiles softly and pushes up from her seat, coming to where I stand at the counter and enclosing me in her arms. Her chin rests on the top of my head and I feel her warm breath in my hair as she says, "I want you because you are a special person and I care deeply for you. I know you've had a rough upbringing, and I know you don't need me to be a parent, but I want to look out for you in any way I can." She pulls back and looks at me. "I love you, Shiloh. I just want to keep you safe."

The icy shell around my heart melts a little. "If that's really what you want, we can talk to him, see what it would be."

"He made it sound like it's just filing the right documents with the courts. Not too complicated."

We sit on the couch. "Would I come live with you?" I gesture at the bus. "After this is over?"

"You would," she says with a nod.

I cringe a little in embarrassment, feeling like I should already know the answer to the question I'm about to ask. "Where do you live?"

"I've got an apartment in LA, but I've been thinking of moving to the burbs. We could find something nice in Beverly Hills or Manhattan Beach."

"Sounds nice," I say, thinking of that old show that runs on late night Nickelodeon that Will Smith used to be in.

She pulls me into a tight hug. "It's going to be amazing, Shiloh. I'm so excited to start our new life."

"Me too," I say, trying to decide if that's what the weird ache in the pit of my stomach is.

#

Two hours later, I'm sweating onstage. Several times, Max come up next to me, and I don't discourage him tonight.

We finish our set and when we file off the stage, I glance around backstage for Tro, but don't see him. I tell myself the sinking feeling in my chest is only because I wanted him here to see that he can't tell me what to do.

"So, the party's private tonight," Max says, slipping up behind me. He leans closer, his mouth brushing my ear as he add, "More intimate."

I turn and cut him a sarcastic look. "I don't do intimate."

It's not a lie.

Lilah and I managed to keep to ourselves clean and stay out of the gangs at our school, but what happened in my group home was another story. At any given time, there were fourteen of us living there. A lot of shit went down that none of the Children and Family Services staff ever put into all those reports that went back to Department of Health and Human Services. Girls got raped all the time.

I was thirteen when they moved me out of my last foster home. They put me in a group home to fill the gap of someone who'd just aged out and make room in the foster home for a younger kid. I figured it out fast. Alonzo was sixteen, but he was the toughest guy there. No one messed with him. Which meant, as long as I was his girl, no one messed with me. I let him fuck me whenever he wanted, and in return, he kept anyone else from fucking with me. He aged out the same month as *The Voice* auditions. A few months later, I was in L.A. and I haven't seen him since.

Max's smile becomes more suggestive. "That's because you've never had the right person to do it with."

"And you're that person?" As I ask, out of the corner of my eye, I see Tro, Grim, and Jamie emerge from the back hallway.

I lean in as Max tucks back a strand of hair that's come loose from my ponytail and his fingers linger over the pulse point behind my ear. "You damn well better believe it."

"Wow," I say with a roll of my eyes. "I think my panties just melted."

His eyes flash wide for a second. "I definitely like the sound of melting panties."

"Whoops, I forgot." I push away from him and head for the dressing room. Tro watches me pass and I catch his eye as I add, "I'm not wearing any."

I feel his eyes burning through my back as I move up the hall. I don't know whether he's jealous or just pissed, but either way, I can use Max to my advantage. I just have to be careful. The trick is going to be making Tro believe there's something going on and making sure Max knows there isn't.

When I get to the dressing room, Billie is there, on the phone. She gives me a nod as I riffle through my bag for some dry clothes, then head to the shower. The truth is, I'm pretty sure I'm never going back to the guys' bus again. I'm on tour. This is my big coming out party. I should be partying every night. But I'm getting really sick of people. Even my own. Just like everything else since *The Voice* started, I'm totally out of my element.

But when I'm cleaned up and I push through the door of the dressing room to head back to the bus, Max is there.

"I'm not taking no for an answer," he says.

I raise my eyebrows at him. "Really."

Up front, Roadkill takes the stage, and he waits through the deafening roar of the crowd before saying, "Really."

I take a deep breath then stick my head back into the dressing room.

"I'm going to the guys' bus for a beer," I mouth to Billie, who's still on the phone.

She scowls, but doesn't shake her head, so I duck back out the door. "One beer," I tell Max.

He grins. "That's all I need."

We walk together through the halls to the rear exit and climb on the bus. And he's right, there are only the band, a few of the crew, and a handful of girls.

Max grabs a beer from the fridge and twists the lid off before he hands it to me. "Chivalry is not dead."

I pat my chest and flutter my eyes, "Oh my melting heart."

He grins. "I liked the melting panties better."

"Avalanche!" Aram shouts, slamming a beer glass and a dice into the middle of the kitchen table.

Everyone starts gathering around.

"What's avalanche?" I ask Max.

He gives me a look. "Seriously?"

"Seriously."

He takes my hand and tugs me over to the table. "Just watch."

Aram pour some of his beer into the cup in the middle of the table. "I'll start," he says, picking up the dice. He rolls a five, and the group shouts and starts pointing at each other. He picks up the glass and looks around the table, finally handing it to a skimpily-clad Asian girl on his immediate left. She drains the glass, then wipes her hand under her chin and giggles. Aram fills the glass again then pushes the die to the Asian girl.

Max points at the die as the girl picks it up and rolls it. "So, Aram rolled a five, which meant he could make anyone at the table drink."

The Asian girl rolls a three and giggles again before lifting the cup and draining it. "I'm in so much trouble," she says as she drops the glass in the middle of the table.

Aram fills it. "Yes," he says, giving her a salacious look. "Yes, you are."

"Come on," Max says, reaching over the girl's shoulder and scooping up the die. "Take a turn. I'll teach you as we go."

I give him a wary look before taking the die. I roll it and it skitters past the one, finally settling on two. "What do I do?"

"Pour more into the glass," he says as Aram lifts it for me to reach.

I add beer to the glass and he sets it down.

Max takes the die and roll a five. He grins at me as Aram lifts the glass again. "Drink up," he says, handing it to me.

I do, then make a *fuck you* face at him. The next time around, I roll a three and drink. Max rolls another five and I drink again.

"I think you're cheating," I say, slamming the glass back down and filling it from my bottle.

Three hours later, I'm way past the one beer I told Billie I was having, but I only realize how trashed I am when I get up to pee and can barely walk. I hold the furniture and walls, and when I get to the toilet and sit, the whole bus starts spinning.

When I come back to the lounge, I don't sit because I'm afraid if I do I won't be able to get back up. "I have to go."

Max makes a sad puppy face, but stands and takes my elbow. He pulls me close and whispers, "You could lay down in my bunk for a while."

I shove him away. "Uh-uh. I'm drunk and you're horny. Bad combination."

He smiles. "You're right." He guides me down the stairs and hooks an arm around my waist to steady me as we walk to my bus. There's a second I can't figure out which one it is, and we walk back and forth past the front of all eight buses while I try to sort it out. When I'm pretty sure I've got the right one, I go to the door.

"Thanks…" I say, turning to look at him. "I think."

"Admit it," he says with a smile. "You're falling for me."

I start to roll my eyes, but that causes the ground to shift under my feet, so I stop. I haven't even gotten my bearings when Max presses me up against the side of the bus. His mouth is warm and wet when it finds mine.

I think about pushing him back, but all of a sudden, I don't have enough energy. He'll be done eventually.

He draws away and gives me a blurry grin. "Told you."

"I'm drunk," I mutter. "You took advantage of me."

"Uh-uh," he says with a shake of his head that makes me dizzy. "That was you falling in love with me. You'll definitely know it when I take advantage of you."

"I'm falling not at all in love with you," I say, feeling my stomach churn uncomfortably, and not sure whether it's the beer or what he just said that's making me sick. I turn for the bus. "Go home."

"'Night, Shiloh," he says through a chuckle, then I hear his receding footsteps. But I'm frozen in place.

Tro stands from where he was sitting on the curb a few feet away and shoves his hands into his pockets.

He saw that. I couldn't have planned it any better. So why am I all of a sudden sure I'm going to puke.

"Have fun?" he asks, a definite edge to his voice.

"The time of my life… right up until this second." I stagger a few steps forward. "Now, not so much."

"We need to talk, Lucky," he says, coming slowly toward me.

"I've got nothing to say to you."

He takes a deep breath. "Listen, I never do this, but what I did earlier today was an even bigger asshole move than my usual, so…sorry."

His eye twitches as he says it, as though it's physically painful.

I shrug like it's no big thing, but I know it is. Tro is right. He *never* apologizes. For anything.

The door flies open and Billie is there in her bathrobe. "What's going on out here?"

Tro rubs the back of his neck as he turns to her. "I just fucked up. I wanted to apologize to Lucky and tell her it won't happen again. I have no right to butt into shit that's not mine to deal with." He turns back to me. "You're tough and I know you can handle your shit way the hell better than I can, so I'm going to get out of your way from here on out."

I push past him, needing the safety of the bus. "Thank you."

When I step up, I grab for the handle and miss, and nearly flip over backward, but before my ass hits the pavement, a pair of strong arms are scooping me up.

"I really am sorry, Lucky," he says, low in my ear. His hot breath on my neck raises goose bumps on my skin and tightens my belly.

God, I hate my body for reacting to his touch.

I shake him off. "Then stay out of my life."

He sets me back on my feet. "Your wish, my command."

Billie takes my arm to steady me as I climb the stairs. When I turn back to where Tro just was, he's gone. Disappointment sinks in my chest because the truth is, I have no fucking clue what my wish is.

CHAPTER 9

Tro

We play Detroit and then two shows in Chicago before we have a day off, and every time Lucky and I cross paths, my heart lodges in my throat and I can't breathe. I don't know what the fuck is wrong with me and I need to figure it out before I start self-destructing, so I take my free day to fly to my place in Austin and try to pull my shit together. It's been a while since I've been here, but of all my places, this is the one that feels most like home.

The cab drops me on the curb outside an old green Victorian and I trudge up the stairs to the attic apartment. I unlock the door and push through, then tug off my hoodie and look around the dusty place.

It's small and in a rundown neighborhood, but it was the first apartment that was all mine. I started renting it when we finally began getting steady work. I bought the whole building from the owner two years later when we signed with our label and the real money started rolling in. In the great room, just inside the door, the ceilings taper from ten feet at the peak in the middle of the house to four feet near the walls, and the windows are dormered. The kitchen is along the wall to the right, just a long counter with a stove and sink in it, and a wooden table splits the kitchen from the rest of the room, where I've got an old leather couch I picked up at a yard sale and a newer TV and sound system bolted to the wall next to my overflowing CD and DVD racks. Beyond the TV in the back is my bedroom, where I'm sure the queen bed sheets are still in the tangle I left them in a few months back, last time I was here. Next to the bedroom door is the bathroom.

All my old shit is here, including my Harley, parked in the garage. I grab the keys off the hook over the kitchen counter and pull my skull cap down from the rack, then lope back down the stairs.

I yank on my helmet as I duck into the garage. A second later, I'm rocketing down the street. I take the straightest line out of the city, skirt past Lake Travis at the outskirts of civilization, then wind it out. I keep my head down and just go. Speed sharpens everything, and right now I need to think. I'm used to living outside the lines and pissing people off, but I just keep fucking this Lucky thing up.

So, I'm going to do what I told her in Toronto. I'm going to back off.

But the scene at the bus that night keeps playing on a loop in my head—Lucky pinned between the bus and Max as he kissed her. Oily black jealousy threads through my insides at the image, so I max my Harley and keep going. I'm halfway to Dallas before I turn back for Austin.

I make it back to the apartment in one piece and stow my bike in the garage. When I turn the corner at the landing to the third floor, I see there's a blonde in skimpy denim shorts and a black bikini top sitting on the step near my door.

A slow smile spreads over her face when she sees me. "Hey."

"How ya been, Kate?" I say with a nod.

"Good." She stands and runs her palms over her hips, all sweet Texas molasses. "I thought I heard someone up here, and then your Harley goes screaming out of the garage and I knew."

I make my way up the last few steps toward her. "Just here for tonight. Got a show in Minneapolis tomorrow."

Her smile grows. "Well, then, lucky me for catching you."

I reach the top stair and she steps into my arms. She feels right there; the only woman who ever has. Which is a little fucked up since she's the only woman to ever be there that I haven't fucked. That's partly because she's the only real friend I have and I don't want to screw it up. But mostly it's because Emmy, her grandmother who has rented the apartment below me since the dawn of time and raised Kate there, owns a rifle and will fill my sorry ass full of buckshot if I touch Kate.

"How have you been?" she asks into my neck.

I take a deep breath and pull away. "Fucked up."

She starts down the stairs and grabs my hand on the way, pulling me behind her. "Then good thing I'm here to straighten you out. Drinks are on you."

She's straightened me out more than once, and literally saved my life in the process. It was after we'd cut our first studio CD, but before our label picked us up that my old man found me here. He never said how he tracked me down and, in the end, I guess it doesn't matter. What does matter is what happened when he got here. He said he'd kill me if he ever found me.

He wasn't joking.

We jump back on my bike and head to the food trucks on Rainey Street before ending up at our favorite bar. The bartender drops two beers in front of us and looks at me a second before sliding a bar napkin in front of me with a pen. "Wasn't gonna be a dick and do this, but my girlfriend will shit if I get her your autograph."

I sign the napkin and slide it back to him without a word.

"There's no girlfriend," Kate says, scowling after him. "That's going to show up on eBay tomorrow along with the shot he just took from his phone of you signing it."

Nothing gets by Kate, which is part of the reason I trust her. She reads people, including me, better than anyone I've ever met.

She props her elbows on the bar and rests her chin in her hand. "So tell me the whole, sad story."

"I can't stop making an ass out of myself. You got a cure for that, doc?"

She smiles. "You've made millions making an ass out of yourself."

I shake my head and swirl the beer in my mug. "This is different."

"Who is she?"

I look up at her and find that knowing expression on her face that always precedes her sorting out all my shit. "She's just this kid I'm touring with."

"Shiloh Luck."

I feel my eyes widen. "Yeah."

Her smile turns cynical. "Don't look at me like I'm clairvoyant. I saw some stuff on Twitter a few weeks ago."

I take a long swallow off my mug. "So you know some of the shit I've pulled."

She nods. "Why don't you fill me in on the rest."

"I just…" I shake my head. "I can't even explain why, but I feel responsible for her."

"Because this is her first time on the road?"

I lift my eyes out of my beer and look directly into hers so she hears everything I'm saying. "Because I've wanted to fuck her since the second I met her."

"You fuck *everyone* the second you meet them and never think twice. Why is she different?"

I rub at the sweat on the back of my neck. "She just is. She's got so much fucking talent, but she's young and...I get that she's tough, but I don't think she's as confident as she lets on. She's just sort of feeling her way through this whole thing and people in this business are fucking sharks, able to sniff out even one drop of blood in the water. They'll eat her fucking alive and spit out her bones."

"Why don't you think she's as confident as she seems?" she asks, but I get the sense she already knows.

I fist a hand in my hair and lean on my elbow. "I saw something that first day—something I've never seen her show anyone else. Hell...if she knew I was there, she wouldn't have shown me. But I saw it. I know it's there—this vulnerability. I just want to protect her."

"Have you talked to her about how you feel?"

"I've told her all the guys in this business, including me, are whores. I've told her to watch her back with her manager and producers. But everything I do only makes things worse. Mostly because I'm a fucking moron."

She shakes her head and all that Kate wisdom shines out of her eyes. "I didn't ask if you talked to her about what you *think*, Tro. I asked if you talked to her about how you *feel*."

I rest back in my seat and cross my arms. "And how is that?"

She presses back in her seat, a smug smile on her face, as if she's just won fucking Trivial Pursuit or something. "You're falling for her."

I blow out a laugh. "You don't know what the fuck you're talking about."

But that's a lie, because Kate always knows what she's talking about. And now I know it too by the way my gut knots at the thought.

She runs her finger along the rim of her glass. "I knew there was someone the second I saw you on the stairs."

I knock back the last of my beer, then slam the glass on the bar. "What the fuck are you talking about?"

"It's in your eyes, Tro. There's not much you can keep secret when your eyes tell the world everything."

"That's bullshit. I've got plenty of secrets." A chill runs up my spine as I say it, because Kate's the only one who's caught a glimpse of my biggest one.

I see in her eyes we're thinking the same thing when they darken. "Okay," she says, but I know she's not giving in. "Fine."

"And besides, even if you were right, there's the age thing."

One blonde eyebrow goes up. "Does that really matter? The heart can't count. There's no math in love. No equation. You love who you love."

"I don't deserve to love anyone," I say with a shake of my head.

She gets all cynical again. "That's really what you're going with?"

"It's all I've got. And it's the truth."

She drains her glass and holds it up to the bartender as she sends me a huge, fake pout. "Poor me, the oversexed international rock star. I'm rolling in cash, but I don't deserve to be happy, so everybody feel sorry for me. Boo fucking hoo."

My jaw tightens. "You know it's more than that."

She flops wearily into the back of her seat. "Shit happened to you a long time ago. Shit happens to everyone. Get over it."

"It was a little bit more than shit, Kate. You should know. You got to pick up all the fucking wreckage."

She leans toward me on her elbows. "And I'll do it again if I have to. But you can't hide behind stupid excuses like you don't deserve shit." She shoves my shoulder hard, nearly knocking me off the stool. "Man up."

The bartender brings our refills.

"So what's going on here?" I ask once he's gone. "How's your grandma?"

A sad smile quirks her mouth. "She died two months ago."

"Fuck!" I say, my mug stopping halfway to my mouth. I lower it to the bar. "Christ, are you okay?"

She shrugs. "Getting there."

We spend the rest of the night talking about Emmy and the rest of her family and she doesn't ask me about Lucky again. She's said her piece and there's no point beating that horse.

When we get back to the building I walk her to her apartment. She lifts up onto her tiptoes and presses a kiss to my mouth. I've been tempted in the past, but tonight, despite that the threat of getting my ass shot is no longer looming large, I'm a little surprised to find there's no temptation.

"'Night, Kate."

She smiles. "Don't be a stranger."

I blow out a humorless laugh. "They don't come any stranger."

She lets herself in and when I hear her deadbolt click into place, I head up one flight to my place. And sleep like a rock for the first time since I met Lucky.

#

It hasn't stopped pouring since we got to Minneapolis, and it's cold in the middle of fucking July. This is why I hate the Midwest. It can do this for days. But, finally, when we come out of the arena a little before midnight, the rain's stopped.

The guys load in the car back to the hotel, but I decide to walk. It's less than a mile and I'm feeling antsy. Too much time in planes and hotel rooms, I guess.

I wave at the guard as I pass through the security gate onto the street, then pull up my hood and shove my hands in my pockets.

I woke up in Austin yesterday with the beginnings of a song in my head. I'm not quite sure what it is yet, but the electricity in my veins tells me it's something. I stop in the middle of the bridge I'm crossing and brace my hands against the rail, staring down at the churning river below.

Because I've had something else on my mind since Austin too.

I think Kate's right. Maybe I really am falling for Lucky. For the first time I can remember, I'm thinking past the first fuck. I care whether she gets hurt, especially by me. I've never been so unclear in my own mind as far as what my motivations are, but what I've unraveled from the chaos in my head is that what I want most is for Lucky to be happy and safe. Which means I need to stick to my word and back off.

I shove off the rail as a mist begins to fall. By the time I get to the hotel, despite the fact I'm soaked, I feel about a thousand pounds lighter. Now that I know what I need to do, my gut is untwisting and I feel like I can breathe for the first time since I met Lucky three weeks ago.

I walk into the suite and the party's already well underway. The crew has managed to round up a couple dozen girls and it looks like no one's feeling any pain.

"Gunner!" Grim shouts when he looks up from the lines he's doing off the glass coffee table and sees me. "Got a big fucking fat one with your name on it over here!"

I start that direction, but I'm only halfway there when a girl wraps herself around me from behind. "I've got your name on me too," she says low in my ear.

I glance over my shoulder and find a reasonable hot blonde I've never seen before. I grab her by the ass and plant one on her, grinding all up the front of her.

But my heart's not in really it.

I let her go and back away toward my bedroom door. "I think I'm gonna lay low tonight—crash early and get some sleep for a change."

Grim looks up at me with raised eyebrows. "You all right, man?"

I give a one shouldered shrug. "Just not feeling it."

He smirks and springs off the couch, grabbing the girl I was just on. "More for us."

I turn for my room without looking back and close the door behind me, then flop onto the bed and stare at the ceiling. I close my eyes and listen as more notes begin threading through my brain. They form into a melody and I get up and mark it out on the pad of hotel paper next to the phone, then hum it out loud. I tweak it a little, then go to the corner and grab my guitar. I totally have that juiced feeling I get when I'm onto something real. My heart starts pounding with an electric current when I begin to get a feel for what this song's gonna be.

I pick and jot, tweak and hum, and with every new line I feel more amped. Before I know it, the sun's coming up outside my window.

#

It takes me another week to finish it. I stick with my plan and steer clear of Lucky through our sweep of the Midwest, but she's always on my mind. Because this song is hers. When I sit down with my guitar and play it, my blood is electric.

It's the best fucking thing I've ever written.

CHAPTER 10

Shiloh

It's been over a week since Tro apologized to me, and since then, I've only seen him a few times in passing.

But I've listened to his openings from backstage every night. He's still wild, because I don't think he knows how to be anything else, but he hasn't said anything about me to the audience beyond telling Louisville last night that they'd already seen the real deal, and now they were stuck with the second string.

And the whole time, all I could think about was what Tro said would happen when we got to Kentucky on *The Tonight Show*. I know he was a joking. The legal age of consent is sixteen in nearly every state we've been in so far. But still…I can't deny that, totally against my will, thoughts of Tro doing to me what he does best have been filtering into my dreams at night. I wake panting and tangled in my sheets, my heart galloping so loud I can't believe it hasn't woken Billie.

I'm behind the curtain tonight when Tro, Grim, and Jamie come out and start their pre-show pump up. It's my birthday and I know Billie's arranged a "surprise" party on the bus. Max and the band headed out without a word right after the show, and I'm sure they're all waiting with a flaming cake or whatever.

I watch as Tro, Grim, and Jamie get their headgear wired. As they storm the stage, Tro glances my way.

I didn't know he saw me here.

He smiles and sends me a little salute, but then his smile fades and he just stares, as if trying to find something he lost in my face. Jamie hits the drums and the stage lights flash. Tro rubs the back of his neck then steps onto the stage to a roar.

The floor shakes with percussion and bass as the guys gear up for their first song. I decide staying tonight was a bad idea and turn to exit backstage, but within the first few notes, the tune morphs into "Happy Birthday."

"St. Louis!" he yells and the crowd cheers. "Did Lucky just tear this place down?"

Another roar goes up from the crowd.

"If you fucking missed it, you fucking missed the show of the century! That girl's got the stuff!"

Jamie woots into his mic and ups the percussion as the crowd yells.

"It's Lucky's birthday today, so let's fucking blow the roof off this place!"

They launch into "Happy Birthday" and the stage monitor engineer turns from his soundboard and grins at me. "Go!" he says with a nudge of his chin at the stage.

I shake my head, but a second later, two of the backline guys who I recognize but don't really know are pulling me toward stage left.

When Tro sees me, he stops singing and smiles, letting the crowd take the vocals. He comes over and grasps my hand, towing me to center stage.

They get to my name and the entire crowd sings out, "Happy Birthday, dear Lucky!"

There's a second I want to be pissed. But then I see Tro's smile, feel his hand in mine, and I can't be mad. There's nothing malicious in the look he's giving me. For the first time, I don't feel like he's undressing me with his eyes.

But just as they're finishing the song, he grabs me by the waist and lifts me so my feet are, like, three feet off the ground, and holds me up in front of the crowd like I'm some kind of doll.

"Don't forget this girl!" he shouts when the applause dies down. He sets me on my feet. "Next tour, we're going to be fucking opening for her."

I remember Billie saying the same thing the day I met Tro…without the expletive, of course.

I start off the stage, but Tro grabs my hand again. "Happy birthday."

My heart kicks at the sincerity in his gaze. Jamie holds up a fist for a knuckle bump, and I bump him on my way off stage, but then I catch Grim's glare and realize he wasn't totally down with this addition to their set list. I scramble off the stage, but instead of leaving right away, as I'd intended, I tuck into the corner near the door and listen to Roadkill's first song.

Maybe Tro's more than what he seems, because there was a tenderness in his gaze I wouldn't have thought he was capable of. I watch as they wrap their first song, then can't make myself leave before the second. But, finally, halfway through the third, I turn and head to the parking lot, jogging to the bus.

The door hisses open and I'm not even up the stairs before Billie starts singing "Happy Birthday." When I round the corner into the front lounge, the guys line the couches and Billie's in the kitchen holding a cake aglow with seventeen lit candles. Everyone joins in and Max takes my hand and leads me to the table, where Billie's sets the cake.

She scowls at our intertwined fingers, then gives me a warning gaze.

I shrug and untangle my hand from Max's, then blow out the candles.

"Thanks, guys," I say, swiping my finger through the frosting and pressing it into my mouth.

I go to the fridge as Billie cuts the cake and find only soda. I glance around, at what everyone else is drinking, and when my eyes lift from the Coke in Max's hand to his face, he gives me a shrug. I grab a Diet Coke and go sit between Max and Chipper.

"Surprise," he says as Billie hands paper plates of cake around.

I roll my eyes.

His arm slips over my shoulders. "We didn't fake you out?"

I take his hand and unwrap his arm, dropping it in his lap. "You might have slipped in a kiss when I wasn't looking, but don't think it means you're getting any."

"See, right there," he says, pointing at me. "You're thinking about us going there. You can't deny imagining it." His smile grows impish. "Have you been fantasizing, Lucky?"

"Don't call me that," I snip, because he hit a little too close to home. I have been fantasizing, just not about him.

He holds his hands up in surrender. "Wow, okay. Sorry."

The guys eat cake, go back for seconds, then thirds, and when it's gone, one by one they start trickling out the door.

"Where's everyone going?" Billie says when she notices.

"Somewhere there's beer," I say, holding up my Coke can.

She splits a stern glance between me, Max, and Chipper, who are the only ones left. "You boys need to remember she's only seventeen."

"Of course," Max says, his face all sincere concern. "We'll look out for her."

She looks at him a second longer, then flicks her wrist in a shooing motion at the door. "Go. Have fun."

Max pulls me up and the three of us skip down the stairs.

When we get to the guys' bus, everyone is huddled around the TV watching some baseball game with their drink of choice. Tonight, it's just the band and some of the backline crew. No girls who don't belong here.

I drop into an empty spot on the couch and Chipper hands me a beer. "Hope Billie's not too pissed."

I shake my head. "She's thinking about applying for legal guardianship, so I think she's decided she needs to start acting more parental."

"Wow," he says. "That's sort of a big deal, right?"

I shrug. "It's really only for a year, and I think she's just doing it because it will make things easier for her if I'm in L.A."

When the game finishes, one of the guys puts in a DVD. I'm nursing my beer because I'm not going to let Max get the upper hand again tonight. Some of the crew starts to head out to their own buses when the movie ends, and when I look outside, I see people start to pour out of the venue onto the street. The clock on the microwave says it's after eleven.

"What do you say?" Max says, reaching into a cup on the counter and holding up a dice. The wicked gleam in his eyes tells me he's hoping for a repeat of the other night.

I scowl at him. "You told Billie you were going to look out for me."

He nods slowly as his eyes rake down my top. "And I take that responsibility very seriously. I plan to look out for every inch of you."

I feel my face scrunch. "Do you ever listen to yourself?"

"You can't tell me it's not working. Face it, you want me."

I lean in a little. "You *are* kind of making me love you…"

His eyes light as he sticks a finger in the air. "Ah-ha! She admits it."

"Like a big brother," I add.

His face wrinkles in disgust. "You'd kiss your brother?"

I just give him a look.

His expression clears and something sparks in his dark eyes as he leans closer. His face is an inch from mine when he finally stops and lifts a hand to stroke my cheek. "Okay, then. I just have to step up my game."

I grab him by the T-shirt and pull him closer. "You can step up anything you want," I whisper in his ear. "It's not going to get you into my pants."

"It's not your pants I want into…yet. It's your heart." His black eyes somehow grow darker in the dim lighting as he grasps my chin softly and forces me to look into them. "You *will* love me by the end of his tour. I guarantee it."

I push up from the couch. "I should head back to my bus."

"Uh-uh," he says, catching my arm. "Not while it's still your birthday."

I tug my arm out of his grasp and keep moving, but just as I get to the stairs, the door of the bus hisses open and Tro steps through.

"Heard this was where all the cool kids were hanging out."

Max is past me in a flash, blocking the stairs. "Sorry, dude. Closed party."

Chipper brushes past me on his way to slug Max upside the head. "You're a fucking moron, you know that?" He yanks Max out of the way. "Come on in, Tro. You're always welcome on our bus."

Tro glances at me, as if waiting for my okay.

"I was just heading out, so—"

"I thought we just determined you were staying till your birthday is over," Max cuts in.

I spin on him. "No, *you* determined that. And I told you to go to hell."

"You never told me to go to hell," he says with a shake of his head.

"In my mind I did."

"Come on, Lucky," he pleads, grasping my elbow.

"You need to listen to the lady," Tro says through a tight jaw.

I turn and he's just behind me, his eyes fixed on Max's hand on my arm. "I've got this," I tell him with a warning glare.

He holds his hands up in surrender and that's when I notice what looks like a rolled paper with a ribbon around it in his hand.

I spin on Max. "And I told you not to call me Lucky."

"Fine," he says, his glare nearly slicing Tro in half. He backs away, then turns and disappears into the back of the bus.

"Didn't mean to cause a problem," Tro says low, just for me.

"You didn't." I shoo him down the stairs and follow. "And don't get used to coming to my rescue, because I don't need your help."

He huffs a laugh. "I'm past thinking you do." He holds up the roll of paper in his hand. "I actually need yours."

"Is it a present?" I ask.

He smiles a little. "Think of it however you want: a present, a peace offering. I've got the bones of something I think would really work for you."

I slip it out of his fingers and pull off the ribbon. It's music, scratched out by hand onto a piece of hotel notepaper. And the title is "Lucky's Song."

CHAPTER 11

Tro

We get to her bus and it's only as we stand here, where she kissed Max the other night, that I realize I didn't really think this through. I want to play what I've written for her, but I'm not sure I can be trusted if she invites me inside.

She holds the paper up in the direction of the streetlight, but it's too dim for her to get a clear look. When she reaches for the door and pulls it open, my gut knots.

"You know," I say when she starts up the stairs. "You can just let me know what you think after you've had a chance to play it a few times."

"I want to hear it now," she says, glancing over her shoulder at me, irritated.

"Okay…go ahead." Then I see the solution. "Read it over, then Skype me so I can hear you play it. We can tweak whatever you think. I'm Fingers12345."

"Skype?" she asks with raised eyebrows. "Seriously?"

"Just do it," I say, turning for the road. I feel her watching after me, but I don't look back. Because if I do, there's every chance I'm going to cross a line I promised myself I wouldn't.

I hop in a cab and I'm not even halfway back to the hotel when there's an alert on my phone. StageRat292 wants to connect on Skype. I laugh and accept. A second later, there's another alert that StageRat292 is calling. I hit the video icon and Lucky's face appears on my screen.

"It's incredible." She holds up the paper. "You wrote this?"

"It sort of wrote itself." I try to come off like it's no big thing, but that electricity is pulsing through my veins and I don't think I'm able to keep it out of my voice. "Play it for me. I want to hear you do it."

She sets the phone down and I can only see her left arm and the neck of the guitar as she fingers the strings. But when she starts on the lyrics, and her voice comes through the line, I want to climb right through the cyber and kiss the living fuck out of her.

Which is exactly the reason I couldn't stay. For once in my sorry life, I made the right call.

She finishes and picks the phone back up so I can see her face.

"So..." I say. "You like?"

Her eyes go wide. "Jesus, Tro. What do you think?"

"Um..."

"I love it. It's fucking amazing."

I slouch deeper into the backseat of the cab. "That's the kind of stuff you should be recording."

She blows out a derisive laugh. "Like that's gonna happen."

"Have you thought any more about jumping labels?" I ask.

She lowers her gaze. "Not really. Billie says we're close to a new contract with Universal. They're giving percentages and escalating royalties. She says we're not going to do better anywhere else."

"First of all, that's bullshit, and second of all, even if it wasn't, if you record the music you were meant to record, the money will follow."

Her face pulls into a skeptical squint. "That's seriously what you're going with?"

I shrug. "It worked for me."

"Yeah, because you willing to say anything and take off your clothes anywhere."

My turn to laugh. "So you're saying my success has nothing to do with my music?"

She drops the phone and the screen goes black. For a second I think she's gone, but then the phone lifts and I see her cynical expression. "Did you hear me say those words? I just meant that your music is only part of what made you so huge."

"You say you've got a friend who writes?" I say, to derail the in-depth analysis of how I got where I am.

"My best friend, Lilah," she says with a nod. "She's the reason I'm here."

The cab driver pulls up to the curb in front of my hotel and I toss some cash over the seat before getting out. "Let me hear something she wrote."

She sets the phone down again, and this time manages to prop it where I can see both her face and the guitar. Her fingers glide over the strings a few times as she thinks, then start on an up-tempo rhythm that puts what I wrote for her to shame. "This one's my favorite."

I head into the lobby and nearly walk into the wall as I listen, because I can't take my eyes off of the screen. I'm off the elevator and at the door to our suite before she's done, but I don't go in. I feel like this is something private, just for us. I'm not willing to walk in there and let the guys wreck this.

When she finishes, she takes a deep breath and looks at the phone. "She wrote that the last summer we spent at her grandma's."

"It's fucking…" I trail off with a shake of my head because there's not a word. "You need to be recording that shit. I'm serious, Lucky. That shit's going to get you wherever you want to go in this business. Your friend has something special."

Her fingers dance distractedly over the strings in another melody. "She's been my inspiration from way back when we were just kids."

I crack a smile and slide down the wall 'til my ass is on the floor. "You're *still* just a kid, Lucky."

She shakes her head, no humor on that incredible face. "I haven't been a kid for a long time."

My laugh is automatic and more bitter than I intended. "Yeah, I get that."

Her gaze lifts to mine and even through the cyber, it pins me in place, looking for the lie. "Do you?"

I hold her eyes and give her a small nod.

"No one writes much about your past," she says suspiciously.

I lift a questioning eyebrow at her and give her my best smirk. But it's all just to hide the fact that a steel band just constricted around my chest and I can't breathe. "And you know this because…?"

A scowl creases her forehead. "Shoot me, I Googled you."

"So, what did you find?" I ask, my heart speeding in my chest even though I'm well aware of what's out there.

"All your Wikipedia page says you is that you grew up in Alabama, and your mom died when you were three and you never knew your dad."

My heart pounds in my throat at the lie. So far no one's dug deep enough to find the truth and I plan to keep it that way.

"What else does it say?" I ask to get her off the topic of my lowlife old man.

"It says Roadkill started in Shreveport, Louisiana when you were seventeen, and you guys relocated to Austin just before you signed with Universal and your first CD went triple platinum."

"That's just about it," I say dismissively.

Her scowl deepens. "There are a lot of gaps there."

I give her the look that always throws the lady journalists off when they're asking too many questions. "You sound awfully interested for someone who hates me."

"I've been in the public eye for less than a year and my Wiki page is twice as long as yours." Her eyes narrow. "Which makes me wonder what you're hiding."

I blow out a laugh and shake my head. "Everything."

"I don't get how you can do that," she says, throwing a hand up in frustration. "Everyone knows every fucking thing about me, and you seem to have dodged all the hard questions."

"We took different paths to get here," I say. "Yours was very public, and that fucking show you were on used all your 'human interest' crap to drive up their ratings." I lean more heavily into the wall. "I, on the other hand, sort of came out of the blue. So they only know what I tell them."

"Who raised you after your mom died?" she pushes.

"An aunt," I lie.

"What were you doing in Shreveport when you were seventeen if you grew up in Alabama?"

"Washing dishes in a roadside dive." I put on my cocky asshole mask to deflect any more questions. "Grim came in to the diner, ordered a burger, and that was the start of Roadkill.

We traveled around Louisiana for most of the next year in Jamie's old Chevy Crew Cab, played seedy bars for free booze, and the seeds of greatness were sown." I try to read her through the screen, hoping she's satisfied with the tidy bow I'm putting on the story. "It grew pretty fast into respectable bars for actual cash, then opening for bigger local bands on tour, finally to a record contract and…" I cuff out a laugh. "…what do you know, a fucking star is born."

"But why were you in Shreveport? You didn't answer that," she presses. "And your dad was nowhere in all of this?"

I drag myself off the floor. "Listen, Lucky, I gotta go. But think about what I said about talking to other labels. That stuff your friend wrote is fucking magic."

I log off before she can ask any more questions and head into the suite.

CHAPTER 12

Shiloh

San Francisco.

Home.

We're seven weeks into our tour. It's our twenty-fourth show and I'm exhausted. But tonight my best friend Lilah and her boyfriend Bran are coming to the show. It's been so long since we've had any time together and I'm dying to see her.

We drove all night from Portland and pulled into the lot at AT&T Park at dawn, but the day has been full of interviews with the local TV shows and sound checks. That's the part I'm getting really tired of. Onstage, I feel the same energy I always have. When I'm performing, I'm in my zone and I don't worry so much about fucking up anymore. But it's the interviews, where they still ask about my love life and all kinds of other crap that isn't anyone's business but mine, that wear me down. I'm starting to get why Tro doesn't do them.

Max grabs me on the way out the door after the sound check. "The buses aren't leaving till morning, so the guys are all going into the city after the show." He grins at me. "Been a while since we've had a carriage ride. You should come."

"Sorry. I have plans."

He frowns. "Your manager has you on too tight a leash, Shiloh. This is your coming out party. Live a little."

I shake my head. "It's not Billie. My best friend is coming tonight, and I really just want some time to catch up with her."

He throws his hands in the air. "You're really not making this fair, you know. I'm charming and loveable. You should be out of your mind falling for me by now, but you keep dodging me."

"Don't take it personally," I say, backing away a step. "I don't do love."

He looks stricken. "But everybody loves me."

Now's the time. I take a breath and get serious. "Look, Max, you're a really cool guy and all, but…" My hand moves in a circle between us. "…this just isn't going to happen."

All the play leaves his expression. "You know Gunnison's only giving you the time of day because he wants into your pants."

I raise my eyebrows at him and smile a little, trying to lighten the blow. "And that's different from you, how?"

His eyes remain hard for a second, but then he shakes his head as his jaw unclenches. "You really have no fucking clue what you're missing, Lucky. I'm seriously all that."

I decide to let the "Lucky" slide. Everywhere I go, people are calling me that. It's like trying to stop a boulder rolling downhill. "I'm sure you are."

He gives me that cocky smile and a small nod, then heads backstage. "See you tonight."

"See you tonight," I say, turning for the door. I hurry back to the bus because Lilah and her boyfriend are supposed to be here any minute, and when I get there, they already are.

"Oh my God!" Lilah squeals when I step into the bus. She slams into me.

"Got a call from security," Billie says with a smile. "Thought you wouldn't mind if I let them in."

A big guy in jeans and a dark blue T-shirt, with a longish dark hair and tattoos up his arms stands back near the couch with his hands in his pockets and his head lowered. Lilah told me her boyfriend was ex-Marine and older, but she failed to mention how hot he is. When she finally unwraps herself from me, she takes my hand and pulls me deeper into the bus to where he is.

"Lo, this is Bran."

I shake his outstretched hand. "It's great to finally meet you."

He nods. "Congrats on all your success."

"Thanks."

Billie comes over with an envelope and pulls two lanyards out. "These are your backstage passes," she tells them. "They need to be worn all the time or security will likely remove you."

"This is so amazing," Lilah says, looping hers around her neck. She looks at me and shakes her head a little. "I can't believe this is your life now." She holds up a hand as her eyes widen. "I mean, I totally can. I always knew this would happen for you, but..." She makes a vague gesture at our surroundings. "I can't believe it."

I smile and pull her down on the couch. "God, I've missed you. How have you been? Tell me everything."

She glances at Bran. "I'm good."

She sounds unsure, and for a second I wonder if Bran is hurting her or something. But then she elaborates. "I've been to see my mom in jail."

"Oh," I say as understanding dawns.

Lilah and her older sister Destiny showed up at my group home one night when Lilah and I were fourteen. They were soaking wet and covered with soot, but neither of them would tell me exactly what happened. The next morning, Destiny told me that their house burned down. Their parents were methheads and ran a lab out of their kitchen, so it wasn't really a surprise that they'd blown up the house, but the cops had hauled their parents to jail. That meant that Lilah and Destiny were on their own.

They managed to stay out of the system even though Destiny was only nineteen. But Lilah and Destiny never once went to see their parents in jail. Until now, apparently.

"How did it go?"

"Did you know my father died in the fire?" she asks.

I feel my face go cold. "I thought he was in jail with your mom."

"Me too."

We've texted each other hundreds of times since I left for *The Voice*, but I'm just now realizing it's all been about me. She's wanted to know about everything, from recording the CD, to where I was living, to how it was to tour with Roadkill. She must have been saving this for our face to face.

I shake my head. "Jesus, Lilah." It seems like a pretty huge discrepancy, dead and jail, and I want to ask how she didn't know, but Bran's eyes find mine and in them I see his concern. There's more to the story than the fact her dad's dead. I want to ask her, but Bran's look tells me now might not be the time.

She nods slowly, trying to put things together in her head. Behind her, Bran slides closer and rests his hand on her shoulder. She lifts her hand and lays it over his.

"Are you okay?" I ask.

She nods again. "I'm getting there." Then her face brightens and she looks around. "So, tell me everything!"

"Why don't you catch up over lunch," Billie says. "I've called a car for you. Go get something to eat, but remember you need to be back for costuming and makeup at six."

We find a pizza place that the driver recommends and we catch each other up on everything over pepperoni and mushrooms. My first release was Lilah's song, so she's made some money from that.

"Enough that Destiny and I moved out of our crap apartment to somewhere Bran thinks is safer," she says with a glance at him.

"It's in my building," he says, a smile ghosting over his face. "So, yeah. It's safer."

"No one messes with Bran," she says with a wily smile.

"Maybe someday I'll get some time off and I can come out there," I say. I'm still having trouble picturing Lilah in the sticks, but she seems happy.

We get back to the bus just in time for me to head over to the dressing room.

"Your passes should get you just about anywhere," I say, giving Lilah a hug on my way into the arena. "You can just walk around or whatever. I'll see you backstage before the show."

At seven I'm onstage, and Lilah is dancing with Bran in the wings through the entire show. When I get to my finale, "More Than Nothing," I drag her onstage with me.

"This is my best friend, Lilah Morgan," I tell the crowd, "and she wrote this song. She's amazing and I hope I get to record more of her songs for you."

I make her stay out here with me through the whole song, and when we come off, Bran is waiting for her with the most incredible smile. There's no doubt from that look how proud he is of her.

Which makes me so happy.

Billie grabs me as soon as we hit the curtain. "You've got a quick interview," she says, pulling me toward the hall to the dressing rooms.

"I'll be right back!" I call over my shoulder to Lilah.

By the time they're done with me and Billie cuts me loose and heads back to the bus, Roadkill is already on stage.

I come up behind a dancing Lilah and grab her hand. "Let's go."

"Uh-uh," she says, tugging back. "I'm backstage at the concert everyone wants tickets for. I'm not going anywhere."

"Fine," I say and keep walking. "Meet me at the bus after."

She grabs my arm. "And so are you."

I bunch my hands on my hips. "Why would I want to do that?"

"Have you stayed for Roadkill's show before?" she asks with a tip of her head toward the stage.

I shake my head.

"You get that people are paying scalpers a grand a ticket to see this show, right?"

I glance toward the stage, where Tro and the guys are just hitting their stride on their next song, and take a deep breath. "I'll see if I can find some chairs."

She grins and starts dancing to the music. "I won't need one."

I sit next to Derrick, the stage monitor guy, while Lilah dances. After the song, Bran pulls her to him and kisses her. She sways in his arms for the next three songs.

Bran brought Lilah to L.A. for *The Voice* finals. I've seen tapes of the show, and when I'm singing my original song, the one Lilah wrote, the cameras cut to Lilah in the audience and caught her and Bran in the middle of a life-altering, Earth-moving kiss. Turns out, I found out later, that was the night that Lilah finally gave into Bran. She'd been fighting her attraction for months because Bran had dated Lilah's sister and Destiny was still into him, but also because Bran was twenty-six and he didn't know Lilah was only sixteen...which he found out the next night while they were in the audience for the results show.

But now...I've never seen Lilah so happy. And after everything she's been through with her methhead parents, she deserves it.

I settle deeper into the chair and watch Tro. It's the first time I think I've ever seen him totally sober out there, focusing on just the music. He always sounds incredible, but tonight, he's on fire. His vocals are clear and perfect, even when he's screaming out the lyrics.

I don't realize he knows I'm still here until he takes a few steps my direction and looks directly at me. "What did you guys think of Lucky tonight? That girl's something, huh?"

An appreciative roar goes up from the audience.

He comes closer and beacons me with a crook of his finger. "Come on out here, Lucky."

My eyes go wide and my feet are suddenly lead. I shake my head.

"How'd you like a Lucky exclusive?" he asks the crowd. "Something no one's ever heard before?"

The audience sends the roof off the stadium.

I feel like a rabbit, trapped in the headlights of an oncoming Lamborghini. It's coming so fast that no matter what I do, it's going to flatten me.

I glance at Grim and he strums his bass and gives me an annoyed look. Apparently he's about as onboard with this detour as he was with "Happy Birthday" a few weeks ago.

"Go, Lo," Lilah says from beside me and gives me a gentle shove.

I turn to look at her with pleading eyes. When I turn back to the stage, I find Tro right in front of me. He takes my hand and gently draws me to center stage. One of the roadies brings over a stool and sets it up in front of Tro's mic and Tro helps me onto it.

And all I can think the entire time is, this is a huge mistake. He wants us to do a song we've never rehearsed. It's basically a rock ballad—nothing like anything else in either of our set lists. The audience, who came here to hear Roadkill's heavy rhythms and Tro's angry lyrics, is going to totally turn on him.

On *us*.

But then he starts fingering out the notes on his guitar—his song, the one he wrote for me, and a desperate tickle starts deep in my chest. I don't know what it means or exactly what I'm desperate for, but the sensation grows stronger with every note until I'm overwhelmed with need so intense that I feel like my heart is about to cave in.

Tro must have given Grim and Jamie a heads up, and the music, because they slide right in seamlessly. And when they come around to the beginning, I open my mouth and sing his words.

"I walk from what I've left behind
as if it has no hold.
As if the chains aren't forged from steel
and welded to my soul."

Out in the dark of the arena, one by one, lighters begin to glow in the air. By the end of the first verse, as far as I can see, arms are waving overhead to the slow beat. And when I glance at Tro, he's watching me with a quiet intensity that sets off sparklers in my chest.

All of a sudden I can't take my eyes off him. They trace the lines of his face as I sing, and when a light I've never seen there before begins to shine out of his eyes, like a reflection of the thousands of lighters out in the audience, it warms me to my core.

He's not drunk. Or stoned. He's right here with me, and despite the fifteen thousand onlookers, it feels like we're all alone.

Emotion begin to choke off my voice, but I fight it because more than I've ever wanted anything, I want to do his song justice.

CHAPTER 13

Tro

She's a fucking angel.

It's cheesy as all fucking hell, but it's what's running though my mind the entire time I'm listening to her sing my words. She turns them into something bigger than what I wrote.

I want to keep her out here. Close.

But the song comes to an end, because that's what they do, and she slips off the stool. For a moment, she holds my gaze, but then she's gone, retreating to the wings.

I can't keep my eyes off her for the rest of the set. I'm pretty sure this is the first time she's stayed to hear us play. I know it's probably because she's got people here with her, but I can't help hoping it's at least partly because she's feeling the same draw I am.

When we head to the dressing room to change between sets, Lucky stands as we pass and gives me a small smile.

And right then, with that gesture, Earth's magnetic poles shift and up turns to down.

I fucking float into the dressing room, the whole time thinking about Lucky and me in the studio, recording that track.

Jamie rips his shirt off and beats his chest like a gorilla before tugging on a fresh T-shirt, but Grim's uncharacteristically quiet.

"Everything cool, man?" I ask.

He looks hard at me. "I'm just not sure what the fuck we were doing out there at the beginning of that set."

"Just wanted to try something new," I say. "The crowd seemed into it, so I don't get the problem."

"I'm not saying it wasn't good, man, but what the fuck's going on with you and that little girl." He tugs on a dry shirt. "I mean, if that's your grand fucking gesture or whatever—"

"We gotta go," I say, pulling on a shirt and heading to the door. Because it kinda was, but I'm not sure I'm ready to admit that yet.

But before I'm out the door, Grim has a handful of my shirt and is yanking me back. "Keep your fucking head on straight, Gunner. Remember who your fucking audience is."

I yank myself out of his grasp and turn for the stage, my Lucky buzz totally dead.

CHAPTER 14

Shiloh

Tro doesn't look at me on his way back to the stage, and their next set is full of their loudest, angriest stuff.

Lilah finally wears out near the end of the set. She's a big ball of sweat when she comes over and sits in my lap. "This is crazy!"

I can't help the smile. "Having fun?"

"Oh my God! This is the most amazing thing that's ever happened to me."

I glance to where Bran's watching show. "The *most* amazing thing?"

She follows my gaze and smiles. "Okay, the *second* most amazing thing."

"Are you in love?" I ask, clasping my hands around her waist.

She drops her head back onto my shoulder. "I am so in love I don't even think there's a word to describe it." She brings her gaze back to mine. "Give it a few weeks and you'll know what I mean."

I scrunch my face at her. "I'd need to find a guy first."

She nods toward Tro, onstage. "You already have a guy, Lo. He's so fucking into you it may as well be tattooed across his forehead."

I pfft her and shake my head. "You have no clue what you're talking about. That's Tro Gunnison. He's into anything with a vagina."

She rolls her eyes. "You've always been so blind to what other people think about you."

The stage lights flash through the colors in quick succession and the crowd roars as Jamie starts the drum intro to "Insane."

"Which is why I'm still sane," I say, shoving her up.

She looks at me a second longer before going over to dance with Bran.

We stay through the encore, and I see why everyone says Roadkill is a tour band. I have to admit their live show is incredible. All three of the guys are total showboats, playing to their audience and leaving it all out there.

Tro heads straight for me when the stage lights dim, toweling off his face and neck. "Surprised you're still here."

I flick a wrist at Lilah. "Only because Lilah wanted the full Roadkill experience."

Tro turns to her with raised eyebrows. "The songwriter friend?"

"Lilah, this is Tro Gunnison. You might want to shield your eyes or get one of those mirror scopes they use to watch solar eclipses, because his ego might blind you if you look directly at him."

She's bouncing on her toes a little, unable to contain herself. "Oh my God. It's amazing to meet you. You guys put on a crazy good show!"

His smile is as cocky as ever. "Thanks."

"You wrote that song?" she asks. "The one you did with Lo?"

"Lo?" he says, glancing at me. "That's what you call her?"

Lilah nods. "We used to call ourselves LoLah when we played in San Francisco. Get it?" she asks, then stabs a finger into my arm. "Lo and Lah," she finishes, thumbing her own chest.

"Well," he says, "all I know is Lucky needs someone with talent writing for her, and she says that's you."

"Her stuff is kickass," I interject before Lilah can put herself down. She knows she's good, but she might not be willing to admit that to a bona fide rock star.

But when she smiles and nods, I know I didn't need to worry. "Kickass," she repeats.

Jamie comes by and chest bumps Tro. "Heading back to the hotel. You coming?"

Tro turns to me. "What are you guys doing now?"

I look at Lilah and shrug. "We might just go back to the bus and hang out."

"When is your bus heading south?" he asks.

"Not till morning."

He looks up at Lilah. "You guys mind if I hang out with you?" He nudges his chin at Jamie and Grim, and Grim cuts Tro a glare as they disappear out the back door. "Otherwise I've got to go back to the hotel with those dicks."

"Yeah," she says with a questioning look at me. "That would be cool."

"Awesome," Tro says, flashing her his killer smile. "Maybe I can hear some of your stuff."

I can tell she wants to be more excited, but she's holding it back while she tries to read me. I guess I don't blame her. Partying with Tro Gunnison has to feel like a pretty big deal to her.

When I look at Tro, he's waiting for my answer. "As long as you promise not to fuck with my girl," I say, nodding at Lilah. "Her boyfriend is an ex-Marine and he'll filet your ass if you touch her."

He cuts Bran a grin. "Wouldn't want to disrespect a national hero."

I stand and we walk toward the hallway to the dressing room.

"I'll find you guys after I get cleaned up?" he says, plucking his sweaty T-shirt off his chest, and that's all it takes for my eyes to glue to his pecs.

Damn.

"You know where the bus is?" I ask, pulling myself together.

He nods. "See you in a few."

"Kay."

He heads up the hall and I turn to find Lilah grinning at me.

"What?"

"Tattooed," she says as Bran punches through the door to the hallway that leads to the parking lot.

We get to the bus and Billie's at the dinette with papers strewn in front of her and her laptop open, talking on the phone. She's always putting out fires for one of her many clients so it doesn't surprise me to see her working so late. She gives us a wave and I gesture that we're heading to the rear lounge. I grab three beers out of the fridge on our way through the kitchen and Billie scowls at me, so I hand them to Bran.

"So, you and your manager have this bus to yourselves?" he asks, glancing at the bunks we're passing on either side of the narrow hallway on the way to the back of the bus. There are six of them, but three are covered with my clothes.

"Yeah. The band is together in another bus."

I open the door into the lounge, where there's a horseshoe sofa around the back facing a big screen TV next to the door we just came through. My guitar is propped in the corner and I've got a snapshot of Lilah and me at her grandmother's tucked into the window casing.

On the other side of the door is a bar with a stocked fridge. By stocked, I mean snacks and sodas. Billie won't let me keep beer back here, I guess because she wants to think she has control over how much I drink.

Billie hardly ever comes back here, so this is my sanctuary. I mostly play Hearthstone and text Lilah and some of my old *The Voice* friends when there's decent cell service. Max texts me a lot, but I'm trying not to encourage him, so about half the time, I ignore them. Sometimes I play some of Lilah's and my old stuff and picture myself back in San Francisco. I'd say it's lonely, but the truth is, I like being alone.

I go to the cupboard and grab bags of Cheetos and Doritos, tossing them on the low table in front of the couch. I pull down a tub of Red Vines and set it in front of Lilah. "Had them pick those up for you."

Bran cracks open a beer and hands it to me, then does the same for Lilah before opening his.

"Pretty glamorous," Lilah says, looking around as she and Bran settle into seats on the couch.

I shoot her a cynical look. "I've always been glamorous."

She laughs, because it's so not true. Lilah's been at my side through every foster home, the group home. We've been there for each other when no one else was. She's the only person I've ever shown my insecurities to. She's the only person who's ever met the real me.

"So, where to next?" she asks, pulling my guitar into her lap and picking at the strings.

"We're heading south, L.A. and San Diego, then we cut back through Denver and Texas on our way to Florida, where we wrap up."

"How many shows all together?" Bran asks.

I click on the TV and find a rerun of *The Big Bang Theory*, then mute it. "Forty in nine weeks."

"How's your voice holding out?" Lilah asks, bringing her hand to her throat with a cringe.

"So far, so good. We usually have a travel day in between shows, so that helps."

"God, Lo," she says, looking around again. "I always knew you'd make it. Ever since that first time we sat on that bus stop bench singing Bob Dylan."

I bust out laughing. "Yeah, that was a big day. Was it four dollars and seventy three cents we made?"

She shakes her head. "It was the way people looked at you. We were, what, nine? Ten? Even then, you had that…whatever. That intangible thing that makes people stars."

"Wow, that was deep," I say, then take a long drink from my bottle. "I'm not drunk enough for that yet."

She slugs me in the shoulder, then her fingers start moving over the strings. It's a song I haven't heard for a while—one of the first Lilah wrote. I start singing the melody and she slides in with the harmony.

And, God, it gives me shivers.

This is what I love about music, how it transcends everything and cuts to the root of a person. To their soul.

We're halfway through the song when a knock on the window behind my head makes me jump. I turn and see Tro just stepping down from where he must have climbed up on the wheel to reach the window. He points at the door up front.

I get up and when I open the lounge door, I see the sliding door to Billie's bunk is closed and the light's are out up front. I tiptoe past and go to the front to open the door.

"Hey," he says.

I look past him and see people still trickling out of the stadium.

I step back and as he moves past me and notice his hair is damp and he smells like soap. I picture him in the shower, then wish I didn't when my insides begin to buzz.

The door closes and I realize we're just standing here and staring at each other when he reaches up and combs a hand self-consciously through his dark curls. I've never seen Tro self-consciously about anything. I didn't know he was even capable.

"Billie's sleeping," I whisper, shaking off the goose bumps and grabbing a few more beers from the fridge.

He nods and we head to the back, where Lilah and Bran are waiting.

"Hey," Bran says, standing and shaking Tro's hand before taking a beer from mine. "Great show, man."

"Thanks." Tro shoots a glance at me. "Think it was our best so far."

Bran slides into his seat next to Lilah. "The girls were just putting on a show of their own."

Tro's eyes widen and slip to me.

"Get your mind out of the gutter," I say. "We were just playing some of Lilah's stuff—songs we used to play in the BART stations and whatever."

"Don't let me interrupt." He gestures to Lilah to continue as he takes the seat next to me and cracks open his beer. "Please."

She thinks for a second, then starts on one that was probably our best moneymaker back in the day.

When we finish, Tro stands. "Come on."

I lift my eyebrows but not my ass. "Where?"

He raises an eyebrow at me. "There's got to be a BART station nearby, right?"

Liliah's eyes widen as she splits a glance between us. "Seriously?"

Tro locks eyes with mine, and in his gaze, all I see is boyish mischief. The player is nowhere to be found. A warm feeling spreads through my chest at the thought of being back in my territory, where I know the deal.

"Let's do it," I say, standing and towing Lilah up by the arm.

She grins and packs my guitar into the case.

We're as quiet as four people on a tour bus can be, sneaking past Billie's bunk. I grab a jacket off mine on the way by, remembering how cold it was when I let Tro in. He pulls the hood up on his hoodie as we step out into the cool night.

"Yeah," I say, giving him a look. "That's inconspicuous."

He grins at me and takes off jogging toward the security gate. Lilah's on his heels, carrying my guitar, but Bran waits for me to lock up.

He gives me an unsure smile. "This is crazy, isn't it?"

I bust out laughing when I think about it. "That's Tro Gunnison," I say pointing after them. "How good are you at crowd control?"

He scratches his head. "Armed insurgents, I've got covered. Not so sure about rabid fans."

I smile and take off after Tro and Lilah. They're waiting just outside the gate for us.

"Thought you went soft on me, Lucky," Tro says with a wink.

I shoot him a glare. "Just shows how little you know about me."

He looks up the street past the stadium. There are still people milling on the sidewalk outside the exits, but the constant flow of fans has slowed. "So where to?"

"This way," Lilah says, leading us up Battery Street.

Tro and I don't talk as we walk, but he stays close by my side. When we get to the station, we lope down the stairs and Lilah uses her pass to get us all through the turnstiles. It's warmer down here, but I take a second to scope things out before lowering my hood.

There are a dozen or so people on the platform, and most of them are in one of two groups, huddled together chatting.

Chances are at least some of these people are coming from the stadium.

I move to the bench in the middle of the platform and Lilah follows. We sit and she pulls out my guitar, laying the case open at our feet, just the way we used to when this was how we made our living.

Bran slides onto a bench just across from ours and Tro stands at my side.

"Let's see this subway magic," he says with a nod at Lilah.

She smiles and starts in on one of my favorites. A few heads turn our direction with the sound of the guitar, but just as fast, they go back to their conversation.

Until I open my mouth.

With my first line, more heads turn, and by the time she kicks in with the harmony on the chorus, there are a dozen pairs of curious eyes perusing our small group. I watch the whispers pass around the circle, and several of them point to Tro.

He's grinning ear to ear as he watches us, seemingly oblivious to the fact that everyone here is staring at him. When we come back around to the chorus and he starts singing along, that's the open invitation. Despite the fact that a train is just pulling into the station, the group nearest us comes over and stares at him with wide eyes and goofy grins. A couple and one of the singles get brave and join the circle. The train doors open and no one gets on. Some of the passengers on the train look out curiously, and then I hear an "Oh my God!" followed closely by a "Go, go, go!" as a stream of girls exit the car nearest us and stampede over to where we sit.

We finish the song and Lilah starts plucking out the melody to the new song Tro wrote. "Do I have it right?" she asks as he smiles.

He nods. "You picked that up fast."

She shrugs as she plays. "I've always just played by ear."

When she comes back around, he starts singing the lyrics and the gathering crowd squeals and presses closer. On the second verse, I join in with harmony.

And fuck, I've got the shivers again.

Tro slides onto the bench next to me and his strong arm hooks around my waist as he sways us to the rhythm. I expect him to remove it when we finish the song. He doesn't, and I shiver again.

It's cold down here. That's what I tell myself anyway. But it's really Tro. I don't want to feel anything at his touch except disgust. But I have that same sense of longing, a deep aching need, that I had while we were onstage, and I don't want him to take his arm away.

Lilah plays her way through all our old material, and when Tro catches onto a chorus, he sings along. I haven't felt so light since *The Voice* started. This is my home, where I belong, and despite the press of listeners, I lose myself in the sensation.

But my phone buzzing in my pocket brings me back to reality.

I pull it out and find two things. It's six o'clock in the morning, which means we've been down here for nearly five hours, and Billie is freaking out.

"I've gotta go," I say, texting her back.

The gathered group, many of whom are the originals, protest, but Tro stands. "Yeah. My flight's in a couple of hours."

Some of the girls ask Tro to sign their boobs and he obliges with a shrug at me. And right then, it strikes me how out of character that reaction is. In the last seven weeks, I've seen him sign plenty of body parts, and never has he been so reserved.

Lilah puts my guitar away and wraps me in a hug. "I was wrong," she says, her eyes watching Tro with the girls. "He's not just into you. He loves you, Lo."

My heart skips and I feel my eyes widen. "Tro Gunnison doesn't love anyone but himself."

She scowls at me. "How can you miss the way he looks at you? Especially onstage tonight when he was playing the song he wrote for you. He would have melted right into you if he could have."

I shake my head. "You don't know him. He's not like that. There's not a genuine bone in his body." I gesture to where he's signing an enormous boob that is fully out of the shirt and bra. "He's all sex and show."

Her eyebrows go up and her gaze turns skeptical. "Maybe it's you that doesn't know him."

"I know him," I say, but when he backs away instead of putting the boob back into the clothes, which is the way it usually goes, I wonder.

Lilah has me in her arms again. "This has been so amazing, Lo. God, I miss you."

"Me too," I say, and am surprised to find myself suddenly near tears. "Sometimes I really don't know what I'm doing, you know? This is the only place I've ever really felt like I belonged."

Her eyes widen as she shakes her head. "Oh my God, Lo. You are amazing out there, on the stage. *That* is where you belong."

I give her a weak smile as Tro finishes with his girls and comes up behind me. "Thanks."

A train pulls into the station and I give Lilah one last hug before she and Bran load on. As Tro and I head toward the exit, I can't believe how hard it is to climb the stairs. The last time I walked out of here, I was getting ready to go to L.A. for *The Voice*. I didn't really think about what that meant, other than I had a chance to live my dream. But now the hollow place in my chest aches, knowing this part of my life is gone forever. I never thought I'm miss my old life, but I do.

Tro leans into me and wraps an arm around my shoulders when we reach the street. "Your friends are pretty cool. This was the best road night I've had in a while."

I know about the parties in their hotel suites and the girls, so I'm having a hard time believing him, but I don't argue it.

"Lilah's the best. I don't know Bran very well, but he makes her happy, so I know he must be a good guy."

He watches the sidewalk unfold in front of us as we walk and gives slow nod. "You and Lilah went to school together?"

"Yeah. She's been my best friend forever."

"So…she's your age?" he asks, and I see his mind cranking out the math. Bran is an ex-Marine, which makes him a lot older than her.

"A few months older, but…yeah."

He nods again and looks like he wants to say something else, but then he gives his head a small shake. And I really wish I could read his mind, because I have a feeling there's way more going on in there than anyone gives him credit for.

CHAPTER 15

Tro

"So, really," Lucky asks, watching her feet on the sidewalk, "what's the deal with your family?"

My feet stall and I pull a smoke from my pack, lighting up. "You're not going to let that go, are you?"

She gives her head a solemn shake.

"Why do you care so much?"

"I guess I just want to understand why you turned out to be so…" She trails off and waves her hand in a circle at me.

I size her up for a long second, deciding how much I can trust her with, then start walking again. "Let's start with you. There's more to your whole story than just showing up and auditioning for *The Voice*."

She frowns at my deflection, but answers anyway. "Like I said, my life is all over the internet. No secrets."

"So, give me the Cliff Notes."

"My crackhead mother left me in a McDonalds bathroom when I was a few days old. They say it's a miracle I'm alive. That's why someone thought it was clever to put the last name Luck instead of Doe on all my paperwork. I was in foster homes for a while, but it's hard to adopt out a crack baby, I guess, because everyone's pretty sure you're going to turn out moron or something. When I started high school, they moved me into a group home in the city." She shoves her hands in the pockets of her jacket and shrugs. "Technically, that's where I still live."

"So, how does that work now that you're a rockstar? Like, who signed your contract and where does all the money go?"

"Thanks to Billie, the State's not stealing all my money, if that's what you're asking. She got a lawyer and we got everything set up in a trust. The State is the custodian, but the lawyer worked it out so that they can't access the accounts without me knowing."

I nod. "Glad someone's looking out for you."

"Billie's been great. She's got my back." She gives me an inquisitive lift of her eyebrows. "Now your turn."

I take a deep drag and blow a stream of white smoke into the cool early morning air. "I took off from home when I was a kid. It was a bad situation. I ended up in Shreveport because that's as far from Mobile as the money I had would take me, and it was far enough that I didn't think anyone would find me."

A deep crease forms between her eyebrows. "So you were running from your family?"

I nod.

"When you say bad situation...?"

"I got beat up a lot. Nearly ended up in the hospital the night I left."

"Who would...?"

She leaves the noose dangling, so I jump into it. "My old man."

Her eyes widen when she puts the pieces together. My cover story is I never knew him. "Did you...I don't know, ever fight back or whatever?"

I shake my head. "Make love, not war. I fucked his girlfriend instead."

Her face freezes in a mask of shock, and I regret opening my mouth. I don't even know what compelled me to say any of this to her. But now I feel like she has to know the rest of the story.

I lower my gaze and take another drag, watching my feet. "She was patching me up the night after my old man beat the living shit out of me, cleaning the blood off my face with a washrag. I grabbed her and stuck my tongue down her throat. I don't really know why, except at the time I felt so fucking helpless and I guess it felt like revenge. But when she kissed me back instead of pushing me away..." I trail off with a shrug, wondering why the fuck it was this story, of all of them, that decided it needed to be told.

"Did your dad know...what happened?" she asks, some of the shock on her face dissolving into sympathy I don't deserve.

We reach the security gate into the lot where her bus is parked and I lean against the post. "I didn't wait around to find out. I took off before dawn."

"As in...forever? You just left home?"

I nod. "I've never been back to Mobile. Not even on tour."

"So, have you talked to your dad since?"

This is deeper into my history than I've ever gone—more information than even Grim has. If I don't stop the bleeding, I'm going to hemorrhage every bloody detail of my sordid past out all over Lucky. Despite my gut telling me I can trust her, I'm not willing to take that risk.

Her phone buzzing in her pocket saves me from having to. She pulls it out and sends a quick text. "I've gotta go," she says when she looks up at me, and there's something a little mournful in the words.

"See you in L.A.," I say, backing up the sidewalk.

She swings around the pole to the other side of the chain link fence and looks back at me. "Barring a bus crash, I'll be there."

A smile I can't stop curves my mouth. "Can't kill an angel."

Lucky grabs the fence and doubles over laughing. "Did you really just say that?"

I rub the back of my neck and feel the cringe on my face. "Yeah...that was pretty lame, wasn't it?"

"Um...yeah."

"I'll have to do better next time," I say, scratching my head as I back away a step. "See you tonight."

"Have a good flight," she says, lifting her hand in a sort of wave. Or maybe it's the signal to stop, because something in her eyes is giving that definite vibe.

"No such thing," I say, still trying to read her. Because, fuck. If she's feeling what I am...I've never wanted to kiss someone as much as I want to kiss Lucky right this second.

We both just stand here, three feet apart, staring at each other for a long moment before I finally lift my hood and turn to the main road to look for a cab. Because if I stand here another second, staring at that face, I won't be able to stop myself.

As I walk, our conversation replays in my mind. What is it about that girl that makes me want to spill my fucking guts?

I shake my head at myself as I wave a passing taxi down. Whatever it is, I need to tame it before I let her in too deep.

#

Me and the guys are stretched out in a corner of the airport at a gate where there's no flight scheduled when my phone rings. I pick it up when I see the number.

"Hey, Freddie. Long time."

"Got your text," he says. "So you're telling me Shiloh Luck is thinking about jumping labels? Because I'd fuck my grandmother to get her over here."

"She's having some creative differences at Universal," I tell him. "But I'm telling you, Fred, I just heard some shit last night that would make you come in your pants. You know her lead single, 'More Than Nothing?'"

"The one she sang on *The Voice*," he confirms.

"I just sat a BART station last night with her and the girl who wrote that, and these two are pretty fucking amazing. This kid, Lilah, can write the shit out of anything. Lucky wants to do her songs, but her producers are forcing her down the pop lane. She's not feeling it and I'm pretty sure she'd consider going anywhere that would let her do what she wants to do."

There's a pause. "You know I'd need to hear it before I could make any kind of commitment in that direction."

"I totally get it, man. I do. But I can't fucking believe Universal vetoed this shit. It's smart and original and kicks fucking ass. She'd be unstoppable with these tracks."

"When can she talk?"

"I haven't said anything to her 'cause I wanted to be sure you were on board first. Let me talk to her and I'll get back to you."

"All right," he says. "Give her my direct line and tell her to call when she has a chance."

"Her manager is Billie Sinclair. You might be hearing from her instead."

There's another pause, longer this time. "Tell me you're not serious."

A stone sinks in my gut. "What the fuck did you do, Freddie?"

"Billie. We've got…history of a personal nature, if you catch my drift. Let's just say she might not be too receptive with the idea of moving her client over to me."

I blow out a slow breath. "You fucked her."

"For six months," he says. "She didn't take it so well when I stopped."

My hand goes to the back of my neck and rubs at the knot forming there. "You're the perfect label for what Lucky wants to do."

"I'd cut off my fucking right nut to get her. And I'm thinking that's pretty literally what it would take to get Billie to bring her over; my right testicle hanging from a chain around her neck."

"Let me work on her. In the meantime, I'm going to send some tape from last night over so you can hear this shit for yourself. Try not to cream your shorts, man."

He laughs. "Can't make any promises."

"That's what got you into this fucking mess, you cocksucker."

I disconnect and loll my head back on the seat, wondering what Lucky's doing right now.

#

The next time I see her is after our sound check in L.A. We're heading out the back just as she and her crew are coming in, and I can't deny the change in my heart rate at just the sight of her.

Christ, she's beautiful.

L.A. is way warmer than San Francisco and she's in a white tank top and short black skirt, and it's everything I can do to rip my eyes away from those legs.

"Hey," I say as our paths cross. "You got a sec?"

She glances over her shoulder at the rest of her band, filing through the door. Max hesitates and cuts me a glare before following the rest of them in.

"Yeah…okay," she says.

There's a second when those deep whiskey eyes connect with mine that my synapses fry and I can't remember a fucking thing I was going to say, but then parts of the thought drift into my consciousness like feathers loose from a pillow.

"There's a guy I've worked with some, Freddie Palmer over at A&M. I think he'd be perfect to produce the stuff you want to do. I talked to him yesterday and he's—"

Her expression turns instantly to stone. "Wait…what? You already *talked* to him? Why would you do that?"

"Just wanted to feel him out to see if he was interested before I mentioned it to you. I think his exact words were he'd cut off his right nut to sign you. And he's interested in hearing Lilah's tracks. This could be perfect for you."

I'm talking too fast, because with every word she shakes her head a little harder and I want her to hear this before she totally shuts me out.

"I don't want your help."

"Seriously? Because this is an amazing opportunity."

Her glare slices through me. "Seriously."

I can't even get my head around a single reason that makes sense why she won't even talk to Freddie. "Why not?"

"Because I don't want to owe you anything."

And there it is. In that once sentence, she's shot me down on every level. That's what she thinks of me, that I'm doing this for some quid pro quo. "Listen, Lucky. I think you've got something. The shit I heard the other night, Lilah's music, you would go big with that. You need to record it. If Universal won't let you do it, you need to find someone who will. I just made a call. If it works out, it's because of you. You owe me nothing. Just talk to the guy. See what you think."

She scrutinizes me for another agonizing minute. "Fine. Text me his number." She rattles off her number and I'm having trouble punching it into my phone accurately because my fucking hand is shaking.

I'm shaking because a girl is giving me her number. What the fuck is wrong with me?

"Got it," I say, attaching Freddie's contact info and texting it to her.

Her phone buzzes. "Got it," she repeats.

And then I remember. All this persuasion, and here's where I probably kill the deal. "Oh, and you might not want to mention this to Billie until you talk to him yourself."

Her gaze grows hazy with suspicion. "Why?"

"I guess they know each other."

Her expression hardens again. "If Billie doesn't trust him, neither do I."

I rub the back of my neck. "Look, Lucky, I could get you some other names, but I really think he's your guy. He does what you want to do and he's really good at it. Just give him a call."

She turns toward the door and disappears inside without another word.

CHAPTER 16

Shiloh

I've stared at both numbers for the last two days. Tro wants me to call this Freddie guy, but what the fuck kind of name is Freddie. And if Billie has an issue with him, then it's not going to happen anyway.

But then there's also Tro's number.

I've had his Skype name, but somehow having his actual number feels so much more personal. I'm pretty damn sure none of his hook-ups have it.

Ever since he stood on stage that first night at Madison Square Garden and told eighteen thousand people he was going to fuck me, I've been one hundred percent sure that's all I was to him. A hook-up. And then when I didn't give in, a challenge. But now…it feels different between us. Something fundamental has changed.

And then I realize.

I like him. Not, *he's so hot* like, but as an actual person.

There's something real inside him that he doesn't want anyone to see. He hides it behind layers of flash and show, but he let down the front and I started to see what's underneath the other night.

And I like the guy I saw there.

I look at his text again. Freddie. He really thinks this guy knows what he's doing. Never in a million years did I expect to trust Tro with anything, especially my career, but I suddenly realize I do.

I hit the number before I can change my mind.

"Freddie here," a voice on the other end of the line says.

I almost disconnect, but instead, I take a deep breath. "Hi. My...um...friend, Tro Gunnison gave me your number...said I should call you?"

Jesus, I'm already fucking this up.

"Is this Shiloh?" he asks, his pitch a little higher. "He told me he'd pass my number along to you."

"Yeah...hi."

"Hey, it's great to hear from you. Thanks for the call."

There's a pause where I think I'm supposed to say something, but I don't have words.

"So, anyway, he sent me a few tracks and I think what you've got going—"

"Wait..." I interrupt. "What did he send you?" That asshole didn't mention sending tracks.

"Some stuff he said he recorded in the subway with your friend?"

I take a deep breath, because every nerve in my body is suddenly on fire. "Okay."

"I think this stuff is gold, Shiloh. I would absolutely be interested in hearing everything this friend of yours has written. And as far as the tracks I heard, they'd definitely be a go. I think this could be huge."

"So...you'd let me have some say in which tracks we went with?" I ask.

"I can guarantee you right now that if the rest of what you have is similar to what I've heard, I'd let you take your pick."

"What about on the studio tracks? Would Lilah have a chance to audition for lead guitar?"

"I can't see why not," he says. "I can't make any guarantees there, but we'd sure as hell listen to what she's got."

I feel like I'm about to float right off the floor. But then I remember Tro's warning. I can't do this without Billie. And I mean that literally. I have no idea what I'm doing. She handles everything business. "Tro says you and Billie have some bad blood?"

There's a short pause. "If you're interested in pursuing this, let me give her a call and see what I can do."

I swallow. "Yeah…okay. I am interested."

"Great," he says. "That's really great, Shiloh. You're playing the Staples Center again tonight, right?"

"Yeah. And then we have a day off before we're in San Diego," I say, the tiniest flicker of hope tickling my heart.

"Excellent. Let me see if I can work something out with Billie to meet before you leave southern California. Hopefully we'll have a chance to talk in person very soon."

"That would be great," I say. "Thanks."

I disconnect and press the phone to my forehead. "God, please," I whisper into the quiet of the bus. I don't pray, but I sure as hell am now. Because I want this…Lilah and me together again, doing our music. Nothing could be better.

#

"How about if, instead of taking it up and connecting the bridge, we go low instead, right there," Tro says, pointing to the bit of scrap paper we're jotting notes onto.

I strum the strings, working though the chord progression and find he's right. It works, but it's unexpected. "But then, on the backside, we can bring it back up so it ties into the chorus here." I work the strings as I explain and Tro nods along with the beat.

My phone buzzes and I pull it out of my pocket. After our show, I told Billie I was staying for Roadkill, but they finished playing over an hour ago. The venue is nearly empty, but Tro and I are still in Roadkill's dressing room, playing with melodies.

"Billie's wondering where I am," I say, setting his guitar aside and standing from the floor, where we've sort of set up camp. There are bowls of chips and a few scattered beer bottles from our impromptu picnic.

"I'll walk you back," he offers, even though the buses are just outside the back doors.

"I think I can manage to get there on my own," I say.

He ignores me and stands, brushing crumbs off his jeans. He shoves his hands in his pockets and we head toward the rear exit. "You should really call Freddie."

I wasn't planning on telling him until he talked to Billie, because I'm trying really hard not to get my hopes up in case this explodes in my face. "I did."

He looks at me. "How'd it go?"

"Good," I say. "He's going to try to set up a meeting with Billie and me before we leave SoCal."

He nods a little. "He's a really good fit for you, Lucky."

"Why didn't you tell me you'd sent him tracks?"

His eyes are a little wide when they flick to me then back to the floor. "Guess I didn't want you know I'd taped some of your stuff. Feels a little stalkerish."

I give him a hard look. "Only if you play it over and over while doing unspeakable things to yourself."

He fights the smile that tugs at the corners of his mouth as he punches open the door. "Don't think it hasn't crossed my mind."

We start across the lot toward the buses, and when he takes my elbow gently in his grasp, the slow burn that started under my skin as we were working flares into a bonfire.

"So…what's the deal with you and Max?" he asks as we pass their bus, where there's clearly a party raging.

I glance through the front window and just make out Max in a crush of female bodies in the front lounge. "He thought he was going to make me fall in love with him."

"Working?" he asks, his grip on my arm tightening slightly.

"I think he finally gets I'm not hooking up with anyone on this tour," I say. "Too awkward."

We reach my bus and he lets me go, but his eyes don't. "Good to know."

I open the door to the bus and Tro watches me up the stairs. "We should finish that song," I say, trying to keep the tickle of desperation I feel out of my voice. Tonight some inky layer of Tro sloughed off and something shiny winked out. I want to see more of whatever that was.

He nods. "Definitely."

"Night." I close the door, and when I turn, Billie is staring me down from her usual spot at the table. I think she's going to lay into me about being with Tro, but instead, she stands and plants a hand on her hip. "Why am I getting a phone call from Fred Palmer?" she says, shaking her phone in the air with the other one.

"Did you talk to him?" I ask.

"No! He's pond scum, Shiloh. I got a message from him saying he wanted to meet with us tomorrow. Why would he even think you might be interested in moving to A&M?"

I cringe. "I kind of called him."

She throws a hand in the air. "Why would you go behind my back and do that?"

"I just wanted to talk to him about doing Lilah's music. He's heard some of it and he says he really likes it."

"Just because he says it, doesn't mean he'll do it, Shiloh. People say all kinds of things in this business that they don't mean. Promises mean nothing until they're signed in blood on a contract."

"Why can't we just talk to him?" I ask. "See what he has to say?"

Her neck is red and it's starting to creep up to her ears. "No. We're not talking to him." She turns for the bunks. "I'm going to bed."

The rush of blood through my ears is so loud I can't hear anything else. What if this was my only chance to do Lilah's music?

I flop onto the couch and yank my hair, trying to think of ways to talk her down. But as my blood pressure settles and my mind stops spinning, I remember that this is Billie's gig. She knows this business. She's always had my back. I trust her, and she obviously doesn't trust this Freddie guy.

If Billie's this adamant, maybe I'm the one who's wrong. Maybe this guy was too good to be true after all.

Have I gotten soft, trusting too easily? Because I trusted Tro on this without even questioning it. I trusted Freddie to be honest and true to his word and I've never even met the guy.

Billie said way back at the start of the tour that I needed to grow a thick skin, and Tro basically said everyone in this business is out to fuck each other.

If I'm going to survive out here, I need to toughen up. And that means trusting no one.

CHAPTER 17

Tro

I'm fucking juiced. The notes that Lucky and I were working on cycle through my head all the way back to the hotel. It's that feeling I have when I'm onto something. What we've got so far is seriously good, but for the first time, I'm not convinced the electricity playing under my skin and running through my veins is because of the music.

Because the high from spending an hour one on one with Lucky is more intense than anything I've ever gotten from booze or drugs, and way the fuck more addictive.

I'm still in the fucking ozone when I walk into the suite. The party's lower key tonight, the standard guys and just a handful of girls. Jamie's speakers are playing and he's dancing slow and making out with a girl who's standing on the coffee table, which brings them to just about the same height.

"Dude!" he says when he sees me. "Where the fuck you been?"

I cross toward my bedroom. "Just hung back at the arena to work on some shit."

Grim scowls up at me from the couch as I pass. "Let me guess—you were with the mutt."

My feet stall and there's a second I can't even process what he means, but then it slams into me. How did I never see that Grim was such a fucking bigot?

Blood rises in my face as I turn to face him. "Her name is Shiloh," I say, realizing that may be the first time I've ever used her actual name.

He blows out a disgusted laugh. "Call her whatever you want, she's nothing but tight, calico pussy," he says, grabbing the crotch of the girl sitting next to him. "At least tell me you're hitting that. Because otherwise, you're just fucking babysitting."

All I can think about is smashing his ugly face with my fists. I can't see past that image to find fucking words.

Jamie must see it in my eyes, because he's off his girl in a flash and has a handful of my T-shirt. He glares down at Grim. "Let's just back the fucking train up here for a sec."

Grim looks like he's going to rise to the fight, but after a minute of stare down, he just gives his head a disgusted shake. "You need to pull your fucking head out of your ass and remember what you're here for."

He shoves the girl at his side off and stands, then slams through his bedroom door.

"What the fuck is up his ass?" I ask Jamie, pissed that fucking Grim killed my buzz.

He lets my shirt go and looks at where Grim just vanished with a shrug. "It's fucking Grim. Could be anything."

I give his chest a shove. "That shit you did tonight on the bridge of "Insane" was seriously fucking animal. You should do that every night."

A grin eats his entire face. "It fucking just came to me. That was crazy, right?"

I smile back. "That's why you're the best."

He claps my back as I head past him into my room. When I get there, I close the door and drop onto the bed, staring at the ceiling and trying to find my Lucky buzz again.

#

Over the last week and a half, I've been finding more and more reasons not to be in the hotel suite with Grim. And most of those reasons are Lucky.

Which is exactly Grim's issue. I don't know why he hates her, but he takes every opportunity he can to make sure I know it. And tonight, he made sure she does too.

We're in Atlanta, our last stop before we wrap up our North American tour in Miami two days from now. Which means I only have two days left with Lucky, and I'm not going to squander a minute.

I haven't missed any of Lucky's shows since L.A., and tonight I was standing in the wings, waiting, when they wrapped their final set and she came off stage. She smiled and came over when she saw me. I fist bumped her. "You broke them," I said with a grin, indicating the rabid crowd, still cheering her. "Not sure they'll even stay for Roadkill now."

I didn't even know Grim was there until I heard him behind me. "Not bad for a trained monkey," he'd said, stepping out of the shadows. He glared Lucky down then headed over to get his sound gear wired.

Our show was pretty rough. Shit just wasn't jelling like it usually does. It wasn't really Grim, and I don't think I was fucking up either. It was just that we weren't pulling together as a unit the way we usually do. We weren't feeling each other. It was strained, and I'm pretty sure the crowd heard it in our music.

So, I'm in Lucky's bus after the show because I don't want to go back to the suite. Billie was in bed when I got here, which is probably good, because I'm still pretty pissed that she sabotaged Lucky's best shot at being able to do her stuff. Freddie called me last week. Said he'd gotten a call from Billie.

"She wants me to stay the hell away from her clients," he said. "Especially Shiloh."

Billie is Lucky's safety net. She trusts her, and I know trust doesn't come easy for Lucky. I don't want to be the person to pull that out from under her, so I haven't said anything.

Lucky and I are in the back lounge, and she's working her fingers over the strings as we play with chord progressions.

"Why do you lie to everyone about your father?" she asks, as if she's asking if I want a Coke. But when her eyes flash to mine, I know she's been holding onto that one for a while, waiting for her chance to ask.

I press into the cushions of the couch. "He was a lowlife drunk. Swore he'd kill me for what I did, and I believed him. I changed my name so he couldn't track me down. Never occurred to me then we'd get big enough that anyone would ever care where I'd come from or who my parents were."

"But you got huge," she says, "and everyone wants to know. How have you kept it hidden this long?"

"I don't do interviews. And I give them plenty to talk about that has nothing to do with then and everything to do with now." I lower my gaze as I say it and rub the back of my neck, for the first time feeling a little uncomfortable about my diversion tactics.

Lucky lets it slide, thankfully. Her eyes scrunch. "So, the thing about your mom dying when you were three...?"

"That part's true."

"And your father raised you," she says, putting the pieces together.

I nod.

"What do you think would happen if he found you now?" she asks, her fingers still working absently through progressions on the strings.

"I don't know."

Her eyes lift to mine, and I'm so close to telling her he already found me. Something deep in my core wants to. But I grind a heel into it. Crush it. I'm not ready to go there, even with Lucky.

"Maybe you could talk to him," she says. "He might have cooled down by now."

I blow out a humorless laugh. "Not likely."

"So you won't even try," she says, irritation bleeding into her words.

I get where it's coming from. Here's a kid who's never had any family. "Listen, Lucky. I get how this probably looks from your perspective. But there are some people, family or not, who are just fucking toxic. You just have to walk away."

She shakes her head and her focus shifts to her fingers again. "So what if we extend the bridge into the third chorus and add a solo there."

I can tell she's not buying it, but I'm happy for the change of topic, so I don't press my point. "Yeah...that could work."

#

I wake to bright sun in my face. When I open my eyes, I find I'm still in Lucky's bus. I'm stretched on the couch and she's thrown a blanket over me. But she's nowhere.

I rub my eyes, then sit up and fish my phone out of my pocket. It's totally blown up, with text and call notifications all up the screen. And when I look at the time, I get why.

Our flight to Miami leaves in twenty minutes.

"Fuck!" I hiss, springing to my feet. "Fuck!"

I scan through the most recent texts. There are a few from our tour manager, but most of them are from Jamie. This isn't the first time one of us hasn't been at the hotel when we were supposed to leave, so we've worked out a contingency plan. Jamie has all my shit. Says just to meet them at the airport.

That isn't going to happen, but at least I don't have to go back to the hotel.

I grab my hoodie off the coffee table and am tugging it on just as the door to the lounge slides open. I'm hoping for Lucky, but it's Billie who's standing there, all bristle and sharp edges. Her mouth is pursed into a small circle and her gaze is hard.

It doesn't take a rocket scientist to surmise that she's not happy I'm here.

"I'm glad you're awake," she says, stepping through the door and closing it behind her. "Shiloh's sleeping, so this is my chance to tell you to stop thinking you know what's best for her career. She has a professional who's taking care of that."

I raise my hands in surrender. "I just thought she might be happier with—"

"See…" she says, pointing a sharpened finger at me, "that's exactly what I'm talking about. It's not your place to 'think' anything about Shiloh or what would make her happy." She gives me the once over. "As a matter of fact, you don't have any place at all when it comes to Shiloh. She may not seem young, but she is."

This woman has been fawning over me since we met at Rockefeller Center at the beginning of all this, handing me business cards and giving me her pitch. I guess she's pretty pissed I gave Lucky Freddie's number.

I nod. "I get that, and I haven't touched her." I scoop the paper with our notes on it and hold it up for her to see. "We've just been working on some things."

Her eyes narrow slightly, but before she can say anything else, the door behind her slides open and Lucky steps through, rubbing the sleep out of one eye. Her copper hair sticks up at every angle and there's a sudden rush in my groin at the image of waking up next to this in my bed.

Through the sleep haze, her eyes flash bright when she sees I'm still here. "Hey."

"Hey," I say and try to keep the flood of sparks I feel in my chest from bleeding into the word.

"What's going on?" she asks, her eyes moving between me and her manager.

I glance at my phone again. "I just missed my flight." I zip my hoodie. "Gotta get to the airport and see if they can get me on something else today before our tour manager blows a gasket."

"You should just ride with us," Lucky says.

But where Lucky's face lights at the idea, Billie's does the opposite.

"I don't think that's a good idea, Shiloh," she says, her sharp gaze daring me to contradict her.

Lucky looks at Billie like she has two heads. "Why not? We're going to the same place."

"He's got his things at the hotel, and he's already paid airfare." Billie's excuse is lame, and it's obvious she knows it by the look on her face, but she just keeps going. "He's got until tomorrow afternoon to get to Miami. The airline will be able to rebook him before that."

"You're coming with us." Lucky's words are clipped and decisive. She says them to me, but they're clearly meant for Billie.

"Okay," I say with a nod. "Thanks."

Billie turns and heads up front, clearly not happy at being vetoed.

"Maybe pissing her off wasn't a great idea," I say, settling back onto the couch.

Lucky goes to the cupboard and pulls down a box of cereal. "Want some?"

A laugh erupts out of me at the sight of Lucky holding up the box of Lucky Charms.

"What?" she says, smoothing down her hair self-consciously, as if she wasn't perfect.

"Just…" I shake my head as my smile fades. "Nothing."

God, she really is perfect. My eyes skim over the body under the oversized black T-shirt that hangs to mid-thigh, all firm curves and contours. They follow lower, along the lines of a pair of legs I've pictured wrapped around my waist (or my head) in every fantasy I've had for the last two months. She's fucking killing me.

"Yes or no?" she ask, irritation creasing her forehead.

"Yeah, thanks."

She pulls down two paper bowls and fills them, then unearths a small carton of milk from the fridge in the bar.

"When's the bus scheduled to pull out?" I ask as she hands me a bowl and spoon.

"No clue," she says, setting her bowl on the table and dropping onto the couch. "But when we start moving, you'll know."

We eat and sometime later, as Lucky's putting *Ironman 2* in the DVD player, the bus starts moving.

"It's been a while since I've done this," I say, looking out the window as we leave Atlanta behind.

"Billie says this is a lot cheaper than flying," she says, stabbing her thumb into the remote and zipping past the previews. She looks at me. "I never realized the artists have to pay their tour expenses. What the fuck is that all about?"

I shrug. "Just the way it's always been. But the label does most of the promotion."

"Still." She sets the remote down and slouches into the corner of the couch, propping one leg on the coffee table. "I know what I get for royalties and they're making a shit-ton of money off me. The least they could do is pay for my fucking bus."

"You can negotiate some of that shit," I say, unable to keep my eyes off the lines of her legs. "We get a flat rate for each appearance versus a percentage of ticket sales."

"Because you're you," she says, her voice full of sarcasm.

"And you're you."

It takes me a second to realize the conversation's stalled, and when I lift my gaze to her face, expecting to see it facing the TV, it's facing me instead.

"See something you like?" she asks with a sultry smirk that's begging to be kissed off her face.

"I've always liked everything I've seen," I answer honestly, my eyes taking a sweep of her body. "I've never pretended I didn't."

Her nipples pebble under the thin cotton of her T-shirt and my dick notices, responding in kind.

But the last few weeks, Lucky and I have gotten close. We've spent most of our free time together and it hasn't been about sex. I can't speak for her, but for me it's been about finding what I love in this business again.

The way Lucky loses herself when we're working, her pure love of what we're creating, has made me remember what playing onstage meant to me before it turned into a three-headed snake. There are so many distractions that it's easy to forget that it's really all about the music.

But here, with Lucky, I remember.

CHAPTER 18

Shiloh

The movie's playing, but Tro's eyes haven't left me in the last hour. Every time I glance his way, he seems to be studying me. Usually it's my face his eyes are glued to, but I've caught him other places too.

I'll admit to teasing him a little—letting my T-shirt slide up my thigh so the trim of my blue lace thong shows at the side of my leg; pulling the thin cotton a little tighter across my chest when I feel his gaze on my nipples, which have been tight for the last hour with his gaze.

I will also admit to liking the attention. I'll admit to the heavy ache low between my legs, and the bubbles in my chest, and the fact that my panties are becoming increasingly wet.

I will admit to wanting him.

Just not out loud.

I remember thinking Tro was the enemy when we started on this journey. Now I realize so much of what he does is to hide the parts of himself he doesn't want anyone to see. But some of those parts are pretty damn incredible. I know who he is, so I have no fantasies that he wants anything other than sex from me, but I've decided I want to give it to him anyway.

I've never been the kind of girl who expects a fairy-tale romance. I don't need to be swept off my feet. I don't need promises or declarations. I don't even need tomorrow. But I need to be in control of where and when it happens.

So, tonight, if it goes there, I will fuck Tro Gunnison on my terms.

When I look at him this time, his eyes are on mine. I hold them for a second before letting mine trace the lines of his neck tattoos until they disappear under the brushed cotton of his T-shirt. His nipples tighten at my perusal as my eyes trail lower, over tight pecs, and I feel mine pull into stiff peaks in response. The ridges of his eight-pack abs crease his shirt and I want to run my tongue along them. And, lower, a substantial erection strains against his jeans.

If Billie wasn't likely to walk in here unannounced at any second, when and where would be here and now.

"How many women have you fucked?" I ask him, my eyes still on the bulge of his jeans.

"A lot."

I lift my eyes to his face and fire burns out of those dark eyes into mine. "Put a number on a lot. Best guess."

He shakes his head and he's unable to hold my gaze as he answers. "Maybe five hundred."

"When did you lose your virginity?"

His eyes lift to mine again. "You already know that story."

"Your father's girlfriend," I say, figuring that must be what he means. "When you were seventeen."

He nods, but then his gaze grows curious. "What about you?"

"Virginity? Or how many?" I ask.

He tips his head. "Both."

"I lost my virginity when I was thirteen."

His eyes widen a little.

I shrug it off. "Self-preservation. You do what you have to do sometimes. There was just that one for two years, then one more last year, during *The Voice*."

"So...two," he confirms.

I nod slowly and send him every watt of my stare. "So far. But I'm planning on changing that very soon."

I've shocked him silent. He just stares at me for a long moment before saying, "Lucky guy."

"You bet your sweet ass he is," I reply, turning back to the TV.

And if I felt his hot gaze on me before, now it's a fucking blow torch.

CHAPTER 19

Tro

When the bus pulls up to the venue in Miami, I say goodbye to Lucky and get the fuck off. Where Lucky's gaze has always been a flame thrower, warning me off, today it was still flaming, but in a whole different way. Something major shifted in her between last night and this morning, and I've spent the last eight hours trying to see past her skin to what's going on inside. I've also spent the last eight hours trying to tame my raging boner. It's not working. Lucky sends that *fuck-me* look my way, you damn well better believe my cock is going to obey.

I've got the worst fucking case of blue balls I've ever had.

Instead of taking a cab to the hotel in South Beach where I know the band is, I walk to the Intercontinental that's only a few blocks from the venue and check in. I send a messenger service to South Beach for my stuff and text Jamie to tell him they're coming.

I have nowhere to be until sound check twenty hours from now. I'm going to spend that time talking my cock down and keeping some perspective. I've made it nine weeks without touching Lucky. That's not because I haven't wanted to, but because I decided weeks ago that when something finally happened with her, it wasn't going to be a onetime thing.

I call room service for a burger, planning on laying low until tomorrow. If I only see Lucky at the arena, surrounded by people, then I'll be able to head to Europe after the show with a clean conscience.

At least that's my plan until I get the text.

Where are you? she wants to know.

I think about ignoring it, but in my gut, I know it will eat me alive all night if I do.

Two blocks down Biscayne at the Intercontinental, I text back.

There's a pause, then, *Room number?*

Fuck. If she comes here, and I have her alone in this room, I can't be held accountable for what I'll do to her if she gives me that look.

Planning on a low key night, I say, hoping that might be enough to her put her off.

I want to finish the solo riff before you go.

The song. Christ. It's good, much better than anything I could pull together on my own, but I'd forgotten all about it. *I trust you to work that out on your own. Or maybe Lilah can help.*

I want you.

Those three words go right to my dick.

2217, I type on the jolt of adrenaline flooding my bloodstream.

On my way.

I jump in the shower, because I stink, then hate that I don't have anything clean to put on. I pull on my jeans commando and am just toweling dry my hair when there's a knock.

I look out the peephole and find a big black guy in a red vest and white shirt.

"Room service," he says.

I pull open my door and he wheels the cart through…just as Lucky steps off the elevator. She's cleaned up too, and dressed to fucking slay in a tight button-up blouse and a short white skirt. Not her typical loose T-shirt and shorts.

I take a deep breath and sign the tab. The guy passes Lucky on his way up the hall, and his head turns to catch the back of her as he passes.

She stops in my door. "I get the hotels," she says, looking past me into my room. "This is nice."

I step aside and as she passes, her typical scent of soap now mingles with vanilla and something earthier that grabs at my balls.

"What's for dinner?" she says, lifting the lid off the plate.

"You hungry? We can split that," I say, gesturing at the burger, "or I can order up something else."

In answer, she picks the burger up off the plate and takes an enormous bite. She wipes the back of her hand across her chin to catch the drip of mustard, and fuck, that's hot.

She sets the burger down and goes to the window that looks back toward the arena where we'll play our final show tomorrow. "So, this is it," she says. "The end of the road."

I move to her side and follow her gaze. "Not for you, Lucky. This is just your rocket launcher. Everything from here is going to be straight up, so I hope you're not afraid of heights."

She presses a palm to the glass and just stands there for a long minute before turning and gazing at me with eyes full of…everything. I see determination and vulnerability, longing and lust, hope and fear. "Then why does it feel like the end."

Before I even know I've done it, my hand is on her face, my calloused thumb gliding over the flawless caramel skin of her cheek. My fingers weave into her hair and I draw her slowly toward me, giving her every opportunity to pull away if she doesn't want this.

But, God, I hope she doesn't.

Closer.

Her sweet breath feathers over my face and I close my eyes with the rush.

Closer.

Her fingers trail over the lines of my bare chest and abs, setting my skin on fire.

Closer.

Some of the softest lips I've ever felt brush across mine.

My tongue slips out of its own accord and strokes her lower lip, desperate for a taste of the only thing I've wanted for weeks. She meets it with hers, just a quick caress, and then her mouth is gone.

I open my eyes as I draw away and find her watching me with unsure eyes—that same vulnerability I saw the day we met. But then they harden and the sass I also saw that first day cracks like a whip out of her mouth. "What the fuck was that?"

"Our first kiss."

My heart is galloping in my chest as I wait for her to digest that.

I can see her walls that had been coming down over the last few weeks clicking back into place. I expect something like *And our last* out of her mouth, so when she steps into me, pressing that body I've craved so hard since I saw her that first day all up mine, no one's more surprised than me. Her eyes flash heat into mine. "That isn't how you kiss your hookups. I want what you give everyone else."

"I don't kiss them at all, Lucky. I just fuck them." I give my head a solemn shake. "You don't want what I give everyone else, because it's nothing."

She presses up on her tiptoes, winding her fists into my hair and taking my lower lip between her teeth, tugging it hard. "I do. I want you to fuck me the way you fuck them. Fuck me hard and then leave."

Fuck me if I'm not hard as stone for her in one second flat. Her face tucks into the crook of my neck, and God, she's soft. The tip of her nose glides up my neck, and then her mouth finds my ear. Her tongue laps softly along the lobe and a shudder racks my whole body before she grabs it with her teeth and bites down hard.

"Fuck," I growl, lifting her by the ass and pinning her against the window.

Her breath is hot in my ear and becoming heavier, matching mine. She hooks her knees over my hips and through my jeans, I can feel all the wet heat between her legs.

My heart pounds harder knowing she wants me.

I grab her chin hard and pull her face to mine, kissing her like she's my last breath. She tries to pull her face away, but I don't let her, and finally she relents. Her tongue plunges into my mouth and wrestles with mine. She starts grinding herself against my hard cock, and even through my jeans, I feel the electricity crackling between us.

Something that had been growing inside me over the last few weeks dies as it hits me that this is happening and there's no fucking way I'm going to be able to stop. As I yank her off the window and carry her to the bed, I realize it's my conscience. I wanted to do this right. I wanted something real with Lucky. But at this second, as I throw her onto the bed and tear her underwear off, I realize I was never capable of that.

I'm not a good person.

This is what I do.

After weeks of blue balls I finally have her where I've wanted her since the moment I saw her backstage at *The Tonight Show*, and I'm going fuck her raw.

Her mouth migrates across my stubbled cheek and she nips my lower lip between her teeth. I close my eyes and hold my breath, because at this rate, I'm going to come before she ever gets me out of my pants. But when her tongue glides out and traces my lips, I nearly lose it. I realize my grasp on her hips could crush bone and lighten my grip. Her mouth seals over mine and her hand finds my straining cock through my jeans. She strokes and pulls a groan from the animal deep inside me. As her fingers work the button of my jeans, I slip mine between her legs. She opens for me, and she's so fucking hot. So wet.

My fingers tease at the opening to everything I've needed for weeks before plunging inside. She moans into my mouth as her pussy contracts hard around my fingers.

She has my button open, and as she inches down my fly, the beast is freed. Her fingers wrap around me, stroking, then lower to cup the family stones.

I break our kiss and hold my breath, talking myself down before I come in her hand.

She presses my jeans lower and lines her hips up under mine. "Give me what you give them," she groans, all sex and desire.

But she's not them. She's Lucky.

The rush is followed instantly by a flood of something dark. Dread twists through my gut and I can't breathe. I sit back on my heels, looking down at her. This isn't how it was supposed to go.

All I've wanted for two months was to fuck this girl. In forty-eight hours I'm on a plane to Amsterdam. This is probably my last shot.

MIA STORM | 161

But as Lucky takes my cock into her hands, the dread flows darker and thicker, like tar through my black insides. Despite the fact that I'm about to explode with need, I find myself pulling out of her grasp and backing off the bed. I stand and stare down at her, my face, no doubt, reflecting her confusion like a mirror.

Never in my life have I stopped a woman from fucking me, and I can't even explain why I'm doing it now, except Lucky isn't like all the others. I want more from her than just a quick fuck.

I tuck my protesting cock into my jeans and zip. "We can't do this, Lucky. I'm leaving the day after tomorrow for two months."

"Which is why we should do this *now*," she says, pressing up onto her elbows.

Already, I'm second guessing myself. What kind of fucking moron am I, letting all *that* slip through my hands?

She shifts onto her knees, right in front of me where I stand at the side of the bed, and bunches her fists on her hips, all kinds of challenge and sex in her dark gaze. "This is a one-time offer."

I feel my head shaking as that conscience I nearly killed just now makes a resurgence.

"Is it because of my age? Because you know this isn't a big virginity thing," she says.

"It's not that. It's…" I trail off with a shake of my head, trying to shake a coherent thought loose. Because I have no fucking clue why I'm doing this. "It was supposed to be different with you."

Her scowl deepens. "You're a real piece of work, you know that? For weeks you've been slinging innuendo at me, and when I finally give you what you've been begging for," she says with a disgusted flick of her hand at that incomparable body, "*now* you don't want me?"

Her rant hits home, and I suddenly understand. I *do* want her. But it's not just her body I want. I want that smart mouth and sharp wit. I want those eyes that see things in an entirely different light and that mind that thinks in ways I can't begin to untwist. I want to lose myself inside the incredible person she is and find out what makes her tick.

I want everything she is.

And fucking her now, before I leave for two months in Europe, is not going to get me any of those things.

"If we do this now," I say, rubbing my neck, "then all it will be is a quick fuck. That's not what I want from you, Lucky. When I get back, whatever you want from me is yours."

She blows out a disgusted snort. "You mean whatever's left of you after you've fucked your way across Europe?"

I shake my head, and this time it's on purpose. "That's not going to happen."

Her arms fold skeptically over her chest. "Really?"

"Really."

"Why?"

It's like someone poured a beer down my throat then shook me. My stomach's all fizzy knots. "Because I have a hunch there might be something here," I say with a wave of my hand between us. "Because I want to find out if my hunch is right."

"So, when that hot French girl gets down on her knees and unzips you…?"

"I'll tell her to get the fuck up and grow a little self-respect."

Lucky's eyebrows shoot up. "She starts sucking you and you're going to push her off?"

I take a step toward her. "There is one girl I want more than I've ever wanted anyone, and I just pushed her off. Frenchy's got no prayer."

There's a second where I think she gets me...that she sees I'm, for once in my pathetic life, not totally full of shit.

But then her eyes narrow. She scoops her underwear off the floor and drags them up her legs. "You are so full of shit." She's off the bed, yanking open the door before I can react. She slams out into the hall and I start to go after her, but what's that going prove. The only thing that will show her I'm serious is to keep my dick clean on the road. Which is something I've never even considered trying before.

I watch her load into the elevator and vanish. And now that she's not here, piercing my soul with that knowing gaze, reminding me what's at stake, I feel like the lowlife snake I am.

What if I can't follow through?

CHAPTER 20

Shiloh

It's sort of awkward going home with Billie. On the bus, it wasn't *her* house. It was our hotel room on wheels that *I* was paying for. As much as she was trying to be the "parent," I didn't feel accountable to her when we were out there.

But this place is all hers. She keeps saying to make myself at home, but I don't feel like I belong here.

It's on the eighteenth floor and out my floor-to-ceiling bedroom window is an old white building that Billie says is the L.A. County Library main branch. All of the rooms are large and open, and full of stuff that looks really expensive. Everything is leather or antique, and everywhere I look, there are crystal vases and art on the walls that I can't make any sense of. I'm not even sure the painting in my room is hanging the right way. Looks to me like it's upside down.

I've spent the last week since we got here staring at it, trying to figure out what it's supposed to be. It keeps my mind off what happened between me and Tro in that Miami hotel room.

Sort of.

I haven't even gotten out of bed yet and it's two. After living under a microscope and sharing a bus for the last two months, having my own space feels amazing, so I've just kind of stayed in here. My laptop is open on the bed and I slam it shut, hating myself for opening it in the first place. But I had to know. I flop onto my stack of pillows and stare out the window.

Tro is in Brussels. Or he was last night. But the picture on my screen is from Paris the night before. I didn't need to translate the caption. I already knew what it said. "Tro Gunnison, sampling Europe's finest."

I turn my face into the pillows and scream. God, I hate him.

I take a deep breath and sit up, pulling open the laptop again. In the picture, Tro is sitting on a barstool in a club. An actress who looks familiar but I can't place is wrapped around him from behind. She's got her chin on his shoulder and her hands splayed on his chest. Tro looks like he's talking to someone out of the shot, but I have no doubt he took that actress back to his hotel and fucked her.

Because that what he does with everyone but me.

But I'm not jealous. This is Tro. He's a manwhore. I knew that going in.

I slam my laptop closed again and nearly throw it across the room, but my stomach growls and I decide to focus my efforts on feeding it instead. I pad to the kitchen and find Billie sitting on the couch, on the phone, as usual.

"I need that in writing, Phillip." She glances at me and nods and I realize she's talking about my contract. "As far as Shiloh's concerned, if we don't get some creative control it's a deal breaker."

"*Full* creative control," I say, remembering my conversation with Freddie as I grab a box of cereal from the cupboard.

She frowns at me as she jots something in her notebook. "Put all of your points on paper and let me look them over."

I pour milk on my Apple Jacks and take the bowl back to my room. I shove the laptop to the bottom of my bed with my foot as I stuff my earbuds in. I mean to turn on my latest playlist, some really cool stuff I found by this Finnish band I stumbled on by accident, but instead I click on the recordings Tro made in the subway with Lilah last month. When I'm done eating, I set my bowl down and lay back on the bed and close my eyes as goose bumps pebble my skin. If Billie gets what we're asking for, I'll be recording this stuff for real. And maybe I can even get Lilah to play the studio tracks.

I roll on my stomach and smile into the pillow. LoLah, together again.

I start making plans in my head as the fantasy takes shape. Lilah will move to L.A. and we can get an apartment together when we turn eighteen. We'll hang out and give each other shit like we used to. And we'll write more music and she'll play on all my CDs, and next tour, it will be her and me sharing a bus.

But then the notes of Tro's song start and I feel my throat tighten.

"Do I have it right?" I hear Lilah say.

"You picked that up fast," he says, his rough around the edges silk voice tugging at my insides like a fishhook.

I don't miss him.

I won't.

I click the music off and text Lilah. When she doesn't answer right away, I get up and take my empty bowl back to the kitchen.

"It looks like we're going to get most of what we're asking for," Billie says, "plus much better royalty terms."

My stomach jumps. "They're going to let me pick the music?"

"You'll have a voice, Shiloh. It's unrealistic to expect they're ever going to give up the final say."

"Why?" I spit. "I'm the artist. I'm the one whose face is on this stuff. It should be my choice."

"But they're the ones financing it. They're the ones promoting it. They're only going to do that if they're passionate about what you're doing. It has to be a product they think they can sell."

"Well, then, they're fucking it all up. Because the songs I wanted to do would be selling ten times better than the crap they gave me."

She closes her laptop and pushes up from the couch. "You'll have veto power, Shiloh. If there's a track or two that you don't want, we can probably get them pulled. That's more than most new artists get."

I shake my head as her words sink in. "That's not creative control. That's being a…" What did Grim call me that night in Atlanta? "…a performing monkey. There has to be a label that would let me sing my own songs," I add when I remember what Tro said.

She shakes her head gently. "You don't want the reputation of being difficult so soon in your career. Phillip and Universal have been more than fair with this new contract. Appearing ungrateful would be a mistake."

"I'm doing Lilah's songs," I say, not even caring I sound like a five-year-old having a tantrum.

"We'll work on that." She picks up a stack of papers from the coffee table. "I've set up a meeting with a lawyer to talk about pursuing guardianship, if this is still what you want."

"What about school?" I ask cautiously. There's some swanky private school Billie wants to register me for. I didn't really think that part through when I agreed to this. With Lilah gone from my old school in San Francisco, there's no real draw to go back, but I missed my junior year with *The Voice*, so I've got two more years. Going to a new school for my junior and senior year doesn't sound like fun.

"I thought we could go over to talk to McCall Academy tomorrow. It's in Beverly Hills, one of the top prep schools in the country."

What's my alternative? Go back to the group home? "Yeah. Okay."

"Great," she says, pulling the stack of papers in front of her together. "Maybe we can go shopping for new school clothes for you after."

I shrug. "I don't need much."

She tucks the papers into a folder and stands. "You know what? Let's not wait. Let's go right now."

I look down at my baggy T-shirt. "Right now?"

"Sure. Why not?"

"Um…give me a sec to change."

I go to my room and find a pair of leggings and a clean T-shirt, then comb my fingers through my kinks and tug them back into a ponytail. When I come out, Billie tucks the folder into her briefcase and locks it, then slings her purse over her shoulder and stands.

"This will be fun," she says. "Girls' day out!"

We head to her car, a white Mercedes that still has the new car smell, and I wonder if she bought it when I started making money. She gets fifteen percent of everything I earn, which, based on the original contract, didn't look like it was going to be much. But the CD is selling better than projected and we've gotten some endorsement money, so cash flow has been good.

She calls the school on the way to say we're coming.

When we get there, I discover what money buys. Where only half the kids in my old high school got lockers because the doors were ripped off most of them or they were falling out of the ancient walls, this school has rows of polished wooden lockers lining the pristine, marble-tiled hallways. We meet with the principal, and Billie explains the situation.

"I've been lead to believe that it shouldn't take long to obtain guardianship," she says. "Will we have to wait until then to enroll her?"

"Unless you have someone within Child and Family Services who is authorized to do so, I'm afraid so," Principal Lewis says. "But in the meantime..." She leans down and pulls some paperwork from her drawer. "...you can certainly start on the paperwork so we're ready to go when the time comes. And if you can fill out the financial disclosure, we can run all that information through the system and pre-qualify Shiloh."

Billie nods. "I can assure you there is money in Shiloh's accounts to cover tuition for the first year."

I feel my eyes go wide. It didn't occur to me until just this second that I'd have to *pay* to go to school. I mean, seriously? Who does that?

Billie takes all the papers and we stand. The principal gives us a brief tour on the way back to the front doors and assures us that celebrity will not be an issue, but then as we're leaving asks if she can take a picture with me.

We load into Billie's car. "I'd be fine with public school," I say as we pull away.

She lets out a strained laugh. "Maybe once we find a place in Beverly Hills, but you don't want to mess with the public schools in L.A. They're dangerous."

"Can't be any worse than where I come from," I mutter, slouching into my seat.

She glances at me, then back to the road. "This is your opportunity to leave all that behind, build a better life for yourself. You need to invest in your future, Shiloh."

There's a moment of sudden, overpowering home sickness, even though I never had an actual home. I look at

Billie and remind myself that through everything, she's had my back. It's been nine months and so far, she's never steered me wrong. "Okay."

She navigates us through city traffic to the Neiman Marcus, but I don't really find much I can wear. Billie models a few new dresses for me and picks two. We check out and head home.

"I know this is going to take some adjustment, Shiloh," Billie says on the way up the elevators, "but I really believe it's going to be awesome. She shifts the shopping bag into her other hand and takes mine. "You are so good for me. I think we will be really good for each other."

"I know, Billie. I know everything you've done for me and I don't mean to seem ungrateful."

She pulls me into a hug. "You don't, honey. I'm just so glad we're doing this."

"So am I." *I think.*

CHAPTER 21

Tro

It's the end of the first week of our European leg and I let Jamie talk me into doing Paris after the show. It's a closed party at a bar in one of the seedier neighborhoods, but you'd never know it looking around. All the beautiful people are here.

Including Amilia Beauchene.

"Hello, Tro," she says in the accent that grabbed onto my balls and didn't let go the first time I heard it two years ago.

We met on Roadkill's first European tour that summer. We had two shows in Paris and when I wasn't on stage, I was in Amilia's bed. I thought I heard something about her getting married last summer to some director, but when she glues herself to my back and whispers, "I've missed you," in my ear, I'm thinking maybe I heard wrong.

"How have you been?" I ask, making some space between us.

She pouts her full red lips. "So so. Mostly bored."

"Sorry to hear that," I say, realizing the accent does nothing for me now.

She presses against me again and her eyes spark as her hand slips to my package. "But I have a feeling things are about to get exciting."

I close my eyes and try to remember what it was about her, other than the accent, that drove me so crazy. But all I see are Lucky's big, whiskey eyes set in flawless skin the color of caramel. And all I feel is a sick pit in my stomach, knowing it's not her hands on me.

"Listen, Amilia," I say, drawing away. "I'm not really feeling this tonight. But, I think you should hang out and have fun, get to know some of the other guys or whatever."

I leave her standing there and head to the bar, intending to get another beer. Instead, I just keep moving, right out the door onto the sidewalk. I walk for a few blocks before a cab happens by. I wave it down and head back to the hotel.

On the way, I pull out my phone. I open Skype and stare at the status circle next to Lucky's name. I've watched it alternate between yellow and green night after night as the party raged in the suite outside my room. Every time it's turned green, telling me she's right here, right now, I've wanted to reach through the cyber and grab onto her.

And right now, it's green.

I start to type before I can change my mind. There's no doubt that I'm that girl's worst nightmare, whether she knows it or not, but she's woven herself into the fabric of my mind. She's part of every thought I have—the first thing on my mind when I wake up and the last thing before I go to sleep.

But that's not what I say. I also decide not to say anything about Amilia. Keeping it on the professional side is less likely to scare her away or piss her off right now. So I just say that, since Freddie didn't work out, I've got a few more producers' names and numbers if she wants to talk to them.

But I want to say so much more.

I want to say that, totally against my will, I've fallen hard for her. I want to say I miss her smile and her frown, her sass and her fire, her voice and her talent. And her touch. God, I miss that most of all.

There's not a day that I don't relive every kiss, every caress, from that night in my hotel room. But I don't regret not going the extra step. I didn't handle it as well as I probably should have, but I was right to stop her. She thought she wanted what I give everyone else, but what I said was true. I give them nothing. I want Lucky to have an actual piece of me—a part of me I've never given anyone before. If it happens between us, it's going to be because she gets that she's not just another fuck. She's going to know how much I care about her.

And the only way she'll know that is if I spend the next two months showing her.

I hit the send icon and wait. Her status circle is still green. She's there. But as much as I might want to, I can't make her reply.

The driver drops me at my hotel, and when I get to the room, there's still no reply. I check again and her circle's gone yellow, indicating she's let the app go dormant.

So I guess I have my answer. She doesn't want to talk to me.

I drop onto the bed and only realize I've dozed off when the sound of people in the next room filters through my door. Sounds like Grim and Jess have brought the party home with them.

I drag myself up and shuck off my jeans, pulling my phone from my pocket to check again for Lucky. Still no reply. I crawl back onto the bed and bury my face in the pillow just as the door clicks opens. I sit up as a pair of scantily clad bottle blondes slip through.

"Grim want us for you," the shorter one with enormous tits says in a heavy French accent, unbuttoning her top. "He say..." She trails off and looks to the other one for help.

"He want you get the dick from *pantalon*," she says, pointing at my package, "and make some French pussy before go too long."

"Before go too *late*," the shorter one corrects. She comes closer, dropping her shirt to the floor. There's no bra. "He say we come here to fuck you. He say we no can go if we no fucking."

I haul myself up from the bed. "Go out there and tell Grim that I'm sending you back to him with my compliments."

The taller one follows her friend closer, a deep crease forming between her brows. "You no want?"

"Not tonight, doll," I say, taking one of each of their arms in my grasp and escorting them back to the door. "If you want to fuck someone, you can fuck Grim."

"He get fucking," the shorter one says, and when I get them to the door, I see she's right. He's got his head lolled against the back of the couch with both hands twisted into the hair of the curvy black woman whose head's bobbing between his legs. Grim's always been into public displays, so this is pretty normal for him.

"Thanks for the offer," I say, depositing the girls outside my door. I scoop up the shirt from my floor and hand it to the half naked one. "I'm just not feeling it tonight."

Grim's head lifts at the sound of my voice and he cuts me a look. "Get your fucking rocks off, Gunner. Your fucking cock's screwed on too tight."

I give him a shake of my head.

The girl between his knees continues to work it as he glowers at me.

"That's it, baby!" Jamie calls over the music.

I tear my eyes away from Grim's and find Jamie headed toward the door of his adjoining room, toting a giggling Amilia under his arm like a ragdoll.

So, at least that worked out.

I close my door and head to the corner of my room for my guitar. There's been some new lyrics threading between my brain cells the last few days and they finally feel like they're ready for a tune.

As I jot down the bones of what I have in my head onto the hotel notepad near the phone, it starts to take shape. I play the notes and listen, then make some tweaks. That electric current starts in my chest and soon I'm buzzing all over with it. I lose myself in the process and the noise from the suite fades away until it's just me and the music. Finally, as the first light of morning begins to streak through my window and paint the wall yellow, I lay back and doze with notes and words braiding themselves into patterns in my dreams.

#

It's after noon by the time I pull myself out of bed. When I head out into the suite to brew a cup of coffee, there are still a few stragglers passed out on the couch. Just as the coffee maker sputters out the last of my cup, Jamie's door opens and Amilia comes out, smoothing last night's dress over her hips. She detours when she sees me and swipes the coffee cup from my hand, then turns and slams out the door without a word.

Jamie comes out as I'm brewing another cup. He grins ear to ear when he sees me. "It's always better with a fucking movie star," he says, then gives his balls a scratch through is boxers. "You don't know what you're fucking missing, dude."

But I do. I know exactly what I'm missing. And the truth? I don't miss it at all.

CHAPTER 22

Shiloh

Billie was a little frustrated that the first time the lawyer was able to meet with us is over a week after we visited McCall. School started Monday and she's spent every day since muttering about how far behind I'm going to be.

"Have a seat," she says when she shows the guy into the family room, where I'm on the couch watching TV. "Can I get you something to drink?"

"Water would be perfect," the lawyer, a fairly hot Hispanic guy about Billie's age, says as he takes the chair across the coffee table from me. "You must be Shiloh," he says to me as Billie turns for the kitchen.

I click off the TV and nod.

"I'm Christian," he says, reaching across the table for my hand.

I shake it.

He looks at me curiously for a second. "This must all seem pretty overwhelming to you, after living your whole life in the system. But it should go smoothly as long as you're sure this is what you want."

Billie sets Christian's water on a coaster in front of him and sits next to me. "We've talked about it and I think we're both excited for this," she says, then squeezes my knee. "Right, Shiloh?"

I nod again. The truth is, I'm way more nervous than I thought I'd be. I don't even know why except so much has changed in the last year, and now it feels like the only thread connecting me to who I really am is about to snap.

Christian reaches for his briefcase and opens it in his lap. "There's paperwork, of course, because anytime you're dealing with the courts, that's the case," he says, as he thumbs through the folders inside. He pulls one from the stack, then closes his briefcase in his lap and uses it like a desk. "We have the guardianship petition, and the guardian consent form..." He reels off several other names as he lifts forms one by one from the folder and sets them in a pile on the coffee table. He looks up at Billie. "Because Shiloh has substantial monetary holdings, you'll actually need to file for guardianship of an estate, which takes a little more paperwork. Most of these are for you, as the adult, but there are a few places Shiloh needs to fill in information too. Where we need your information is marked with yellow sticky tabs, and Shiloh's is marked with pink."

I've always hated pink.

"How long will it take for all of this to go through?" Billie asks.

"The part that often holds things up in cases like these is the court requirement of giving notice to all relatives or agencies involved. In Shiloh's case, where there are no known relatives, that should go quickly. Once the papers are filed with the court, they'll set a date for a hearing. Depending on how busy family court is, that could take anywhere from a few days to a few weeks."

"Then how long until we hear?" Billie presses.

"In an uncontested case, if the minor agrees to the guardian, the judge will often make his determination at the time of the hearing."

Billie's nodding the whole time Christian is explaining. "So it may only take a few weeks?"

"It's possible." He quirks his head at Billie. "Is there a hurry?"

"We need to get her registered for school at McCall Academy, and we can't do that until I'm her legal guardian."

"McCall," he says, raising his eyebrows and turning toward me. "Aiming high."

"There's no reason Shiloh shouldn't have the best," Billie says a little defensively. "And I'll feel better to have my guardianship official as soon as possible so there aren't any problems with the Department of Health and Human Services."

Christian sorts through the forms he's pulled. "Unless a foster family complains, there shouldn't be an issue, as long as we're working toward getting the paperwork filed." He turns to me. "My understanding is that your last residence was in a group home in San Francisco?"

I nod.

He scrutinizes me for a moment, his eyes narrowing slightly. "You seem very quiet, Shiloh. Is everything okay?"

I need to actually open my mouth and say something. "I'm just nervous, I guess."

"But this is what she wants," Billie interjects with an exuberant nod. "We've talked about it several times," she repeats.

Christian keeps me pinned in his gaze. "I'd like to hear that from Shiloh, if I could."

I nod again. "Billie's great."

"And you want her to be your guardian?"

"Yes."

He looks at me a second longer before laying the papers in front of Billie. "When you have all of this completed, bring it by my office. I'll get it filed with family court as soon as I have it back."

He talks her through the process and I feel myself getting smaller and smaller every time he uses the word "minor." I've never felt so much like a kid in my life.

Which makes me wonder what the hell I thought I was doing with Tro. He's no kid. He's six feet, two-hundred pounds of pure sex. And unlike the conversation happening across the coffee table, he makes me feel all woman.

But I'm not. I can't sign my own contracts, I can't register myself for school, I can't rent my own apartment. Hell, I can't even rent a car. The whole world looks at me and sees a kid. Everyone but Tro.

My phone buzzes in my pocket. I know it's probably Lilah responding to my text, but my hand's shaking as pull it out of my pocket. Billie and Christian wrap up their conversation and Billie gets up and sees him to the door as I flip my phone and look at the screen.

Any progress on that solo?

The reason I gave for going to Tro's hotel room three weeks ago. My heart slams against my ribs as I read his text again.

Heat rises in my face and I close my messages. I don't even want to think about that night. Tro Gunnison, who sleeps with anything with a vagina, turned me down. He's probably texting me from some German woman's bed.

I set my phone down, but then pick it up again and do what I've been forcing myself not to for the last week—type his name into my browser. It opens a list of links. The news feed at the top has the most recent stories. I click on the first link and am hit in the face with a picture of a devastating redhead sitting on Tro's lap in a Belgian night club, her face in his neck.

I click to the next article down, which has a picture of the guys onstage in Madrid last night, pyrotechnics lighting the stage behind them.

The next article has another picture of him and a woman, this time groping each other in a dark corner of another night club. This article's in English, so I read the first paragraph. Princess Silvia of Bulgaria.

My intestines wind their way around my stomach and tie themselves in a knot as I close the browser. He knew he had French movie stars and Bulgarian princesses waiting for him in Europe. No wonder he didn't want me.

But I hate that I hate he's fucking Europe when he wouldn't fuck me. I don't want to care.

I watch Billie come back from the door, and from the smile she gives me, I'm surprised she doesn't offer me a cookie and pat my head.

I've never felt younger than I do right now.

CHAPTER 23

Tro

"Thank you, Barcelona!" I shout into the mic after our second encore.

The stage lights dim and I jog off the stage. We hit the wings and Jamie gets both Grim and me in a headlock and jams us together. "Let's fucking burn this city down!" he yells over the dying applause. "Spanish booze, Spanish pussy, all fucking night!"

I don't say anything, but just like every other night in the month and a half since I left Lucky behind, I'm really not feeling it. I've let Jamie drag me along a few times to keep the peace with Grim, but I always bag out early and head back to the hotel alone.

We leave the roadies to their work and head back to the dressing room.

"I'm gonna shower," I say, tugging off my sweat-soaked T-shirt and pulling another one from my duffel. "You guys go ahead. I'll catch up to you."

What I'm really going to do is go back to the hotel and work on the song that's been eating my brain over the last six weeks. Had a chunk of lyrics come to me while we were onstage tonight and I want to get it down before I forget.

Grim cracks the top of a new bottle of Jack. "We'll wait." He doesn't add the "you fucking pussy" but it's clear in his expression as he drops into a chair and takes a swig.

This isn't the first time I've used that excuse to ditch the after-party. Since the shit in Paris with Amilia, I've tried to avoid the public eye whenever I can. I don't know if Lucky's even paying any attention, but the thought of her seeing shots of women grinding up on me leaves an ache in the pit of my stomach that no amount of TUMS seems to touch. I've been chewing them like candy. Still, my stomach's in a constant knot.

I take my sweet fucking time in the shower, hoping they'll get sick of waiting and go without me, but when I come back to the dressing room in fresh jeans, toweling off my hair, they're still there.

Grim shoves the bottle in my face. "Drink."

I tip the bottle and take a swallow. When I go to lower it, he grabs the neck and holds it to my mouth. I swallow the initial flood to keep from drowning in it, and about half the bottle empties down my bare chest.

"What the fuck was that?" I say, shoving him back.

His face pulls into a toxic mix of fury and frustration. "I don't know what the fuck happened to you, but you aren't the fucking Tro Gunnison that our fans come to see. You're like some fucking shadow of that guy. You're losing your edge, man, and I'm going to make sure you get it the fuck back before you ruin us."

Acid rises up in me like snake venom and I strike without thinking. I ram my hand into his solar plexus, knocking him back against the wall. "Maybe I wanna be more than a fucking tweaking waste of space when I'm fucking forty."

Before I even see it coming, his fist ricochets off my left cheekbone. Stars flash in my vision as fireworks go off behind my left eye. I stagger back a step and catch the couch to regain my balance.

In our early days on the road, fights in the seedy Louisiana bars we played weren't uncommon. One or the other of us were always in some kind of scrap. More than once it started when one of us made moves on some local's girl. I've seen Grim nearly kill a guy with those fists without even flinching.

And the look in his eye now tells me he wouldn't think twice about doing the same to me.

"Jesus fucking Christ, Grim," Jamie shouts, stepping between us and grabbing Grim by the shirt. "What the fuck was that?"

"You read the shit they're saying about us?" he asks, ripping out of Jamie's grasp. "They say we're low energy and the crowds are pissed that they're not getting what they fucking paid for." He glares at me. "They say our frontman's lost his edge. That we're just any second-rate band now. Nothing special."

"Everyone gets crap reviews," Jamie says, letting him go. "It doesn't mean shit."

Grim shakes his head. "This is different, man. You see him up there. He's just fucking calling it in. Has been since about halfway through the U.S. leg." He glares pure disgust at me. "Since he brought that little mutt cunt up on stage with us in San Francisco and bled his fucking heart all over her."

There's a second where I picture him dead as my fist swings out. I'm not drunk, so my aim is true, and where his swing didn't take me all the way to the floor, mine does. But he's up a second later, all two hundred pounds of over-the-hill beer gut charging at me. I get another punch off before he's on me and we both go to the ground.

After some clawing and grabbing, I get an elbow around his neck and roll him face down into the floor, a knee in his back. "Don't fuck with me, Grim. You're way the fuck too old."

I slam his face into the floor and pull myself up. Jamie just stares, wide-eyed as I grab my duffel off the chair, yank on a hoodie, and storm out the door. I weave through the hallways and punch out the back door, then wave down a taxi when I hit the street.

I hurl myself in back and when the cabbie looks at me, I tell him to drive. "I don't give a fuck where."

He looks confused for a second, so I yank the wad of bills from my bag and toss it over the back of his seat. It's Euros and I have no fucking clue how much it is, but it's enough that the driver does as I ask.

I watch the city unfold outside my window as my blood pressure slowly comes out of the stratosphere. Fucking Grim. Sometimes I hate that fucking bastard.

Especially when he's right.

I've totally lost my edge. I used to love getting totally fucked up, going out on stage and not giving a shit what the hell happened. Now all I can think is, *What if Lucky's watching?*

I know she's not. She doesn't give a flying fuck about me or what I do. She expects me to fuck my way across Europe. Said so herself.

I'm feeling all kinds of shit for someone who doesn't give a shit about me. She wanted a quick fuck before I left. But she's worth so much more than that. I shut her down and pissed her off, all because I wanted more.

And now I have nothing.

I fish my phone out of my bag and pull up the last messages I sent. Producers and songs. All fucking business. Maybe it's time I came clean.

Thinking about you, I type. *Too much. Fucked up before I left. Wondering if you're still pissed.*

My finger hovers over send for a long time, wondering if I should add more. But since she doesn't seem to be speaking to me, better to start small, see the reaction before I go all confessional.

I send it and wait. But there's no reaction.

The driver takes me up and down random streets for another half hour. Still nothing. I do the math and figure it's five in the afternoon in California. She should be awake.

Maybe she's doing an interview. Or recording.

Or can't stand the fucking thought of me.

Fuck.

Finally, I have the cabbie take me back to the hotel. When I get to the front desk, I ask if they've got a vacancy and check myself into a room on the third floor, away from Grim. I lay on the bed and chain smoke until dawn, staring at the ceiling and working out the lyrics to the final verse of the song that I'm just now realizing is me.

I watch the sun come up. And still nothing from Lucky.

CHAPTER 24

Shiloh

The paperwork got filed with the court and our hearing is tomorrow.

I'm starting to get worried about...everything. I'm not a worrier by nature, but everything is just so fucking out of my control right now. Billie has say over guardianship and my recording contract. Tro has control over everything else.

I can't stop thinking about him, torturing myself wondering what he's doing every minute of every day. I follow their schedule and imagine him onstage at show time. I picture the parties after. But when I get to the part around what would be two or three in the morning where he is, when he takes some groupie, or actress, or princess to bed, that's when my insides turn to stone. Unfortunately for me, that's right around dinner time, and I can't eat. I've lost seven pounds.

But the thing that's worrying me the most is my contract. Whenever Billie takes calls from Universal, she's started leaving the room. When I ask, she assures me they're working everything out and we'll have a contract soon. I can't help but feel like she's hiding something from me. I just don't know what.

So, when she goes out for dinner with a potential new client, I take the opportunity to reassure myself everything's okay.

At least, that's how I justify going through her things.

Her briefcase is locked, but one thing I learned on the streets is how to pick locks. This one's relatively simple and me and two paperclips have it open in just a few minutes. I thumb through the folders inside until I find the blue one she always has out when she's talking to Phillip. On the top is what I first think is my original Universal contract…until I start reading. It's a new contract, dated the week before last. I have no idea what most of it means, but behind it are two more copies, and they're all already signed by my producer.

Under those is a markup of the same contract, with some things crossed out and others jotted in the margins. This one is over a month old, from not long after we got back from tour.

Billie's had my final contract in writing for two weeks. Why haven't we signed it?

Behind the Universal paperwork, there are several yellow legal sheets with scribbles about royalty percentages and endorsement terms, but as I flip to the last one, it only has three lines of numbers. I'm not sure what I'm looking at until, at the bottom, I notice the ends of a staple poking through from behind. I flip the page, and there's a bank deposit slip stapled on the back. The deposit was last week for two hundred and eighty three thousand dollars.

I flip the page back over and look at the numbers again. Account numbers?

If I need cash, I go to the ATM. If I need to buy something, I do it online with my card. I never use my checkbook, so it takes me a minute to find it in the bottom of a box of my stuff. I pull it out and compare the numbers to what's on the paper. And my stomach sinks.

Why does Billie have my account numbers? And what does it have to do with the deposit slip?

There's a customer service number on the checkbook. I call it. After a hundred automated prompts, I finally get to an actual person.

"This is Christina. How can I be of service today?" she asks.

So formal.

"I had a question about my account?" I say, not even sure of what I want to ask.

"Can I please have your account information?"

I rattle off the account number and my PIN, then ask her what my most recent deposit has been. I haven't touched this account since I've been back in L.A.

"Let's see..." she says. "There was an eighteen thousand dollar deposit on June seventh."

That was royalties. "What about other transactions?"

"It looks like check number seventy-six just cleared last week. It was for ten thousand even. And there was another one a week earlier," she adds after a brief pause. "Check number seventy-five, also for ten thousand."

My throat tightens as I thumb through the checkbook and find the top check is number seventy-seven. "And I signed those?" I ask, my voice rough.

"Are you saying you didn't?" she asks, alarmed.

"I might have," I say like an idiot. Not too many people would forget writing ten thousand dollar checks. "Is there somewhere I can see a copy?"

"Your online banking statement will have an option to view individual checks. Have you set that up?"

"Um...no."

She walks me through the steps and when I get into my account and pull up the checks, my breath catches. Blood pounds in my ears as I lift Billie's handwritten paper and compare the writing, but I already know it's hers. Both checks are made out to her.

"Can I ask you about another account?"

"Certainly," Christina says.

I read the number on the deposit slip and wait with a speeding heart through a pause.

"That's not ours," she finally says.

"Thank you," I say and hang up, staring at the papers and trying to make sense of them.

#

When Billie comes home, I'm sitting at the kitchen table with everything from the folder laid out in front of me. I try not to let her see my shake.

"What's going on, Shiloh?" she asks, her eyes darting from the papers to my face. When I don't answer, she moves closer and picks up the stack of contracts. "How did you get this?"

"I broke into your briefcase," I say, holding her gaze.

Her face goes slack. "Why would you do that?"

"Because you wouldn't tell me anything about those," I say, gesturing with a nod of my head at the contracts, still in her hand.

Her eyes fall on the yellow page with the bank information on it and widen. She drops the stack of contracts and scoops up the page. "This is nothing, Shiloh," she says, crumpling it into a ball. "I just needed your account information so we could set up direct deposit for your Universal checks."

"So...you didn't write two ten thousand dollar checks out of that account?"

Her face goes ashen and it's a second before she answers. "It was to reimburse Universal for tour expenses...the venues and travel expenses and paying the staff..."

"Then why aren't the checks written to Universal?"

She lowers herself into the seat across from me. "I wanted to set some money aside so I could just take care of it when the itemization came. It's…I opened a new account for you, just to keep everything separate from your State money. I thought it would be easier."

"Why?" I say, trying to make myself believe what she's saying makes sense. It takes me less than a second to realize it doesn't. "I can write checks out of that account with no problem."

"But if you want me to take care of things for you, I'll need access too. I couldn't do that with your other accounts."

"What's this?" I ask, lifting the deposit slip from my lap. "This is a lot of money. Where did it come from?"

"Universal." She swallows. "It's your cut of ticket sales."

"Why didn't you tell me about it?"

She slams her palms on the table. "Why are you giving me the third degree, Shiloh? I've only done any of this to make your life easier."

"Then why didn't you just ask me to write a check, instead of taking my checkbook and doing it yourself?"

"I…" Her mouth opens and closes a few times before she finds words. "I'm trying to keep things simple for you. I didn't think you'd mind if I took care of this."

I stand from the table and lift my phone. "I'm calling Phillip."

"No!" she shouts, lunging for my hand.

I yank it away. "I want him to tell me how much they're charging me for tour expenses."

"Shiloh…wait," she says, panic thick in her voice. "Just…let's just talk about this, okay? It's late. You can wait for morning to call him when he's in the office. He'll have all the numbers there."

I pull up his number and hit connect.

"Hello," he says when he answers.

I try to keep the shake out of my voice. "Hi Phillip. Sorry to call so late. This is Shiloh Luck."

"Shiloh!" he says as Billie sinks onto the couch with her head in her hands. "Has Billie had a chance to take you through the new contract?"

"Um…no. I didn't know we had one until just now."

There's a pause. "Huh. We had the final draft couriered over a few weeks ago."

My head is a whir of questions, but I close my eyes and breathe, trying to keep my focus. "I really need to ask you about tour expenses. Have you billed for that yet?"

"Didn't Billie tell you?" he asks. "Minus expenses, your cut of ticket sales was two hundred and eighty grand. We just cut that check last week."

"So…I won't owe anything?"

"Hell, no, Shiloh. That tour was pure gold."

When I look at Billie, cringing on the couch, I know.

Me, the kid who used to con all my classmates, just got conned.

CHAPTER 25

Tro

When my phone rings, the sound splits my head in half. I pull my pillow around my ears. My first thought in the morning is always the same as my last thought at night. A heart-shaped face. Whiskey eyes full of fire.

Lucky.

All at once I'm wide awake and grabbing for the phone. The empty Jack bottle I'm sharing my bed with this morning falls to the floor with a thud and I'm relieved to find that's the only thing other than me in my bed.

Last night is a blur, but as I blink my eyes open and they begin to focus, the destruction all around me is enough to know the snippets of memory I have are accurate.

I squint at the screen, knowing who I need it to be. There are things Lucky needs to hear, things I need to say out loud before I self-destruct.

It's not her.

I'm so busy being disappointed at who it's *not* that it takes me a second to register who it *is*.

I hit connect and bring the phone to my ear. "Hey, Kate."

"How's world domination coming?" she asks.

I rub my aching head and take a second before answering to decide if I need to run to the bathroom, or if the feeling I'm about to puke will pass on its own. "Fucking not good," I say honestly.

"Been reading stuff on the internet about a rift in the band. You guys okay?"

I take a deep breath as my stomach settles and drop my head into the pillows. "Not by a long shot."

"Anything you want to talk about?" she asks.

I shake my head as if she can see it. "Just some shit I need to work out."

"You always land on your feet, Tro. No matter what's going on, I have no doubt you will now."

"Thanks. So…" I add when it occurs to me Kate's never called just to shoot the shit, "everything okay there?"

"I'm not sure," she answers tentatively.

I pull myself up to sit with my back propped on the headboard. "What up?"

"There were cops here asking for you a little while ago."

The image of Lucky pressed between me and the mattress, the electric sensation of her skin on mine, her warm, wet mouth devouring me, flashes in my mind. My body predictably responds. Did someone report me? Who would know?

My next thought sends a rod of cold steel through my gut. Grim.

He fucking narced me out to the cops because he thinks me being into Lucky is ruining the band. There's no one else who would pull this shit.

"What did they say?" I ask, trying to tie all the loose ends together in my mind. What would Grim know? What could he have told them?

"Nothing, which really pissed me off. I tried flaunting my feminine wiles and everything. I think they must have been gay."

I smile despite the sinking feeling in my gut. "Musta been. Those wiles are damn near impossible to resist."

"You sound like you're speaking from experience," she purrs, a smile in her voice.

"You better fucking believe it."

"But, seriously, Tro. They looked all business. And when I told them you were out of the country, they got all cagey like they were afraid you might not come back if you knew they were looking for you. They asked when you were coming home and tried to make out like it was no big deal either way, but I could tell they were all worked up over something."

"What did you tell them?"

"I told them if they want to know your schedule, they should Google you."

I huff out a laugh. "Hard to hide when I've got fifteen thousand pairs of eyes on me every night."

"Anyway…I just thought you should know. They told me not to mention to you they'd been by. Which, of course, means I called you as soon as they left."

"Thanks, Kate. You've always got my back."

There's a pause. "Yeah, well…that's what friends do, right?"

"See you in a few days," I say, then disconnect.

My eyes scan the destruction all around me, the evidence of my meltdown last night, and I press my hand to my face. My lower lip's cracked and swollen from where Grim managed to get a right hook off before I made him pay.

I open my texts and check for anything new from Jamie, but there's nothing since three this morning, just after they got Grim to the hospital.

He's gonna be okay, dude, his text says.

So, Grim is going to survive. But the band's not.

I can't do this anymore.

I drag myself out of bed, piss, and then climb into the scalding shower, bracing my hands against the cool tile walls.

We're supposed to play Milan tomorrow night and finish with two shows in Rome. Our tour manager isn't going to let us cancel unless Grim is on his death bed. I don't think I hurt him that bad. So, we finish the last few stops and that's it. My manager's going to fucking blow a gasket when I tell him we're canceling the next studio album. Maybe he can renegotiate it into a solo.

I wrap a towel around my waist when I get out and grab my shit and start to pack. The plan was to spend our free day here in Zurich, then fly to Milan tomorrow, but I have to get the fuck out of here.

An hour later, I'm at the ticket desk at the airport. The agent finds a flight with an open first-class seat and switches me, and when I get to Milan, I grab a random hotel flier from the information desk and tell the taxi driver to take me there.

I order up a bottle of Jack and my only plan is to stay lost until someone thinks to find me. Maybe no one will. Maybe they'll just let me stay lost.

CHAPTER 26

Shiloh

I land in Sacramento and Lilah and Bran are waiting outside security for me. She jumps up and down and waves when she sees me coming, and I wave back.

Bran takes my duffel as Lilah pulls me into a hug. "Oh my God, it's so amazing that you're here!"

"Thanks for letting me come," I say into her shoulder. "I didn't know where else to go."

She draws back and looks into my eyes. "You can always come to me. For anything. Please never forget that, Lo."

I smile. "Same as always."

Bran holds out his hand. "Sorry to hear about how things went down with Billie."

I shake as the knot in my stomach tightens. "I trusted too easily. It won't happen again."

Lilah gives me a sad look, but turns for the doors without saying anything. We head to the garage and I follow Bran to an old black car.

"This is cool," I say, running a finger over the hood.

"Bran's first love," Lilah says, elbowing him in the ribs.

He grabs her and crushes her to him. "Not true. Everything is second to you."

There's a second they just stare at each other, but then Bran seems to remember where they are and that they're not alone. He unlocks the car and pulls the front seat forward so I can climb in back.

I slide into the back seat and expect Lilah to sit up front, but instead, she shoves me over and climbs in next to me.

"Home, Jeeves," she teases Bran.

He smiles and folds his substantial frame into the front seat.

"So...?" she asks cautiously as we pull out of the garage. "Are you really okay?"

I take a deep breath and sink into the seat. "I'm just so pissed. After living my whole fucking life on the street, I can't believe I was so gullible." I shake my head. "You don't expect respectable white people to be fucking con artists, you know?"

She gives me a sympathetic look. "You couldn't have known, Lo."

I shake my head at myself again, because I should have. "This whole thing is all just so new to me. I was totally out of my element when I signed with Billie. And she seemed cool, you know? She looked out for me, made sure the label wasn't screwing me on my contract or promotion or whatever. I just never guessed it was so she could try to steal everything from me later."

"But you found out in time, so that's the thing to remember. Everything's going to be fine."

Other than the brand new Mercedes, which it turned out she did buy with my money (and not just her fifteen percent of it), there was the house in Beverly Hills she'd put an offer on and used my money for the deposit. She promised to get all the money back so I wouldn't call the cops, but I didn't stick around past the place where we closed the account with her name on it and transferred what was left of my concert earnings into mine. I haven't decided yet if I'm going to report her. People should know. But I'm not sure I want to be the poster child for naïve little girls.

"I want to hear everything new you've written," I tell her to change the subject. I don't know where anything with my contract stands right now, but if anyone ever lets me record again, it's going to be Lilah's stuff.

She tells me about a few new songs, and says they're her moneymakers at Bran's bar, where she plays on weekends. "I don't really need the money anymore," she says. "My royalty checks for 'More Than Nothing' pay the rent, but I don't think I could ever totally give up performing."

When she starts talking about school, a deep ache grows in my chest. I love that my life is music now, but part of me longs for what Lilah and I used to have. As bad as it was, living in the group home, trying to survive on the streets, hustling our fellow students for their lunch money, it was home. I don't know where that is anymore.

We take a turn off the windy road that weaves through the hills and come to a small town with wooden plank sidewalks in front of old wooden buildings.

"That's the bar that Bran's family owns," Lilah says, pointing at one of those buildings as we pass. A worn sign swings from chains over the door declaring it the Sam Hill Saloon.

"Wow..." I say, looking around as Bran continues past. "This is so..."

Lilah cracks up when I trail off, unable to find a word that doesn't sound like an insult. "I was the same way when Destiny moved us here. I couldn't understand how anyone would want to live way the hell in the woods. But..." She glances at Bran and her whole face lights. "...you get used to the quiet after a while, and the people are real." She turns and looks at me. "They actually give a shit about each other here. It's sort of nice."

"And everybody knows everybody else's business," Bran adds with a disparaging glance at Lilah.

"Yeah…" Lilah says, her face scrunching. "That part's not always so great, but the rest sort of grows on you."

We pull up to an apartment building on a hill overlooking town and unload. Bran pops the trunk and shoulders my bag. I packed fast, so all I have is a duffel with my jeans and T-shirts, a few pairs of flip flops, and my toothbrush and bathroom stuff. The rest is still at Billie's. I wonder if she's sold it on eBay already.

Lilah hooks her elbow into mine. "Destiny's on a camping trip with her boyfriend, so we have the place to ourselves for a few days."

I feel my eyes widen. The Destiny I remember was pure-blooded city-girl. "Destiny? Camping?"

Lilah smiles. "I told you, this place grows on you."

I follow them up the walk. "So, who's the guy?"

"Someone she met waiting tables at Sam Hill." She leans in and whispers, "Hot firefighter."

They lead me to a first floor doorway and Lilah pulls out her key. "Bran's place is over there and upstairs," she says, pointing farther down the building as she turns the key and opens the door. "We used to live in this fleabag apartment in town over the gun shop, but he made us move up here where he could keep an eye on us."

"Must make it easier for you two to…" I wiggle my eyebrows. "…you know."

She laughs and I swear I catch color rising under the collar of Bran's T-shirt as he follows us in.

He sets my bag on the coffee table and gently grasps her hand, tugging her close. "I've got to get to the bar. Will you be down later?"

She steps into his arms and kisses him, slow and easy, as if it's the most natural thing in the world, and I think again about their age difference. He's ten years older than her, twenty-seven to her seventeen. But watching them together, there's no question that he's good for her. For such a big guy, he holds her so carefully, a hand on her waist and another woven into the hair on the back of her head, as if she's some delicate thing.

I turn my back to give them their moment and take the opportunity to look around the apartment. It's tired and small, but it feels homey. The family room is open to the kitchen and has a couch and a coffee table across from a TV on a stand. It's separated from the kitchen to the left by a short, wide island with two barstools on one end. Next to that is a small kitchen table with three chairs. To the right is a short hallway, the door at the end open to a bathroom.

"We'll be there," Lilah says, and when I turn back to them, they're done kissing.

He holds her a minute longer as they gaze into each other's eyes, communicating more than can be said with words.

He lets her go and backs toward the door. "You should come down for burgers."

She nods. "Sounds good."

"See you in a bit," he says, turning for the door, but he can't make it through without one more glance over his shoulder at his woman. She beams at him and he rewards her with a smile that's one part love and three parts desire.

The door clicks closed and Lilah stares after Bran for a minute before picking up my bag from where he left it on the coffee table and carrying it toward the hallway. "Destiny's gone until Thursday, so her room is yours until then. After that, you can bunk with me."

"I'll figure something out and be out of here in a day or two," I say, following her through a door on the right.

She sets my bag on the double bed and takes my hands in hers. "You will stay here as long as you need or want to, Lo. Hell, I hope you can stay forever." She pulls me into her arms and crushes me in a hug. "God, I've missed you so much."

I wrap my arms around her and hug her back. "Me too."

She really is an amazing friend. She's the only person I've ever trusted completely until Billie. I cringe and shake my head at myself. I can't believe I trusted her so blindly.

"You okay?" Lilah asks, noticing my expression, no doubt.

I drop onto the bed and flop onto my back. "How was I was so stupid?"

"Listen, Lo. You need some time to regroup, and this is a really great place to do that. You can take all the time you need and no one will bother you here."

I roll on my side and prop myself up on an elbow. "I don't even know where to start."

"Where did you start last time?"

I take a deep breath. "With a manager, and we all know how that turned out."

She lays on her side next to me. "So, you'll find a better one this time."

"I don't trust any of them."

"Well, chances are that your next manager won't try to adopt you or whatever, so it won't be an issue, right? I mean, you said all your accounts are in your name."

I flop onto my back again. "I just wish I got this business better so I didn't have to rely so much on other people."

"What about Tro?" she says with an air of caution. "He's got to know people he can set you up with."

I feel my insides harden to cement as images of European beauties draped all over him flash in my mind. "I trust him least of all."

A wry smile tilts her mouth. "He loves you, Lo."

"Which is why he shot me down the night before he left for Europe," I say with a roll of my eyes.

She bolts upright and stares down at me, wide-eyed. "What?"

"I made a serious move and he literally climbed off me and told me it wasn't happening."

"Holy shit, Lo! Tell me exactly what he said."

I cringe a little with the memory. "He said if we did it before he left, all it would be was a quick fuck and that's not what he wanted."

Her face softens. "It sounds like he was trying not to take advantage of you...which seems sort of chivalrous to me. And a little hot."

I stare at the ceiling. "Well, he also said he wouldn't fuck French girls, but he's fucking his way through Bulgaria as we speak, so I'm thinking chivalry is dead."

"You don't know that, Lo. Maybe he's not," she says hopefully.

I tug my phone from my pocket and pull up the picture of him and the actress. "You think?"

She grimaces a little. "You don't really know what's going on there, Shiloh. This doesn't mean anything," she says, handing my phone back.

I open the article with the shot of Tro all but fucking the Bulgarian princess in the corner of a nightclub. "And this?"

Her grimace deepens, because there's no denying the obvious. "Sorry, Lo. I really thought..." She shakes her head. "Have you talked to him?"

"He's texted me, but I haven't answered. What's the point?"

"The point is, maybe he's *not* fucking his way through Bulgaria or any other country. Maybe he's waiting 'til he gets home to be with *you*."

I snort a derisive laugh and glance down at the picture. "You're delusional."

"I might be, but there's only one way to find out. You should talk to him."

I sit up and unzip my bag. "Can I use your shower?"

She looks at me a long minute, not liking my evasion. But finally, she nods. "There's shampoo and whatever in there. Help yourself."

I pull a clean thong and T-shirt from my bag and head to the bathroom. I stand in the hot shower longer than I should, but it's Lilah, so I'm not too worried about being rude. When I come out, she's in the family room watching TV.

"Feel better?" she asks.

I shrug. "A little, I guess."

She grins. "Well, you'll definitely feel better after a Sam Hill burger. People come from all over for them."

I tug on a pair of jeans from my bag, then pull my hair back. "Let's go."

She goes to her room and comes out with her old guitar...the one we both learned to play on. I'm surprised when a lump forms in my throat. That was a lifetime ago. The only reason it didn't burn in the fire that took half Lilah's San Francisco city block to the ground when her parents blew up their kitchen cooking meth was because I'd given it to a guy who owed me money for a gambling debt to restring. That was how he got his parents to cover his ass without them knowing he'd been gambling at school.

She holds it up on her way to the door. "Show time."

It's a short walk to town, and on our way, she fills me in on the locals. Bran's mom owns the bar he works in, and has since before Bran and his sister were born. His parents are divorced now, but Lilah says they still spend time together. "Quality time," she says with a dubious look. "If you know what I mean."

When we walk into the bar, it's pretty quiet, a few groups tucked into the corners and the big-screen TV on the wall playing some baseball game.

Bran is behind the bar, just where Lilah met him—after he'd already slept with Lilah's sister. Let's just say things were complicated between them for a while, and it was only complicated further by the fact she was sixteen and he was twenty-six at the time. But they've obviously worked it out.

"I don't usually play on weeknights," she says as we move to the bar. She grins at me. "But tonight I've got my rockstar best friend here, so it's happening."

We slide onto stools and Bran gives Lilah just about the sexiest smile I've ever seen from behind the beer taps, where he's got a fistful of mugs he's filling. He drops them on a tray and a waitress comes by for them, carting them to a table of guys in the corner.

"What can I get you ladies?" he says, planting his hands on the bar in front of us. With the motion, his pecs flex, and *holy shit*.

"Two burgers," she says with a questioning raise of her eyebrows at me. When I nod, she adds, "And two Diet Cokes."

The waitress comes by the end of the bar on her way to the kitchen and Bran catches her eye. "Tell Jeff I need three burgers."

She nods and disappears through the swinging door.

He pours our Cokes and then comes around and sits on the stool next to Lilah with a beer. He nods at the guitar. "You playing tonight?"

She smiles and glances at me. "I got my partner in crime here, so I couldn't resist."

He looks past Lilah to me. "It's not going to touch your normal payday," he says, "but you're welcome to sing in my bar anytime you want."

We shoot the shit while we wait for our food, and when Bran gets up to pour another round of beers for the table of guys, I notice one of them looking at us. He gets up and makes his way over as the others watch and throw out the occasional catcall.

"So…" he says when he stops between our stools, scratching his elbow nervously. "Has anyone ever told you, you look exactly like Shiloh Luck?"

Lilah shoves his shoulder. "I know! That's what I keep telling her, but she doesn't think so." She looks at me through a frame she makes with her fingers. "I mean, if her hair was just a little lighter, and maybe if her cheekbones were a little more defined and her nose a little smaller, she'd be like her twin, don't you think?"

The guy is nodding along as she talks, way less nervous now that he thinks I'm not who I really am. "Yeah. I mean, seriously. She could totally pass for her." He smiles at me and holds out his hand. "I'm Greg, by the way."

"Lilah," she says, shaking his hand even though it was pointed at me. "And this is Giselle. She's an exchange student from Costa Rica and doesn't speak much English."

The way this guy's eyes go all glassy as they scan down my body, you'd think she just told him I was made of pure gold. "Giselle," he says, sliding onto the stool next to me. "Wow…so, Costa Rica, huh? This must be a big change."

"Take a hike, buddy," Bran says, pounding the side of his fist on the bar in front of us.

Considering Bran's neck is nearly as wide as this guy's waist, the look on his face when he turns and sees Bran is no surprise. His eyes widen and he lifts his hands as if to demonstrate that he's not touching anything he shouldn't be. "Dude, I was just talking to the lady."

"Find a different lady," Bran growls, and the guy nearly falls off his stool and stumbles back to his table.

"He was kind of cute," I say, watching him fill the others in. "What if I was planning on taking him home?"

Bran shakes his head. "Not gonna happen on my watch."

I turn to him. "So now you're my protector?"

"Lilah cares about you, so I'm going to do what I can," he says with a slow nod and a deadly serious look in those intense eyes.

I suddenly see why Lilah went through the hell she did to be with him.

"Okay," I say with a nod. "Thank you."

The waitress drops our plates on the bar in front of us and sets one on Lilah's other side. "Thanks, Carol," Lilah says as Bran comes around the bar and hikes himself onto the stool.

We eat and with the first bite, I see what Lilah was talking about. I never realized a burger could be more than a burger, but this is a little slice of heaven on a plate.

The image of taking a bite of Tro's room service burger in Miami flashes through my head and a cold sweat breaks down my back. I don't even remember what that one tasted like. My mind was on Tro's half-naked body and what it was about to do to mine.

I shake the memory off as Lilah says, "Good, right?"

I can't even stop eating to answer.

I'm licking every last morsel off my fingers when Carol comes for our dishes. Lilah reaches for her guitar and Bran mutes the TV and sets a beer mug on the bar in front of us. He slips a ten in from his pocket to get the tipping started. There are more people now than when we came in, but just barely, so I get what he was saying about the payday.

"Play me one of your new ones," I say as she begins strumming.

She does and I close my eyes and listen. Lilah's every bit the singer I am, but her real talent is in finding combinations in her head that totally work, but don't seem like they should. After the first, she does another that I haven't heard, but then segues directly from that into one of our oldest, and I can't help but to sing along.

The guys in the corner all start shoving each other and pointing. By the next song, one of our subway favorites, some of them are out of their seats and standing near the bar.

"You're no fucking exchange student," Greg says, and he's clearly drunker than he was half an hour ago.

"No entiendo," I say, pulling one of the only things I ever learned in Spanish class from the recesses of my mind.

Bran is out on his feet. "If you're here to tip the ladies, then be my guest. Otherwise…"

He doesn't even need to finish before the kid is backing off. "Christ, man. I'm just want to know if she's really Lucky?"

At his use of Tro's nick name, acid rolls up my throat from my stomach. "Don't call me that."

He turns toward his buddies. "It's fucking her! I told you!"

Bran takes an annoyed breath, then gets in the guy's face. "You want to sit and listen, you'll have a story to tell all your college buddies. You want to make a scene, you'll get your ass tossed. Up to you."

"It's really her, though?" he asks, squinting past Bran at me. "I'm right, right?"

"That depends," he answers. "Can you behave yourself?"

Greg nods emphatically.

"What do you have in your pocket?" Bran asks.

He pulls a wad of cash from his pocket and a twenty falls to the bar. Bran scoops it up and slips it into our jar. "Perfect. Now sit down and listen."

The guy and his friends go back to their table. Lilah plays another of our oldies and we sing. When we've run through most of our old repertoire, she starts on the song Tro wrote—the one he made me sing onstage when we played San Francisco.

I feel my throat constrict and I can't sing.

"Go ahead," she coaxes.

I shake my head and am surprised to feel tears sting the corners of my eyes. I don't cry. Ever.

But after everything with Billie, the thought of Tro, how he showed me a side of himself that I'd never even guessed at, makes something deep in my chest ache. It turns out nothing in that life was real. But, in my heart, I wanted Tro to be.

CHAPTER 27

Tro

The stage under my feet shakes with the thunder of the crowd as the last notes of our encore echo through the cavernous space.

I pump a fist in the air. "We love you, Rome!"

Another roar goes up as the stage lights are doused for the final time this tour. Tomorrow afternoon, we film a video in Pompeii, and the next morning we're on a plane home.

That is if Grim doesn't kill me in my sleep tonight. Which I'm pretty sure he's been plotting since I put him in the hospital.

He's got two black eyes and three stitches across his left cheek. He's wearing them like a badge of honor. The doctor said with his concussion he shouldn't be playing, but he is. All night he's cut me glances and I know what that fucker's thinking. Him dying on stage would be his final fuck you.

We pile off the stage and I don't even have to make an excuse tonight. No one's spoken to me since Zurich. Grim and Jamie gather up the sound guys and they're talking about where they want to start the party as we spill out into the night. They all load in the car and Jamie sends me a plea in his gaze. He's like Switzerland, trying to be neutral, but I know he's pissed.

I turn and head up the sidewalk, happy for the walk.

"You're a fucking pussy!" he yells as the car speeds past me, but there's none of Grim's malice when he says it.

I don't turn around. Or slow down. He might be right, but I really don't give a shit. Better a pussy than an asshole, which is what I've been for the last few years.

When I get to the hotel, I head straight to my room and close the door. I find my guitar in the corner and my fingers run automatically over the strings in the song that's imprinted on my brain. I tweak the few notes tying the bridge to the chorus, then jot them down along with the last line of lyrics. As I look it over, I have the sudden, overpowering need to play it for Lucky.

I open Skype and stare at the yellow status circle next to Lucky's name. She's blown off my texts. She doesn't want to hear from me. Me blowing up her Skype isn't going to change that.

I set my phone down and play the new song straight through for first time.

"The beast isn't content to admire from afar.
It dwells deep inside, the child of obsession.
The taking begins, insidious and perverse.
Suffocating me with enduring possession.

"The living façade that others despise.
Ravaging my soul, watching through my eyes.
The lower I am, the higher its rise,

nestled in pillows feathered with lies."

This song's not my normal thing—slower and more ballady than what my fans want. But it's more my song than anything else I've ever written. I twist through the rest of the lyrics from the birth of the beast through its evolution, and as I sing of its demise, I wonder how I'm supposed to survive without it to hide behind. With the beast banished, what's left?

But that's what the last three months have been about: trying to find the guy behind the beast—the guy deep inside me who Lucky seems to see when she looks at me. I'm not sure if that guy even exists, but if he does, that's who I want to be—someone who might be worth Lucky's time.

The guys come back somewhere around four, bringing the party with them. I ignore the noise and keep playing until I have it perfect. Somewhere around six, everything outside my door but the music finally goes quiet.

I get up and survey the destruction in the suite. There are several unwrapped women passed out on the couches, and a few of the crew scattered on them and the floor. Grim and Jamie aren't among them, so they must be in their rooms.

I click off Jamie's iPod and head back to my room. I flop onto the bed and close my eyes.

When I open them, it's because my phone is vibrating. I jerk awake and look at it. Every fucking time, I can't help hoping for Lucky.

It's never her.

This time, it's our video guy, texting with a change in time. He says he's over at the site and the weather and lighting will be better if we push filming back an hour. Says he'll switch the car he's sending for us to one. I look at the time and find it's after eleven.

Got it, I text back, then close the screen. It opens to Skype, the last app I had open before I crashed. And Lucky's status circle is green. I do the math in my head and figure it's got to be three in the morning where she's at. For a long time, I just stare at the green circle, feeling it tug at me the way it always does.

I promised myself I'd give her space if that's what she needed. But I feel my resolve wavering.

CHAPTER 28

Shiloh

Bran brought Lilah and me back to her place after closing. That was at two. They slipped into her room a little while later and the apartment's been quiet for the last hour.

But I can't sleep.

I've always thought the ever-present danger on the streets of San Francisco had taught me to read people, but I guess my internal danger meter only works for thugs and rapists. I never saw Billie's scam.

Phillip called tonight while we were playing. I saw the message on our way home. He took the decision out of my hands and reported Billie to the cops. I honestly think I'm more pissed at myself than Billie for letting her make a fool out of me, but that doesn't mean I don't hope she rots in jail.

I sit up and lean against the wall. There's a full moon outside the picture window that looks toward nothing but a brick wall across the street. I stare out the window and try to figure out what comes next. Lilah says I can stay here as long as I need to, but sooner or later Children and Family Services is going to find out I'm not living with Billie anymore and force me back to the group home. I haven't lived there since I left for *The Voice*, and I'm not sure I'm equipped to survive there anymore. I'm softer now than when I left. I feel like I've lost my street edge. The shit with Billie was bad, but there are *real*, hardened criminals in the system who will figure out how to get what they want from me if I'm not careful.

Through the wall next to me, I hear a rustle of sheets and then the creak of bedsprings. There's a whisper, then the low rumble of Bran's reply. Lilah obviously waited until she thought I was asleep to wake her man for some playtime.

I get up and tiptoe to the window, away from the wall, hoping to give them some privacy, but there's nowhere in this tiny apartment I can go that I don't hear them, all soft whispers and low moans as he loves her.

And it makes me think of Tro.

I hate that with everything else going on in my life right now, I still spend hours watching the status circle next to his Skype avatar change from green to yellow and back, but I can't help it. It's the only connection I have to him. I slip my phone off the charger and open the app.

And there he is.

As always, the big green circle indicating he's online makes my heart jump. He's here. Right now. And so am I. We're here together, but so very, very far apart. I haven't found the courage to type in a message. I can't even think of what I'd say. He's off doing Europe. The last thing he wants is to hear from the stupid little girl he rejected before he left.

I read through our message thread from before he left for the hundredth time and a tear dampens the corner of my eye. How can he seem so different when it's just me? I know who he is. I always have. Celebrities and royalty. That's who he's been fucking for the last two months. He said I could have whatever I wanted from him when he got back, but out of sight, out of mind, I guess.

I click it over to my music app, because I'm not going to cry over him. I press in my earbuds and choose a playlist from before the tour started—one that has nothing Tro ever sent or played for me on it, then crank the volume to block the sounds from the bedroom. I'm just losing myself in some classic shit when there's an alert. I look at the lit screen of my phone and see it's Skype.

I've got three Skype contacts: Billie, who I doubt has the balls to contact me after what she did; Lilah, who's pinned between the mattress and two-hundred-thirty pounds of ex-marine right now, and Tro.

When I open the app, there's a new message indicator next to Tro's name on my list. I pull up our convo thread and see a new video message loading.

My heart is slamming against my ribs as it finishes loading and opens. Tro is sitting on the floor, his back against a white wall and his guitar in his lap.

"Been working on something," he says into the camera, and God, he looks tired. His scruff is on the long side, so it's been a while since he trimmed it, and his dark hair is all over the place, but his eyes are clear. He's sober. "Thinking maybe it should be the opening track of my first solo studio album. See what you think."

There's nothing twisted or complicated about the melody. It's simple and pure and straightforward. But as he begins to sing, I realize it's because the lyrics stand on their own and he didn't want the meaning to get lost in too much glitz.

I listen to him sing about the death of the beast and the rise of the heart…how life isn't a battle, but a dance. When the video ends, his status circle is still green.

My fingers hover over the screen for a moment, and then I start to type. I read my message over twice before sending it.

What do the guys think about you going solo?

The alert for a Skype video call sends my stomach into a freefall. I pull my earbuds out and find it's quiet in the bedroom next door now.

I open the bedroom door and skitter through the family room, stepping out into the hall. I leave the door open just a crack so I can get back in and skip down the first flight of stairs, sitting in the landing away from people's doors. My finger shakes as it taps the icon to answer. The next second, Tro Gunnison's incredible face fills my screen.

"Isn't it, like, three in the morning there?" he asks.

I go for annoyed so he won't see how nervous I am. "Yep. So why the hell are you calling me in the middle of the night."

"Because you responded to my video message, which meant you were awake."

"Maybe you woke me."

He gives a slow nod. "If I did, I'm not sorry."

I shake off the goose bumps. "What do you want, Tro?"

"Your opinion. Seriously," he adds when he must notice my face screw into a frown.

"You didn't answer my question. What do the guys think about you going solo?'

His expression goes solemn and he turns his head as he scratches the top of it. That's when I notice the split on the corner of his lower lip. "I don't think it will surprise anyone at this point."

"What's going on?" I ask cautiously.

"Grim doesn't think my heart's in it anymore," he says, his eyes finding mine again through the screen. "Thinks I'm distracted."

"He did that to you?" I ask, tapping my lip with a finger.

He nods. "And being the asshole I am, I gave it back tenfold."

"Is he okay?"

Tro looks away again. "Got a concussion. The doc told him not to play, but I think he's hoping he'll die onstage and they'll arrest me for his murder. His final *fuck you*, you know?"

"Wow," I say, my stomach sinking to my toes. Grim mostly ignored me when we were touring, so I never really got a feel for him, but... "I thought you guys were tight."

He shrugs and locks me in his gaze as if we were in the same room instead of half a world apart. "Things change."

I pull my eyes away because, even through the cyber, there's something untamed in his gaze that unnerves me. "So when will you start recording this solo album, do you think?"

"Not for a while. My manager needs to hammer out some contract details, and I need to pull some material together. But I really need some downtime first, so I'm heading home to Austin to kick back for a few weeks before I worry about the rest of it." He shrugs like he's not talking about his whole world turning upside down. "Whatever."

"When do you get home?"

"Tuesday," he answers, and his gaze grows even more intense. "I really want to see you, Lucky. It's been a rough couple of months, not knowing where we stand."

I huff a derisive laugh. "You knew exactly where I stood that last night in Miami."

"I did," he says with an almost nod. "But I don't now. You were pissed last I saw you, and you haven't answered any of my messages."

Everything in me is completely at odds. I ache for him in places I don't want to, but I'm still so pissed. "I have to be the only girl in history to try to get into your pants that you shut down," I hiss through a tight jaw.

His expression shifts into a mix of frustration and anger as he drops his head back against the wall. "Because you're the only girl who's ever tried to get into my pants that I gave a shit about."

There's a noise, then an empty beer can comes flying in from the right and hits the wall next to Tro's head.

"What the fuck, man!" Jamie's voice says from a distance.

Tro chucks the can back at him. "Get the fuck out of my room, asshole."

"It's our last fucking day on the road. You need to drop this hermit shit and come out here and fix this thing with Grim."

The picture is a blur of light and dark as Tro gets up and goes to where Jamie is. "I said, get the fuck out of my room."

There's a slam, then he turns his phone back on himself. "He's a douche."

"And crazy. You haven't been a hermit."

His eyes widen as he moves to the bed and sits against the headboard. "How would you know?"

I shrug and try to make like it's no big thing, but I feel my cheeks warm. "I just saw some stuff."

He grins. "Have you been stalking me, Lucky?"

I roll my eyes. "Yeah, because that's how I really want to spend my time."

"So, tell me what you've seen," he says, and I hate the amusement I hear in his voice.

"The usual."

"Meaning?"

"You fucking every woman in Europe."

He slouches deeper into the pillows. "I suppose that's fair." His head quirks to the side. "Not true, but fair."

"You're denying that actress in Paris?"

He shakes his head. "She went home with Jamie."

"Or the Bulgarian princess?"

A cocky half smile tugs at his mouth. "That almost got me arrested, but it wasn't this trip. Guess the press dredged that one up for something to write about when they didn't think I was getting in enough trouble this time around."

"You're never going to make me believe that there's not groupies in your bed every night."

He raises his eyebrows. "You almost sound like you care."

I catch myself chewing my lower lip and make myself stop.

When I don't answer he gives me a look, then the camera blurs again as he gets up and crosses the room. He pulls open the door and turns the screen out so I'm looking at the living room. Jamie and Grim are packing up their stuff.

"Hey, Grim?" Tro yells into the room.

His head pivots and he glares daggers at Tro. And holy shit. Even with the crappy resolution of the picture I can tell his face is a mess.

"How many women have I fucked this trip?" Tro asks.

Grim just glares at him, then turns and disappears through a door on the other side of the room.

"He's pussy-whipped," Jamie yells.

"Pussy-whipped?" I ask, trying to keep the shake out of my voice. "Whose pussy would that be?"

Tro turns the screen back to face himself and ducks into his room. "I'll give you one guess."

I shake my head. "Sure as hell isn't mine. You didn't want my pussy when you had the chance."

His eyes flash wide, a mix of anger and surprise. "You really think I didn't want you, Lucky? Seriously? Are you fucking blind?"

"My eyesight is just fine," I say, tapping a finger under my eye. "Didn't miss a thing when you rejected me and walked away."

"I have wanted you from the moment I saw you backstage at Rockefeller Center. I fucking fantasize about how you'd feel under me, over me, beside me, every fucking night. I want you more than I've ever wanted anything, Lucky, but I don't even know how to do that—fuck someone who matters to me." He gives a small shake of his head and a disgusted laugh as he drops his gaze from the screen. "I mean, when you never want to let someone out of your arms once they're in them, how does that work?"

My heart is hammering and there are shooting stars flickering through my vision. "What time Tuesday?"

His eyes find mine again through the screen. "I'll text you the flight. You'll be there?"

I nod. Just once, but his face changes the minute my head starts to move. He rolls his eyes up toward the ceiling and takes a deep breath. "Thank fucking God."

"Didn't know you were a believer."

"Wasn't 'til just this second," he says, grinning at me. "But when the big guy answers your only prayer, you got to give credit, right?"

"Well, you seem to be in confession mode, so I guess that makes sense."

His eyes soften. "I should have told you this shit before I left."

"Yeah, well…" I say, "I think maybe you tried, but I wasn't ready to hear it then."

"But you are now?"

I take a deep breath. "Not quite, but maybe by Tuesday."

"Tuesday," he says with a nod. "The only thing I know for fucking sure is the next three days are going to blow."

"Night, Tro," I say.

"Night, Lucky."

I disconnect and stare at the phone before pulling myself up and heading back into Lilah's place.

On Tuesday everything is going to change, one way or another. Which way that goes is going to be up to Tro.

CHAPTER 29

Tro

The flight from Rome to JFK feels like a funeral procession. Jamie and I are across the first-class aisle from each other and Grim is on Jamie's other side. No one talks and Grim is well on his way to cleaning out the entire plane's alcohol supply, tiny airline whiskey and vodka bottles lined up on his tray table like bowling pins. About halfway through the ten hour flight, when he starts slurring a string of expletives across the aisle at me, the flight attendants cut him off. When he wants to climb over Jamie's lap to get to me, Jamie's able to talk him down and finally he passes out.

Jamie nudges my elbow from across the aisle. "We'll get through this, man. By the time we're back in the studio next month, Grim will have cooled down and everything will be fucking fine."

He's trying to sound confident in his prediction, but from the squint in his eyes, I can tell he knows it's most likely bullshit.

I sip my drink then set it down and swirl the ice cubes. "I don't think so, man. I'm just not feeling it anymore, and I don't think you're going to get Grim on board with that plan anyway."

I know he's already got feelers out for a new vocalist for "his" band, and I'm okay with that. It feels like the right move.

Jamie's eyes narrow. "Christ, Gunner. You're saying you're really gonna just fucking walk away?"

I feel my head bobbing before my mouth opens. "I feel like it's time. I've got some different stuff I want to do and Grim is still stuck in the same place he's always been. I don't think he's capable of evolving. As a person or an artist."

Jamie looks toward Grim, on his other side. "Fuck. I can't fucking believe that this might be over."

I drain my glass. "Not over. Think of it as a new beginning. Everybody gets what they want this way."

But, just like Jamie, I know my prediction might be bullshit too. Because if Lucky's not in Austin when I get there, I won't have the thing I want most. The thing I need.

"What about me, man?" he says, his face crumbling. "What the fuck am I supposed to do?"

"Whatever feels right. You can stay with Roadkill, or if you feel like it's time for a change, I'd be honored to have you run my drum tracks. The invitation's open, man. Your choice."

He tips his head against the headrest and rubs his eyes. I know what he's going to choose. As Roadkill's drummer, people know who he is. Backing up a solo is a tough spot to get noticed. "This fucking blows."

We make it to JFK without Grim trying to kill me again and after we clear customs we all head our separate ways, toward our connecting flights. When I get to my gate, I've got an hour to stress over whether Lucky will be there when I get to Austin. If she's not, I just blew up my life for nothing.

But then I realize that's not true. Lucky made me see how meaningless my life really was. Either way, with her or without her, this change is for the best.

But, fuck me, I hope it's with her.

The flight to Texas is only four hours, but they're the longest four hours of my life. When finally we unload in Austin, my chest is so tight I can't breathe. But when I get to the end of the jet bridge, my heart skids to a stop.

Lucky is waiting at the gate.

My feet stall and the guy behind me slams into my back.

"Sorry, man," I say, and when I turn back to Lucky, she's smiling.

It pierces straight to my heart and I feel like a love-struck teenager, complete with rampant hormones. Because the image that takes hold in my mind as her smile fades is her naked body pressed against mine.

"Hey," I say, finally forcing my feet to move.

"Hey," she echoes.

I take her arm and turn us up the concourse toward baggage claim. "How did you get here?"

She breathes a laugh. "My father was too stoned to remember to use a condom."

I smile and shake my head. "Let me rephrase that. I'm surprised Billie let you come to Austin."

"I fired her," she says.

My feet stall again and I spin to face her. "What?"

"It was all bullshit." A disgusted frown twists her face. "I can't believe I didn't spot the con."

The nervous knot in my stomach swirls into a cloud of rage. "What the fuck happened?"

She lowers her gaze, as if ashamed. "She was stealing my money. She only wanted to become my legal guardian so she could get her hands on more."

"Holy shit, Lucky," I say, looping my arm over her shoulder and pulling her close.

"She was writing checks out of my trust accounts and diverted my concert earnings into an account she'd set up in both our names. I didn't even know."

We start walking again, but I keep my arm around her. "She sort of laid into me on your bus that last morning on the road. She was pretty pissed I'd made the Freddie connection for you and she told me to back off." I shake my head. "Her whole reaction was off, but I thought it was just because Freddie'd dumped her."

"Wait...what?" she says, looking at me. She blinks a few times as understanding dawns in her eyes. "She derailed the A&M thing because Freddie dumped her?"

I nod. "According to Freddie."

"She told me he lied and broke promises. I thought she meant *professional* promises." Her face scrunches and she rubs her eyes. "I'm so fucking stupid."

"You're not stupid, Lucky. Shit happens. When you're successful, people screw with you. You just learn and move on."

"Yeah, well..." She shrugs. "Doesn't really make any difference now, except I have nowhere to live and I need a new manager."

"My manager's pretty useless, but I have a few names that might work for you."

She pulls away. "I told you, I don't want your help."

"Jesus Christ, Lucky," I say, right on the edge of losing my shit all over her for being so stubborn. "Just let me do one fucking thing for you."

She looks at me for a long second, and that's when I see the truth in her eyes. She came to me, but she doesn't trust me.

I want to be angry, but I think about her life: abandoned by her mother, jerked around from foster home to foster home. And now her manager, one of the few people in her life she's ever let herself trust, turns out to be a skank. And here I am, the biggest dirtbag to ever walk the face of the earth, and I expect her to trust me? Yeah, right.

We get to the baggage claim and I lean against the luggage cart stand, pulling her with me. "I don't blame you for not trusting me, but I'm not fucking with you. Just let me give you some names. I won't even contact them. You can talk to them and see what you think. If you don't like any of them, then fuck 'em. You can go out and find someone else."

She bites her lower lip as she thinks about it. "Fine," she finally says.

She looks at me a moment longer before stepping between my legs and sinking against my chest. I tip my face into her hair and breathe her in. I'm going to explode with whatever this feeling is, like someone dropped an entire box of Alka Seltzer into my bloodstream.

From the corner of my eye, I see a few people snapping shots. I don't move. After weeks of waiting, I finally have her where I've wanted her since the moment I first saw her, and I'm not going to do anything to spook her.

When my duffel comes around, I push off the stand and yank it off the belt, keeping my other arm firmly around Lucky's waist. We head to the curb and find a cab. My heart kicks when I give the driver the address of my apartment. After everything, Lucky's here. She's coming home with me. I made her a promise before I left. Anything she wants from me is hers. My body, my heart, my soul. There will be no holding back.

She owns me.

Lucky leans against me as we pull away from the airport. Her warm body against my side is doing things to my vitals that I can't control.

I wrap my arm around her shoulders and when she settles deeper into my side, I tip my face into her hair. "What are we doing here, Lucky? Because if this is just a onetime thing, I need to know that up front."

She lifts her head and smirks at me. "So I don't break your tender heart?"

I hold her gaze so she knows this is no joke. "Exactly."

For a long time, we stay locked in each other's gazes, but her pull is too strong and I find myself leaning closer.

She closes the last inch between us and her warm, soft lips brush over mine.

My groan rolls up from the deepest part of me, pure base need. The next second, my fist is twisted into her hair and I'm crushing her to me, devouring her mouth with mine.

She doesn't pull away and I feel the desperation in her kiss matching mine. I spend the next several minutes trying to find a way to crawl right inside Lucky and just live there. When we finally come up for air, I glance out the window and see we've reached my neighborhood. But when Lucky's hand finds my jaw and pulls me back to her mouth, I forget everything else.

"Forty six seventy five," the driver says over the seat as he pulls up in front of my building.

Lucky shoves me away and smiles a wicked smile that turns my insides to molten lava. I toss a wad of cash at the driver as Lucky lets herself out onto the sidewalk, then follow her out of the car. The driver pops the trunk and I shoulder our duffels before grabbing Lucky and throwing her over my shoulder as well.

She squeals as her feet unexpectedly leave the ground, then pounds on my back as I haul her toward the house. "Let me go!"

"Not fucking likely," I mutter as I stride up the walk. I unlock the door and bound up the stairs, and the whole way, Lucky's screaming at me to put her down.

So I do. Once I'm through my apartment door, I head straight to my bedroom and throw her down right onto the middle of my bed, where I intend on taking my sweet fucking time ravaging her pristine caramel body. I dump our bags and her hungry gaze flicks from my face to my straining erection before she grabs the front of my T-shirt, dragging me down on top of her.

And I'm kissing the living fuck out of her.

This is what I've needed since that first second I saw her backstage at *The Tonight Show*, and it feels like some deep, eternal itch is finally being scratched.

CHAPTER 30

Shiloh

He pins me under two hundred pounds of pure testosterone and kisses me. Our mouths devour and our hands conquer, laying claim to each other's bodies in a flood of desire so intense that I'm dizzy with it. We tug at each other's clothing—the last obstacle between us after all this time, and when I feel mine rip in his tight grasp, I shudder. No one's ever literally ripped my clothes off before.

But I understand his need, because mine is overpowering and instinctual. I press him up just long enough to yank his shirt over his head and toss the tattered remains of mine aside. But then I fist my hands into his hair and pull his face back to mine. He's my oxygen. Without his mouth on mine, I'd suffocate.

His kiss becomes more desperate as his hands skim over my hypersensitive skin and he unhooks my bra. My fingers trace all the hard lines of his ripped pecs and abs. Somewhere deep inside me, a dam breaks and a reservoir of need I never knew existed floods through me. I have his jeans open a second later, and when I wrap my fingers around his erection and squeeze, he freezes and holds his breath.

He presses up on strong arms, breaking our kiss and leaving me gasping for him. His fingers weave into mine, pinning my hands next to my head on the mattress. Every nerve ending in me pricks to life when his eyes course over my body like hot coals. His mouth finds my hardened nipple and he gives suck, setting off landmines under my skin. The shockwave travels straight to my groin, and I grind myself against the thigh he's positioned between my legs. He presses his leg harder against me as his fingertips tease my other nipple into a hard peak. I can't help the moan that claws up my throat, and he answers with one of his own, then his hand slips under my skirt and divests me of my thong.

He doesn't waste any time, his fingers dipping into my slick opening, and a feral moan I can't contain comes from the animal deep inside me.

"You have no fucking clue how much I've fantasized about this," he says, slipping his fingers out of me and bringing them to his mouth. Everything south of my waist contracts hard when he sucks my juices off them. He reaches for the drawer of his nightstand and comes out with a condom, which he rips open with his teeth. A second later, he's suited up and ready.

Fuck foreplay. I want him now.

I grab his hair and yank him to me, spreading my legs over his hips. His aim is true and I'm so wet I feel the tip of that thick cock glide inside me. Fireworks go off in my belly as he presses deeper, and, God, he's huge. He hooks his elbows through my knees, supporting his weight on straining biceps, then all at once takes what's his on one deep thrust.

A cry of both pain and pleasure erupts out of me, followed by the satisfied moan of the animal inside.

"Okay?" he breathes.

I look up at him, and along with the lust flaming behind his gaze, there's something deeper. In this second, I know that's a question he's never bothered asking before.

I roll my pelvis, taking him deeper, and smile wicked thoughts at him. "I can handle anything you've got."

His smile turns pure demon and he shifts his hands under my ass, lifting me and driving himself inside me to the root. He thrusts again, hard and deep, and the center of my universe is right there, between my legs. I feel the spring in my belly winding tight again as he brings me to the peak of sensation.

I've never been loud in bed, but I've never felt anything as intense as this. I cry out again, then again when he thrusts even deeper.

"Christ, Lucky," he groans as I grind against him. He lowers himself to his elbows, and his hot breath feathers across my neck as he says, "I fucking knew it would be like this."

My body tells him exactly what I need, and he gives it to me. He moves inside of me, hot and thick, and there's nothing gentle about it. He's all power and need.

Never have I felt so inside out, all my nerve endings on the surface—this crazy, blood-on-fire, synapses-on-overload, overflowing-with-pure-ecstasy feeling. His subtle male scent; the moisture starting to bead on his hot skin; the flex of his biceps under my hands; his firm pressure inside of me, stretching me and filling me in a way nothing else ever has; I take it all in, feeling his essence flow through me in slow waves of bliss.

We fuck hard, and even still, I can't get close enough. He pounds into me, deep and unrelenting, demanding everything I have to offer. I give it to him, because it's always been his. Everything inside me swirls into a hurricane of lust and desire, born on a wave of something deeper and more instinctual. I don't want to fall in love with Tro. He doesn't do love. But like a tsunami intent on my destruction, there doesn't seem to be any stopping it.

My cries grow louder as the animal inside is uncaged and takes full control of my body. And when I come, the sound isn't human. Everything has ceased to exist except the sensations Tro has created inside me. I turn to liquid, flow under him, around him, through him. On a last thrust, he growls, his animal finding mine. I open my eyes, stare into his face as he grimaces with what looks like pain, but I know is pleasure.

He collapses on top of me, panting hard, and I relish the feeling of him there, finally as close as I've wanted him from the start. His eyes open and find me watching. The barest hint of a smile quirks one side of him mouth. I trace it with my fingers. "This is only a onetime thing if that's what you want," I say, answering the question I left hanging earlier.

"Oh, hell, no." He lowers his forehead onto mine and closes his eyes again. "I'm already way the hell addicted."

We lay like this, our sweat mingling on the sex ravaged sheets, until we both have our breath. When he rolls off me, I feel suddenly cold without his blazing heat. He flicks at the unfastened bra, still slung between my shoulders, and tugs the hem of my skirt. "Next time I'm going to take my sweet fucking time and get you all the way naked."

I sit up and slip off the remaining shreds of my clothes. "But now you're overdressed," I say with a nod at his jeans and boxers, scrunched nearly down to his knees now.

He grins and kicks them off, then peels off the condom and drops it in the trash near the nightstand. He settles onto the bed next to me and trails a finger over my lips. "The sweetest fucking thing I've ever tasted." The devil creeps into his eyes and his hand trails lower, down my neck, over my left breast, my stomach, coming to rest between my legs. "Almost."

He gives my sensitive clit a flick and I gasp.

"Fucking honey," he says, barely dipping his finger into my sex and stroking my clit with the slick tip.

I bend my knees and spread them, giving him more space to work.

He takes the invitation, shifting himself down the bed. He watches himself finger me, and with each stroke, electricity crackles under my skin and all my inner muscles contract. He shifts even lower and his tongue swirls over my clit.

"Oh, fuck," I groan, unable to contain myself.

"You taste so fucking sweet," he says, then closes his mouth over me and sucks.

Sparklers ignite in my stomach as a moan vibrates out of my core. He's wired directly to the most instinctual part of me, knowing exactly what I need.

He flicks and sucks and I buck against his mouth. He groans when I grab fistfuls of his hair and press him deeper. He fucks me with his tongue, then flicks my clit, and I cry out again.

"I want you inside me when I come," I gasp, pulling his head back. "Fuck me again."

"There's not much chance that's not going to happen, Lucky, but right now I want to taste all that fucking honey." He swirls his tongue and gives me another suck. "You're going to come in my mouth."

I am. I'm so fucking close. He glides his fingers deep inside and fucks me as he sucks my clit. A second later, I'm arching off the bed and screaming out his name.

I see stars and I can't breathe. But Tro doesn't stop. He sucks again, harder, and I come totally unglued as I come for a second time in thirty seconds.

And he keeps going.

I've heard of multiple orgasms, but none of the guys I've been with had the first clue of how to make a girl come even once. Five orgasms later, I'm starting to get that practice makes perfect. Tro's slept with more women than anyone can count, and he's learned a few things along the way.

I lie panting, unable to catch my breath for a long time as his mouth moves back up my body. He kisses my mouth, slow and deep. "That is how you deserve to be loved."

I'm a wet noodle of contentment, but a little shot of adrenaline causes my blood to sizzle at the word "loved." Is that what we're doing? Is he loving me?

Before he left for Europe, I wanted sex with Tro. He shot me down.

Because he wanted *this*.

He drops kisses along my face and neck, then settles against my side. I close my eyes and for the first time in a long time, I finally feel like I'm where I belong.

#

The next time my eyes open, the fading afternoon light has been replace by the yellow light of a full moon. Tro's hot body is still pressed against me and I lay for a long time listening to the slow cadence of his breathing. Finally, he stirs and his eyes open. They spark in the moonlight when he sees me looking.

"Hey, beautiful. How long was I out?"

I shake my head. "No idea. I just woke up."

He weaves a hand into my hair and kisses me, then smiles. "This is nice."

"What?"

"Waking up to this gorgeous face."

It's only as he says it that I wonder if he's ever woken up with someone still in his bed.

He glides a finger down the curve of my nose. "I'm fucking starving. You hungry?"

"Uh-huh," I say, rolling him on his back.

His eyes flare heat in the moonlight as they follow me down the bed. His cock is already stiffening when I grasp it in my hand and start kneading. I circle my tongue over the thickening tip and he grasps a handful of my hair.

"Christ, Lucky. You're fucking killing me here."

I smile up at him, holding his eyes with mine, then suck his hardening cock deep.

"Fuck," he groans, his head rolling back and his fist tightening.

I glide him in and out and he begins to pump against my mouth. I find his rhythm and work with him, feeling him start to pulse in my mouth.

His grasp on my hair loosens and he stops moving. "How far we taking this, Lucky?" he asks, his voice thick.

I watch him watch me take him deep again. I tighten my mouth around him and move faster.

His groans turn to more of a growl as he gets closer, and minutes later, he explodes in my mouth in a burst of salty heat.

"Fuck," he growls as he unloads into me.

I swallow and suck for a second longer as shudders wrack his body.

He grabs my shoulder and yanks me up his body, and his eyes burn into mine. "Who the fuck taught you to do that?" he growls, all possessive alpha. "I'm gonna rip that fucking cocksuckers dick off."

I can't stop the smile. "You."

He quirks his head at me.

"You were my first," I say.

His arms crush me against his firm chest. "How the fuck did you get so perfect?"

I lay in his arms and he kisses the crown of my hair.

"Any chance you're still hungry?" he asks as his stomach growls.

I laugh and pull myself up. "Let's get you fed. You're going to need your energy."

He grins, a white crescent in the dark of the room. "I like the sound of that."

We dress and I tame my copper lion's mane back into a ponytail. Tro grabs a pair of helmets from the corner of the family room on his way to the door and hands me one. He opens the door and takes my hand. "There's a great sausage place down on Rainey Street. That work for you?"

I can only imagine that my smile looks as depraved as it feels. "Can't beat the sausage I just ate."

He stops short and yanks me to him, planting a kiss on me that curls my toes. Before I even know how it happened, I'm pinned between Tro's body the wall of the landing with my legs wrapped around his waist.

There's the click of a door and Tro sets me down and turns.

"Christ, Tro," a woman's voice says from just around the corner of the hallway, out of my line of sight. "Sounded like something out of *Animal Planet* up there. What gives? You don't usually bring them home with you."

He takes my hand and draws me to the top of the stairs. At the bottom is a very surprised looking blond woman in cut off shorts, a white tank, and bare feet, staring up at me. She's tall and tan and stunning, which means I'm sure Tro's slept with her.

The second I think it, I hate both her and my mind for instantly going there.

"Kate," he says, "this is Lu—"

"Shiloh Luck," she cuts in. "Wow." She steps forward and holds out her hand as we descend the last few stairs to the second floor. "I'm sorry. I didn't realize…" Her eyes shift to Tro and she cracks a smile. "Glad you took my advice for once."

I take her hand and shake. "What advice?"

The warning look Tro throws her is a blow torch. "Not now, Kate."

She pulls me closer by the hand she still has hold of. "I'll tell you later," she whispers loud enough for Tro to hear, then lets me go. "So, where you guys headed?"

"Down to Bangers." He looks a question at me and I shrug. He turns back to her. "Want to join?"

She nods eagerly. "Just let me grab my stuff."

A minute later she comes out with a pair of flip flops on her feet and a bag over her shoulder. "You guys want to ride with me?" she asks, jiggling a set of car keys.

Tro shakes his head. "We'll take the bike."

She nods and skips down the stairs ahead of us. "I'll meet you there."

We reach the ground floor and Tro leads me into a single car garage where a Harley is parked. We climb on. "Hold on tight," he says.

I clasp my arms around his chest and we rocket out of the garage. I press my body against his back, taking the opportunity to soak him in, but before I've gotten enough, we're pulling over. We park and he takes my hand and walks me up the street to an opening in a knee-high white picket fence. Near the road is a red building all lit up with a sign boasting over thirty kinds of sausage and the largest tap wall in Austin. Next to the building are rows of worn wooden picnic tables full of people.

"Popular place," I say, glancing over the crowd and cringing a little at the thought of the ensuing stampede when they spot Tro. "You can still go to places like this?"

He shrugs like it's no big thing. "It's pretty dark back there so I've never really had a problem. But even if I did, it would be worth it. They've got some pretty crazy stuff on this menu."

"Hey, guys," Kate says, jogging across the street toward us. "We good?"

Tro nods and we head in. We're seated near the end of a long row of five picnic tables, and Tro's right. The only light is from strings of small globes overhead.

We order: South Texas Antelope and Venison sausage for Tro, Drunk Chicken sausage for me, and Vegan Tempura Eggplant and Roasted Red Bell Pepper sausage for Kate, and beers all around. The waitress is trying to play it cool, but she obviously recognizes us and doesn't card me.

The waitress turns for the red building and Kate kicks Tro's foot under the table. "How long are you home?"

He rests his elbows on the table and props this chin on his fists. "Not sure. Things are a little up in the air right now."

Her eyebrows go up. "Meaning?"

"Meaning the European leg of our tour was pretty rough. Grim wants me out, and the truth is, I want out too, so…" He trails off with a shrug as my insides turn to cement.

"What are you talking about?" I ask.

He shrugs again. "Shit happens. Grim's got his idea of what Roadkill's supposed to be, and we just don't share the same vision anymore."

"But you *are* Roadkill," I say, exasperated.

He shakes his head. "Not according to Grim."

"Who writes the music?" I ask, anger flooding my words and making them sharper than I mean for them to be. "Who sings the songs? If you were to ask anyone on the street who's in Roadkill, the only one any of them would be able to name is you."

Tro just looks at me.

"Grim can think whatever he wants. You are that band's heart, soul, and lifeblood."

"She's right, you know," Kate says.

"I'm just so fucking sick of it." He rubs a hand down his face. "I know this is a hell of my own making, but I don't want to play the game anymore. I've wasted the last six years of my life on shit that doesn't mean anything." He shakes his head wearily. "I guess I just want something in my life to be real for a change." As he says it, he finds my hand under the table and weaves his fingers into mine.

"I had no idea," I say, shocked that Roadkill may be no more.

He breathes out a weary laugh. "Yes you did. You're the only one who's ever seen past the flash. I think I would have gotten to this same place eventually, but you cut through all the bullshit and made me see what I really wanted."

My heart nearly bounds right out of my chest to meet Tro's. "So what now?

The waitress sweeps by and drops our beers on the table. "Now, we celebrate." He picks up his beer and taps it against mine. "To freedom."

I clink his glass, then Kate's and we all drink.

As I watch Tro I realize all the lines around his eyes have smoothed. He's so much more fluid. So maybe he really is finally free of whatever's haunted him for so long.

And so am I.

What if this could work, Tro and me? What if we could be free together?

CHAPTER 31

Tro

The feel of Lucky's thighs hugging my hips, her arms around my chest, that spectacular body pressed all up my back on the ride home does things to me I can't begin to explain. I've never felt hardwired to another person before, but that's what this sensation is.

When we get back to the apartment, we're not even though the door before we're kissing. It was more than I could handle keeping my hands off her in public. But this is our private sanctum. I can have her here, away from prying eyes.

And I do.

I have her from every side, every angle, every direction, all night long. I never knew what sex could be—how huge. How intense. But somehow, I knew with Lucky it would be different than with anyone else, and I wasn't wrong.

We finally doze as the sun's rays begin to streak my wall, and as I drift off, I decide to take Kate's advice for real. When

Lucky wakes up, I'm going to tell her I'm falling so fucking hard for her I can't see straight.

#

But what happens instead is this—

A pound on the door wakes me from an intense dream about that very conversation, and I jerk upright in bed.

Lucky rubs her eyes and looks up at me, her naked body twisted into my white sheets like cream swirling into coffee.

The knock comes again, and this time, there's a voice. "Trotte Gunnison, this is the police. We have a warrant to search the premises."

My stomach launches itself into my throat. "Fuck," I say, scrambling out of bed. In that second, I realize I don't give a shit what they do to me, but I don't want them dragging Lucky through the mud.

I grab my jeans from the floor and tug them on. "Get dressed and round up all your stuff." I go to the window and yank it open. "Go down the fire escape one floor and knock on the next window down. It's Kate's."

Her eyes are wide with fear and confusion, but she starts grabbing her things from the floor. "What's the age of consent in Texas?" she asks, and I know we're thinking the same thing.

But it doesn't matter.

"You're a California resident, where it's eighteen, and you're over state lines with me."

Her face pales as I speak. "Oh God."

She moves faster when another knock comes at the door. "This is your last opportunity to open this door voluntarily, Mr. Gunnison," the cop says through the door.

I give her one last look, then turn for the family room. I take a deep breath and pull open the door, standing squarely in the opening to keep them from coming in until Lucky's had time to get out. Three large cops stand outside my door, two on the landing and one a few stairs down.

"Sorry, just got back from Europe so my clock's all fucked up." I rub my eyes to make it clear I was sleeping. "What time is it?"

Instead of answering, the two cops closest to me hem me in. "Trotte Gunnison? AKA Trotte Michael Tanner?"

Nobody's called me that in six years and hearing it now freezes my blood.

"What's this about?"

The biggest of the two cops, who outweighs me by at least thirty pounds, gets up in my face. "We need you to come with us to the station."

"Why?"

The older guy in plain clothes on the stairs behind the two uniforms speaks up for the first time. "Because we have some questions to ask you about the murder of Michael Henry Tanner." He steps up onto the landing and the uniform in my face backs off. "He was your father, correct?"

There's suddenly no air. I can't answer.

"I have a warrant to search this property," he says, pulling a folded paper from the breast pocket of his white button-down. He flicks his wrist and opens it in front of me. "Sergeant Garcia will be happy to escort you to the department, if you'd like to wait there."

"He's dead," I say, processing what he said.

The last time I saw him was almost three years ago, right in this apartment, after he tracked me down. We did our best to kill each other, and when I woke up, he was gone and Kate had hauled me into my bedroom and had me mostly cleaned up and bandaged.

"Dead," the plain clothes guy confirms.

"How do you know?" I ask, but I know he's right. I've known it for a long time.

He quirks his head at me, assessing, and in that gaze, I see it. They think I did it. "Because we found his body strapped into the passenger seat of his '99 Chevy pickup at the bottom of Lake Travis two weeks ago."

I close my eyes and rub them. So, just about the time Grim and I were beating the living shit out of each other in Zurich, my old man was fucking with my life one last time.

"Can't say I'm sorry the cocksucker's dead," I say, "but I didn't kill him."

The guy steps closer and his uniforms back off. "You're not under arrest, son, but I do have some questions for you. Anything you want to tell us about how your father died?"

"No fucking clue," I lie.

"Why don't you take a ride with Sergeant Garcia," he says. "We can talk in more detail at the station after I've had a quick look around."

The uniform on my right grabs my arm and he and the other start herding me down the stairs as the older guy steps into my apartment.

And I hope three years is long enough that whatever he finds in there is useless.

CHAPTER 32

Shiloh

At first, no one answers when I knock on the downstairs window. I want more than anything to go back up to Tro's, but I can only get him into more trouble if they find me there. I knock again, harder, and the window slides open a minute later.

"Shiloh!" Kate says. I've clearly surprised her again.

"Tro's in trouble," I say, crawling through the window into what is obviously her bedroom.

She looks toward the hallway. "What's going on?"

"The cops are upstairs. He sent me down the fire escape so they wouldn't catch me in his bedroom."

"Damn." She takes a deep breath and rubs her eyes, then looks at me. "Did you hear what they wanted?"

"I got out of there as fast as I could. If they're arresting him because of me…" I trail off as my face crumples and tears threaten. "I just never thought...but Billie...if she found out I came here, she might have done this."

Kate starts shaking her head as I talk. "They were here a week ago. I don't think it's because of you."

That information does nothing to settle my churning stomach. "Then why?"

"Stay here," she says, turning for the hall.

I don't. I drop my bag on the bed and follow her into a small living room. She goes to the door and opens it, and I hear voices and the sound of feet on stairs.

I move to her side just as Tro is being escorted across Kate's landing flanked by two burly cops. He catches my eye and I'm surprised to see he doesn't look afraid.

Which makes me feel better.

But then he nudges his chin at me and shakes his head, his eyes flashing over his shoulder as more feet thud on the stairs from his apartment.

They vanish around the corner of the landing and head down the next flight just as a heavyset older guy in a white button-up shirt emerges from the stairs to Tro's apartment.

I back into Kate's apartment and go to the living room window, watching the front entrance below.

The hinges creak as Kate closes the door all but a crack. "What's going on?" I hear her ask.

"I'm sorry to bother you, but my name is Detective Stills," a deep voice says. "May I ask you a few questions?"

She nods.

"What is your name?" he asks.

"Kate McGown," she answers.

"This is your apartment?"

She nods.

"How long have you lived here, Miss McGown?"

"All my life."

He pauses and I hear a rustle of paper. "I know this was a while back, but in or around late November of 2012, we believe your upstairs neighbor's father might have shown up here. Do you remember hearing anything unusual? Maybe a fight? Raised voices or sounds of a scuffle?"

She thinks for a second, then shakes her head. "Not that I can think of."

"As I said, it was a while ago," he says. "How well do you know Trotte Gunnison?"

"He's not here much because of his job, but we've been friends since he moved in four years ago."

"Does anyone else live here with you?"

Instinctively, I duck into the corner, even though the door's mostly closed.

"My grandmother passed away a few months ago," she answers. "She was the only one."

"Thank you for your time, Miss McGown," he says, just as Tro and the officers spill through the door onto the sidewalk a story below. "If you think of anything at all, give us a call," the cop adds after a second.

"Okay," she answers and I hear the door click closed.

One of the cops grabs Tro's arm once they're outside, like he thinks Tro might try to run or something. Tro shakes him off and walks ahead of them toward the waiting cruiser. He lowers himself into the backseat, then looks up at the window I'm standing in and waves.

I spin on Kate as the cruiser pulls away from the curb. Her face is in her hand and a business card is pinched between her index and middle fingers. "What's going on?" I ask around my heart, which is now firmly lodged in my throat.

"Nothing," she says, pulling herself together. "There's been a mistake."

"But they were asking about Tro's father."

Her face scrunches into a grimace. "It's a mistake."

Kate must be right. This has nothing to do with me, and whatever they're taking Tro in for is a mistake.

"He'll be right back," I tell myself as the cruiser disappears around the corner at the end of the street. And I pray I'm not wrong.

CHAPTER 33

Tro

"There appears to be a very large residuum of blood in the cracks of your wooden floor, Trotte," the older cop, who it turns out is a homicide detective, says to me. "A large enough area that it might indicate someone lost a fatal amount of blood there.

"And I've already told you some of it probably belongs to my old man," I remind him. "I've told you the whole fucking story. He found me here, we beat the shit out of each other, he hit me over the head, knocked me out, and when I woke up, he was gone. End of story."

"How many times does he have to say the same thing?" my court appointed lawyer asks. When I told them this morning that I thought maybe I should have a lawyer before I said anything, I got the *he-must-be-guilty* look, but I figured better safe than sorry. I can afford anyone I want, but I like this guy. He's only a little older than me, but he's sharp. And hungry. If he gets me out of here with no charges, he makes a name for himself.

"Start from the beginning," the detective says, like he thinks he's going to hear something different now than the last three hundred times I've told him the story.

I take a deep breath and start again. "My dad's favorite drunken pastime was beating the living shit out of me. My first memory is of him standing over me with a strap. Went on all my life. One day I finally decided to fight back. He didn't like that. Nearly put me in the hospital."

The detective looks down at his notes. "August 2009," he confirms. "You were seventeen."

I nod. "His girlfriend found me bloody on the floor and patched me up. I was pissed, so I made a move on her, mostly to get back at my douche dad, I guess. I didn't expect anything to happen, but she kissed me back, one thing lead to another." I shrug. "Left town before the sun came up."

"He knew what you did?"

"Wendy called me, told me he'd figured it out. Guess he beat her up pretty good too. She said he'd sworn to hunt me down and kill me." I shift in my seat. "I saw this guy who looked sort of like a slightly older me at the gas station I'd hitchhiked to. Craig Gunnison. Stole his wallet and went as far as I could on his cash—across two state lines. Used his ID for a while until I could get a fake one made. Got a job washing dishes at a two-bit roadside diner in Shreveport, where I met Grim. We started the band, and I figured I was pretty safe because we were playing lowlife Louisiana bars for cash and free booze. But then we started getting noticed, playing bigger venues. I guess my dad saw my picture somewhere. Tracked me here, tried to make good on his threat, and you know the rest. I have no fucking clue what happened to him after he left my apartment."

"You're contending that you were unconscious when he left?" he asks.

I nod. "He'd grabbed my electric guitar from the stand near the couch and swung it at my head," I say, poking absently at my crooked nose. "He managed to get the amp cord around my neck. That's the last thing I remember."

The stupid thing? I could have taken him out way before it got that far, but I had money by then. Figured I could make the whole thing go away quietly with a wad of cash. I kept trying to talk him down, but didn't realize just how fucking crazy the old man had gotten. Alcohol had eaten his brain by then and he was basically a rabid dog. Nothing more. He wasn't interested in my bribe.

"If he was so intent on killing you, why wouldn't he have brought a weapon? A knife or a gun?" the detective asks.

He did. I managed to kick the hunting knife out of his hand. But telling this cop that truth that will only complicate things.

"You'd have to ask him," I answer.

The cop's mouth presses into a line as he looks over his notes. "What happened to that guitar, Trotte? The one you say your dad hit you with?"

I shake my head. "The place was trashed. I tossed all the broken shit, including the guitar."

"Huh...that's interesting because we found the neck and several other pieces of a guitar in the truck with your father's remains."

Acid rises in my throat, but I swallow it and try not to show anything I'm feeling. They only use shit like that against you. "Maybe he took it with him for some reason."

The detective's gaze hardens. "He was in the *passenger* seat, Mr. Gunnison."

"Maybe whoever was driving came up and got him." I shrug. "I have no fucking clue."

"Unless you have another line of questioning, I'm going to have to insist that this interview is over," my lawyer says. "My client has acted on good faith and been forthcoming with information. His story hasn't deviated or been in any way inconsistent with the evidence you've shared. If you have more, please enlighten us and make the arrest. Otherwise, you have no grounds to hold my client."

The detective gives my lawyer an annoyed look, then stands. "This is an ongoing investigation. We'll be processing evidence from the apartment for the next few weeks." He shifts his stern gaze to me. "You don't have any more trips planned, I trust?"

I shake my head. "Taking a few weeks off."

"Good." He closes his file and pulls open the door. "The blood evidence collected from your apartment was enough to get an injunction to seal it until we're able to complete processing of the crime scene, which could take another twenty-four hours. You'll have to find somewhere else to stay in the meantime. But you're free to go."

CHAPTER 34

Shiloh

I'm curled into the corner of Kate's couch. The TV's on, but neither of us are watching it. It's nearly eight. Tro's been gone for ten hours. Kate's called the police station and they don't have any information.

"That's a good thing," she said after her first call at two. "It means they haven't charged him."

She's not saying that anymore.

I'm so jacked up that the knock on the door sends me through the roof. Kate leaps off the other end of the couch and yanks the door open. The first thing I feel is paralyzing relief. But on its heels, I can't deny the stab of jealousy when she launches herself into Tro's arms.

"Oh my God!" she breathes.

Tro's gaze is a little wild as it darts over her shoulder and finds me. When he sees me, he closes his eyes and breathes a huge sigh. She lets him go and he comes into the room. "Hey," he says with an unsure squint and tip of his head. "Wasn't sure you'd still be here."

I'm finally able to move and I pull myself up from the cushions. "I sort of don't have anywhere else to go."

He nods as he moves slowly toward me. He stops just in front of me, waiting. I can't stand being this close and not touching him, but I force my hands to stay at my sides.

He lifts a hand, strokes a finger along the line of my jaw. "I've never been so fucking glad you're an orphan."

I smile as he pulls me to his chest.

Kate backs toward the kitchen. "I'm going to pull something together for dinner."

When she's gone, Tro cups my face in his hands and kisses me. His kiss is slow and soft and makes my heart ache.

"What happened?" I ask when he draws away.

"They think I killed my old man," he says, "but they don't have enough to charge me. They've sealed off my apartment for a few days, looking for something they can nail me on, no doubt."

"But you didn't do it," Kate says from the kitchen door.

He looks at her and shrugs. "You think that really matters? They've got a body. They have to pin it on somebody, so why not go big and convict a rock star?"

Kate just looks at him a long minute before saying, "You didn't do it," again and turning back to the kitchen.

She boils some spaghetti and we all just pick at it.

"Did I tell you I walked into the garage last week and found the new downstairs neighbor taking naked pictures on your bike?" Kate says when no one talks.

Tro makes a disgusted face. "That fat, bald guy? Jesus."

She shakes her head. "His hot eighteen-year-old daughter."

"Ah," Tro says, then winks at me. "That's different."

The conversation's lighter for the rest of dinner, and when we all decide we're done picking, we clean up.

"I've put Shiloh's stuff in Grandma's room," Kate announces, dumping spaghetti down the disposal. "You guys are staying here tonight."

"Thanks, Kate," Tro says. "I need to sneak up the fire escape and grab some clothes and whatever."

"They won't let you in?" I ask.

"I doubt anyone's up there right now. I'd have to wait until tomorrow and" —he plucks at his T-shirt—"I'm pretty sure I stink."

I step into him and nestle my face into his chest. He smells like sweat and sex. "I'm just going to take off anything you put on, so don't bother," I whisper.

He groans low in his chest. "Yes, please."

I stretch up on my tiptoes and he leans down to kiss me. "We're calling Freddie tomorrow. I want to get your manager nailed down so you can start sorting out your contract."

"Way to kill the mood," I grumble, shoving him away.

Tro and I curl together on one end of the couch, and Kate puts in a movie and sits on Tro's other side. When it's over, Tro takes my hand and leads me to another bedroom at the end of the hallway.

"I'm going to take a shower before we hit the sack," he says.

"Why?" I whisper, pulling him close. "You're just going to get sweaty again."

A cocky smile tugs at his mouth. "I've unleashed your inner nymphomaniac."

I tug his T-shirt off and start on the button of his jeans. Because he has. Despite everything that's happened today, or maybe because of it, all I can think about this second is how Tro felt inside me.

He lifts my shirt as he backs me toward the bed and slips my shorts over my hips. By the time my back hits the bed, we're both naked.

"I don't have protection," he says, his lips brushing mine as he hovers over me.

I tug my bag over from the corner of the bed and riffle through it, coming out with one of the condoms Lilah slipped into it just as I was leaving. "My best friend always has my back."

He smiles as I tear it open. Once it's in place, he takes his time with me, teasing me to the peak of sanity before dropping me over the edge. I bite my lips, trying to stay quiet, but if these walls are anything like Lilah's, I know what Kate's hearing.

I wrap myself around Tro and hold on, because there's not a minute with him that's not a wild ride.

CHAPTER 35

Tro

They let me back into my apartment the next day and tell me not to leave town. When I look around, I realize a lot of my shit is missing, bagged and tagged for evidence, no doubt. I try to send Lucky back to Lilah's place, but she refuses to go until we know what's happening.

What happens is: Eight o'clock the following morning, there's a knock on my door. And this time, the cop on the other side says, "Trotte Michael Tanner, we have a warrant for your arrest."

I wasn't asleep, but Lucky was. I watch her wake to the sound and her eyes pull wide. She grabs onto me, her fingers digging into my arm.

"It's going to be okay," I whisper, then kiss her with every fiber of my being. I gently pull myself out of her grasp and go to the door.

When I open it, it's the same two uniforms who were here before. The larger one reaches for my arm and slaps a cuff on my wrist and the other one rattles off my rights. They shove me into the back of a cruiser and haul me back to the station, where they take my mug shots, my prints, and all my stuff, giving me an orange jumpsuit to put on instead.

My lawyer is there by noon, taking me through everything he knows they have, the most compelling being my busted guitar in my old man's truck, the large quantity of his blood on my floor, and the bit they didn't tell us before: his body was wrapped in the decayed remnants of a blanket from my apartment. A blanket with my hair all over it.

"There's no useable blood evidence in the truck because it's been under water for almost three years," he tells me. "But the cause of death is exsanguination from a knife wound to the back, which they believe supports their theory that he died on your living room floor. They haven't recovered a murder weapon as of yet."

"That's why all my knives are missing," I say with a nod, the pieces fitting together in my head. "So…what happens now?"

"They have forty-eight hours to arraign you, and with this case they'll put it off as long as they can while they scramble to get as much of the evidence from your apartment processed as possible." He looks through his notes, rubbing at the soul patch under his lip as he reads. "They made the arrest faster than they might have wanted to because you have means and they were afraid you'd flee if they waited too long."

"Why would I run?" I ask. "I didn't do it." And Lucky's right here. No way I'm going anywhere.

"Apparently, they're not convinced of that," he says, looking up at me with a skeptic's eye.

I've been arrested more than once on drunk and disorderly and I get how the arraignment thing works. "They'll set bail at the arraignment, right?"

"Maybe. More likely, they'll set a separate hearing for that. Again, if they really think you're a flight risk, they'll try to keep you without bail as long as they can. And it's possible they will try to convince the judge to deny bail altogether."

I feel my head shaking as he says it. "They can't do that."

"It's very unusual for the judge to grant that request. We'll fight it with everything we have."

As he packs up his things and leaves, I'm left with a sinking feeling in the pit of my stomach. Looks like my old man is going to figure out a way to ruin my life even from the grave.

CHAPTER 36

Shiloh

Tro's arraignment is closed. Kate and I go down to the courthouse anyway, and when we get there, I see why. It's a madhouse, news vans lining both sides of the street for the entire block. Reporters mill on the lawn outside, chatting in small groups.

We slip inside and go through the metal detector...and find a sea of reporters in the corridor outside the courtroom as well.

My chest is so tight my heart can barely beat. I keep my hood up and my sunglasses on, because the last thing Tro needs is for someone to spot me here. I shouldn't have come.

But I had to.

I've never felt so helpless in my life. I know there's nothing I can do but make this worse for him, but I need to be here for him even if he doesn't know I am.

There's a commotion in the hallway, and over the heads of the reporters I see them usher Tro through the crowd. The decibel level rises from murmur to cacophony as everyone shoves mics at Tro and asks questions all at once, but Tro keeps his head down and moves with his lawyer and the bailiff, who has a tight grasp on his arm, to the door of the courtroom. It closes behind them and the hall buzzes as the crews all film their snippet for the evening news.

I take Kate's hand and pull her toward the other end of the hall, to where the crowd is thinner and there's an empty bench.

We sit. And then we wait.

"He didn't do it," she says. It's about the hundredth time I've heard it in the last two days. It seems to be her mantra. She seems a little shell-shocked and hasn't talked much, but when she has opened her mouth, nine times out of ten, it's been to utter those words.

It's nearly an hour later when the ripple starts though the hallway and spreads like wildfire.

"No bail!" someone shouts, and suddenly all the crews are filming again.

Kate has been sitting next to me with her head in her hands, rocking herself, the whole time, so it takes me a second to realize she's gone.

She's well into the sea of reporters before I spot her, and I don't dare follow her into the mêlée. When she grabs for the handle of the door to the courtroom, a big bailiff steps in her way. He says something, but she lunges for the door anyway. He grabs her before she gets it open and manhandles her face first against the wall.

And that's when I hear her scream. "He didn't do it!"

The scuffle catches the attention of the reporters nearest the courtroom and they turn their cameras on her. Some of them shrug her off as a rabid groupie and go back to their monologues, but the ones who catch her say, "I killed him! It was me!" on camera run it on the news that evening.

#

Tro's cigarette shakes where he's got it pinched between his finger and thumb. "She kept the fucking knife," he says with a disbelieving shake of his head. "Why would she do that?"

I lay my hand over his on the kitchen table to stop the shaking. "Because she knew this might happen. She didn't want you going to jail for something you didn't do, and she knew that knife was the only proof."

"She shouldn't have done that." He takes a long drag and stares blankly at the table with dead eyes. "I would have killed him," he says through a stream of smoke. "I *should* have. She's only sitting in that jail cell because I didn't do what needed to be done. She was saving my sorry ass."

He's right about Kate saving him. She confessed everything—how she heard the fight and came upstairs. According to her story, when she found them, Tro was unconscious and his father was pulling the amp cord from his guitar so tight around Tro's neck that he was blue. The knife Tro had kicked out of his father's hand was on the floor near the couch. On instinct, she picked it up and brought it down on his back, just to get him off Tro. He fell away and she went to Tro, pulled the cord off his neck and made sure he was breathing. When she turned back to his dad a little while later and realized he was dead, she panicked. She wrapped the body in a blanket and dragged it down to the garage. She went back to Tro's apartment and cleaned it and him. When he came to and she knew he was okay, she loaded his father in the Chevy he'd shown up in and drove him out to Lake Travis.

She did it for Tro, and for that, he will never forgive himself.

I get up and pour him a cup of coffee, hoping he'll lay off the Jack bottle that's open on the table in front of him. I've watched his slow self-destruction for the last three days, since they took Kate in and released him, and it's killing me that I can't seem to reach him, no matter what I do. I set the steaming mug down in front of him. "Drink that."

He doesn't look up at me as he says, "I booked you a flight back to California for tomorrow morning. There's a cab coming at seven."

The blood in my veins turns to ice. "I'm not leaving."

There's nothing of the Tro I spent two months touring with in the hollow gaze that meets mine when he lifts his head. All the playful recklessness that ultimately made me love him is gone. "The only thing that could make this worse is someone coming after you here. It's only a matter of time."

He's right. I've been thinking the same thing. But I need to be here for him. "I'll head back next week."

The shake of his head is so subtle I barely see it, but despair coils tighter around my heart, like a python going in for the kill. "I want you to go now."

"No."

I nearly jump out of my skin when he slams his palms into the table and stands, knocking over the bottle. The only sound for the next several seconds is the contents of the bottle trickling onto the floor, but the venom in his gaze as he stares me down has the intended effect. That python tightens itself one last notch and snuffs out my heart.

"Don't do this, Tro," I whisper.

He turns and grabs his helmet and keys on the way out the door.

And that's the last I see of Tro Gunnison before a taxi pulls up for me at seven o'clock the next morning.

CHAPTER 37

Tro

Kate and I never talked about what happened the night my old man crashed my apartment, but I've always known in my gut what must have gone down. I could see it in her eyes. When you're someone like Kate—someone good—you can't kill a man and stay unaffected. She was never quite herself after that.

Kate got three years for obstruction of justice. Three years of her life gone because I fucked up and didn't finish my old man when I had the chance.

But it could have been worse.

I testified to what my old man was. I told them everything I remembered from when he found me in Austin. In the end, the jury found her not guilty for the actual murder because she was acting in the "defense of others."

It's been all over every fucking place. Internet, news, papers. The media's made into this big romantic thing, where

Kate did what she had to do to defend her lover. I haven't corrected them, mostly because it doesn't matter.

I sent Lucky back home right after Kate confessed and they let me out. I haven't talked to her since. She texted me every day for the first few weeks, so I let my phone battery die. I only plug it in when I need to call for food. And I never check messages anymore.

Last I heard, she's back in California, living with some foster family. Freddie called me and told me that not long after I sent her back. He said she'd signed with A&M and the girls were recording their shit.

Her eighteenth birthday is coming up in a few months, but that doesn't matter either.

I am poison. Everyone who gets close to me gets hurt. So I've spent most of the last eight months living in one bottle or another and ignoring the world.

Every once in a while, I pull out my guitar and play the last song I wrote. I realize how stupid I was to think I'd ever be able to banish the beast inside. Because the beast inside is *me*. Everything else is the lie.

I'm on the couch, three quarters passed out, *Ironman 2* playing on the TV for the thousandth time, when there's a knock. The reporters have been gone for months. No one comes up here anymore looking for a story since I threatened to kill the next person who did. The only people who've knocked on my door in months are the delivery guys I call whenever I'm on the brink of starvation.

I didn't call anyone today. I'm thinking of just letting it happen this time.

"Open up, Tro," a woman's voice says. I know it, but I can't place it.

I drag myself up and open the door. On the landing is Lucky's friend Lilah. As I stare, trying to figure out what the fuck is going on, Lucky materializes from behind her.

She's all in white, tank top and skirt, and her copper kinks are full and loose, like a halo around her head.

My heart thuds to a stop in my chest. Sending her away was just about the hardest thing I've ever done. I couldn't even stay to see her go. "What are you doing here?"

She steps forward. "You don't answer my texts. You don't answer your phone. No one's seen or heard from you in months. I had to know you were alive."

"I'm alive."

Her eyes run over my body, clad only in boxer briefs. "Barely."

I've stopped eating. I've stopped working out. It's been at least three days since my last shower and I can't remember the last time I shaved. I can only imagine what she sees when she looks at me.

"You should go," I say, swinging the door closed. I can't keep looking at her, because seeing her here, this perfect fucking angel in my own personal hell, that's going to be the thing that actually kills me.

She slams a shoulder into the door before it closes and it flies open again, banging sharply off the wall, where the knob leaves a hole. She's through it before I can stop her.

"You need to pull your fucking shit together. I get that things went sideways with Kate and you think you ruined her life, but I'm not going to let you curl up and die in here."

"Too late," I say, going back to the couch for my bottle. I take a long drink, then hand it to her. "Want some?"

She takes it and hands it to Lilah, who goes to the sink and dumps the contents. "You have things to do, Tro. Remember when you told me and Kate you'd wasted the last six years of your life on shit that didn't mean anything?"

I drop onto the couch. "That was a different guy."

"Uh-uh," she says, pushing the overflowing ashtray on the coffee table aside and sitting across from me, forcing me to see her. "That was you figuring out what you wanted to be when you grew up. So grow the fuck up, Tro. Be that person."

I stare at her. Don't know why I expected her to go all hearts and flowers on me, because that's not her style. But this is—right to the point, no dicking around.

"The last time bad shit happened," she continues, picking up her rant where she left off when I don't say anything, "you changed your name and ran away. This time, you're just imploding in on yourself. It's all just different forms of hiding, Tro. I thought you'd finally figured out that that isn't what you want."

"What I want doesn't matter."

She gets all up in my face. "What about what *I* want?"

I blow out a humorless laugh. "I can tell you what you *don't* want." I flick a hand at my face. "Anything to do with this."

"You clearly don't have the first fucking clue what I want," she snarls, "even though you should, you selfish bastard."

I used to get that a lot, but here I am doing probably the most unselfish thing I ever have and she's calling me selfish? For the first time in a while, anger at someone other than myself flares in my gut. "Go away, Shiloh."

When I lift my head and look at her, I expect fury or frustration. What I see instead is pain.

"Don't call me that," she says, her voice breaking.

My heart squeezes up my throat and there's a second I can't breathe. She used to hate that I called her Lucky, but now…

"Come on, Lilah," she says, standing.

For a moment I think I'm getting my wish and they're leaving, but the next second I'm being dragged off the couch by both arms. It's questionable whether, even sober, I could fight them off at this point, but as drunk as I am, it doesn't take much for them to drag me into the bathroom. They dump me in the tub and Lucky cranks the cold water.

It pelts me from the shower head and stings when it hits my skin, but I just lay here, unable to move.

Lucky grabs the bar of soap and leans over me. Water trickles down her loose hair and off her nose as she begins to wash my arms. Her hands feel like silk as she lathers me up, and my heart dies a little in my chest, but still, I don't move. Her fingers work over my neck, my chest, and when she reaches my underwear, she doesn't even hesitate. She tugs them down my ass and yanks them off my legs.

"Um...I'll just be..." Lilah says, backing out the door.

I close my eyes as her soapy hands move over my hips and will my cock not to respond. But it's hopeless. This is Lucky. I've never had any control over what my body does when she's near. Her hand glides between my legs as she cleans me, and by the time she moves from my balls to my cock, it's already stiffening for her.

She strokes me.

I hold my breath with the rush.

Her hand tightens, stroking harder, and when I open my eyes, Lucky's whiskey eyes are blazing into mine.

I sit up and yank her over the edge of the tub so she's straddling me. As the cold spray hits her back, she hisses out a gasp. Through her tank and bra, both stuck to her body now, her nipples tighten. I pull her to me and take one into my mouth, sucking through the fabric and tugging with my teeth like the beast I am.

She cries out and the door flies open.

"Shiloh!" Lilah says. But then she sees us and her eyes widen. "Oh..." There's an unspoken exchange between the friends, and the door closes.

Lucky sits back and peels her wet shirt off her body. The bra comes next. Her caramel skin is pebbled with gooseflesh from the cold water, and it runs in beads down her chest, falling in drops from her hard nipples onto my abs.

Suddenly, I'm not cold. Despite the frigid water, I'm burning alive.

Lucky leans in, and I think she's going to kiss me, but instead, she picks up a razor from the edge of the tub. I watch, barely breathing, as she soaps up my neck and starts shaving me.

Every scrape of the razor, up my neck, across my jaw, my cheek, around my mouth, removes a little more of the rancor that I've gilded myself in. My shield slowly falls away, and when she's done, the armor's off and I'm exposed and vulnerable.

She combs back my hair with her fingers and examines my entire face, and I don't let myself retreat back inside. I hold her gaze when her eyes find mine.

"There you are," she says, the shadow of a smile in her eyes. And this time, when she leans in, her mouth finds mine.

We kiss and her hands familiarize themselves with the new landscape of my body. And when she lifts her hips and pulls her underwear aside, I don't stop her from sinking down my hard length. She fucks me agonizingly slowly and I move to her rhythm, feeling her pump a little more life into me with each downward stroke. When she arches and moans her pleasure, I take the bead of one nipple into my mouth, then the other.

Her pace quickens as her moans become louder and more feral. I lift her and shift so my knees are bent under me and use the leverage to thrust deeper. She throws her head back and groans with her orgasm, and I pull out as I come just behind her.

After she's taken a second to catch her breath, she leans her elbows on my shoulders and gazes into my eyes. "Welcome back."

CHAPTER 38

Shiloh

When I got home from Austin after Tro sent me away, it only took Children and Family Services a week to find me at Lilah's. But instead of sending me back to the group home in the city, they found me a foster home only a few towns away from her.

But today is my eighteenth birthday—the day I've been dying for since Tro bought a house in a little town in the mountains near Yosemite, about twenty minutes from Lilah's place, and asked me to move in with him. He picks me up at eight in the morning and we make a beeline for his place. He scoops me into his arms, bride style, then kicks open the front door and carries me through.

"What are you doing?" I ask, struggling in his arms.

He grins, his whole face lighting. It's been a long road back since Lilah and I found him half-dead in his apartment three months ago. He's started taking care of himself again, and there are times he almost seems back to his old self, but this is the first time I've seen that reckless spark in his eye since before everything happened with Kate. "Practicing."

My insides turn to cement and I squirm out of his arms, my feet thudding onto the hardwood floor. "Don't make me change my mind and move in with Lilah instead," I warn.

The spark fades with his grin, and instantly, I hate myself for saying that. His gaze grows intense and searches mine. "You don't ever think about it?"

I shake my head slowly as I step into him, my fingers caressing down the three-day growth along the line of his jaw. "Right now, all I can think about is what it will take to get you naked."

My diversion works. The devil is back in his eyes as he rips his T-shirt over his head. He toes off his shoes and a second later, he's stepping out of his jeans and boxer briefs. And then he's got me in his arms again. He lifts me by the ass and hooks my knees over his hips, taking the stairs up to his bedroom two at a time, as if I weigh nothing.

This is the room that sold the house. The master suite is the only thing on the second floor: a large room with floor-to-ceiling windows on three sides that look over the woods to the mountains beyond—a view that would make even birds jealous. For miles all there is is serenity. Which has been good for Tro.

I've been here before, of course. Tro has fucked me on this bed at least a dozen times since he bought this place last month. But this feels different. I feel his need in the pound of his blood under my hands on his neck, and in the hard heat of his cock between my legs, as usual. But what's overwhelming me, making it hard to breath, is the intensity of his gaze. He holds me in that gaze as he lays me back on the bed and undresses me, and right here, in this instant, I understand that there is such a thing as a soul mate. Suddenly, I feel closer to him than I ever thought possible to feel to another human being. I see him, hovering over me. I feel him as he enters me. But I *know* him in every cell of my body. And as he takes me, mind, body, and soul, I know in my heart that I'm finally where I belong.

Home.

It's dark by the time Tro is done with me, but I'm not tired. I'm wired. Being with Tro is like being plugged in. We lay in a pool of sweaty sheets, catching our breath.

"You hungry?" he asks.

I left the foster home without breakfast this morning. Not that they weren't good people, but I wasn't going to waste a minute getting here. "Sure."

Tro peals himself out of the sheets and snags his boxer briefs off the floor, tugging them on as he moves to the door. "Think I've got a box of mac-n-cheese downstairs."

I'm suddenly freezing without him, despite the heat the summer sun through the windows has left behind. I pull on my underwear and one of his T-shirts, then pad down the stairs behind him. I slip onto a barstool at the long island separating his kitchen from the large, open living room. Down here, the floor-to-ceiling windows are painted green by all the cedar trees just outside, making me feel fresh and clean despite all the dirty things Tro just did to me in his bedroom.

I watch him knock around the kitchen, and a few minutes later, he's scooping mac-n-cheese onto two plates. He sets them on the island in front of me then goes to the fridge, coming back with two beers.

"I've been working on something the last few weeks," he says, watching his plate as he stirs the food around with a fork. "I'm stuck on this one spot."

My heart skips. I haven't pushed him, but I know getting back to his music will help him so much. "Tell me about it."

We sit and eat, and he takes me through where he feels like it's not quite right. When we're finished, he pulls his guitar from the corner near the window and we settle onto the couch.

"So, it's right here," he says as he strums through a progression leading back to the chorus.

I slip the guitar out of his arms. "How 'bout if you just do this?" I say, modulating it up a chord.

"Shit," he says with a shake of his head. "That's fucking brilliant."

I give him a look. "It's not brilliant."

He takes the guitar back and plays the song through the way I showed him. "Brilliant," he mutters again as he grabs a paper off the table and jots some notes.

I pull the guitar away and lean it against the coffee table, then climb on, straddling him. "You want to know what's brilliant?" I ask, my fingers trailing over his body, still skinnier than it was when we met, but so fucking hot. "This."

His mouth pulls into that lopsided cocky smile that I used to hate. Now, it lights desire like a slow-burning fuse in my heart that works its way to my belly and sets me on fire. I kiss it off his mouth, then kiss him some more. When he lifts my T-shirt over my head, I break this kiss and find the same fire in his eyes as they gaze into mine. I free his cock and he pulls my panties aside, and when I sink down his length, he grabs me and flips us so I'm under him on the couch. He fucks me again, so slow, so deep, unlocking every sensation and making me wonder for the hundredth time what I did to deserve something so perfect in my life. I come twice before he does, and I know that's on purpose. He definitely knows what he's doing.

"Why was that so scary to you?" he asks, trailing a fingertip over my cheekbone as we catch our breath.

I open my eyes and look at him, still on top of me. Still inside me. "Nothing you do to me scares me, Tro. You should know that by now."

He lifts a skeptical eyebrow. "When I carried you over the threshold, you were scared."

At the mention of it, I freeze. I guess I'd blocked that out. "I wasn't scared."

It's not a lie. What I feel lodge in my heart at the thought of marriage…or anything permanent, isn't fear. It's cold, raw terror.

He sees it in my eyes, apparently. "Talk to me," he says, rolling on his side and propping himself on an elbow.

But I can't find words. Panic builds in my chest like a lightning storm, short-circuiting my thoughts.

He leans in and kisses me, and just that begins to calm the storm. "I will never ask you for anything you're not willing or able to give, Lucky. But just know, there's nothing I won't give if you ask."

"So, what are you saying? That *I* have to ask *you* to marry me?"

He nods. "Down the road, whenever you're ready."

"What if I'm never ready?"

"Then we'll just keep doing what we're doing."

I smile, some of the tension softening out of my shoulders, and roll to face him. "Fucking on the couch?"

He smiles back and the devil flashes in his eyes. "And on the kitchen counter, and in the shower, and on the porch, and in the woods, and on my bike. Wherever the fuck I can have you."

I tug him closer. "You can have me anywhere, anytime."

So he does. We start on the couch, but end up on the floor. And again on the kitchen table. And again in the shower. And in between we talk, and write, and sing, and belong. We give a little more of ourselves to each other with every touch, every word. And at dawn, we finally fall asleep in each other's arms.

#

"Let's take Shiloh's part from the bridge," the sound guy Ricky says from the booth.

Tro backs away from his mic and nods at me as the guitar line starts in my earpiece.

He's been in the studio for the last month, working on his first solo album. I told him he needed to focus on his own music for this one, but he never listens to me. He wants the lead single to be the one we wrote together the last few weeks on tour, which is why I'm here today recording.

As I belt out his lyrics, he watches me with eyes that tug at every level of my being all at the same time. I want him. I need him. And, God, I love him so fucking much. My heart swells, then overflows with everything I'm feeling for him, making my voice a little scratchy with emotion. He comes up behind me, wraps me in his arms as I sing, and all of a sudden, I'm more.

That's what we do for each other—make each other something bigger than we are when we're apart.

In the three months since Tro asked the question, I've been thinking more about why I'm so scared of anything permanent. I haven't come up with an answer. But what I know is, with each passing day, I'm a little less scared of something permanent with Tro. He's not the same person I met over a year ago. And I'm not the same person he met back then either. We each cancel out the other's insecurities and doubts. We make each other whole.

When we're not working, we spend most of our time the same way we spent our first day together at his place. We stay up until dawn most nights, writing music, talking, fucking, then sleep until afternoon. We only get dressed when we have to leave the house.

And we're touring again next spring—the Lo and Tro tour. Or as Tro calls it, the Lucky Me tour. Either way, it's going to be my new tracks with Lilah playing lead for me, and I can't fucking wait. I kind of want to send copies of our bank statements to all those high school teachers and guidance counselors who told Lilah and me we'd never amount to anything but a drain on society.

"That was great, Shiloh," Ricky says in our ears as I wrap. "Let's take it from the same spot on Tro's harmony."

Tro doesn't let me go as he sings, and I shiver in his arms with the memory of the weeks we wrote this song—the weeks I wouldn't let myself admit I was falling for him. I never could have dreamed then that we'd end up where we are: Tro without Roadkill and me without Billie. But everything happens for a reason.

Tro and I collided in fiery crash that melted away all the bullshit until we each found the person we were meant to be. The road eventually smoothed out and led us to the place we both needed to end up, in each other's arms making the music we were meant to make.

And this is where I plan to say.

ACKNOWLEDGEMENTS

Many hugs to the incredible team at New Leaf, including but not limited to my omnipotent uberagent, Suzie Townsend, for being the most incredible advocate any author could have, and Danielle Barthel for everything she does behind the scenes. To Danielle Sanchez and the fabulous ladies at Inkslinger, who put up with me for some unknown reason. And my writer friends for all their incredible support.

ABOUT THE AUTHOR

Mia Storm is a hopeless romantic who is always searching for her happy ending. Sometimes she's forced to make one up. When that happens, she's thrilled to be able to share those stories with her readers. She lives in California and spends much of her time in the sun with a book in one hand and a mug of black coffee in the other, or hiking the trails in Yosemite.

Connect with her online at
MiaStormAuthor.blogspot.com, on Twitter at
@MiaStormAuthor, and on Facebook at
www.facebook.com/MiaStormAuthor.